IR

BAD WITCH
BURNING

BAD
WITCH
BURNING

JESSICA LEWIS

Delacorte Press

Text copyright © 2021 by Jessica Lewis
Jacket art copyright © 2021 by Sorin Ilie

Visit us on the Web! GetUnderlined.com

Educators and librarians, for a variety of teaching tools,
visit us at RHTeachersLibrarians.com

Library of Congress Cataloging-in-Publication Data
Names: Lewis, Jessica, author.
Title: Bad witch burning / Jessica Lewis.
Description: First edition. | New York : Delacorte Press, 2021. |
Audience: Ages 14 & up. | Audience: Grades 10–12. | Summary: Sixteen-year-old Katrell
uses her witchy powers to talk to the dead and escape her home life,
but when she disregards the dead's warnings to stop, dark forces begin to close
in forcing Katrell to make some hard decisions.
Identifiers: LCCN 2020043212 | ISBN 978-0-593-17738-9 (hardcover) |
ISBN 978-0-593-17740-2 (library binding) | ISBN 978-0-593-17739-6 (ebook)
Subjects: CYAC: Witches—Fiction. | Magic—Fiction. | Dead—Fiction. |
Good and evil—Fiction. | African Americans—Fiction.
Classification: LCC PZ7.1.L518 Bad 2021 | DDC [Fic]—dc23

The text of this book is set in 11-point Janson MT Pro.
Interior design by Jen Valero

Printed in the United States of America
10 9 8 7 6 5 4 3 2 1
First Edition

Content note: this book contains depictions of child and animal abuse.

For Grandma, who healed me, loved me, saved me.

*And for fierce, restless, broken girls who have fire
in their hearts—stay strong.
Your time is coming.*

BAD WITCH
BURNING

I'm painting Will's nails when she asks me to talk to her dead grandma.

"Didn't we talk to her last week?" I don't look up from my work as I paint a coat of hot pink. Will's nails are short and brittle from nervous chewing, so it takes extra effort to make them look good.

"It's been a month, I think." Her voice is a hesitant whisper. "Katrell, please? I wanna tell her about the contest."

I finish the second layer before looking up at her. Will's eyes search mine, brimming with cautious excitement. She's always been like this—desperately hopeful, but expecting someone to crush her at the same time.

Will's big. Not just heavy, but physically imposing. Five foot ten, huge arms that could hurt someone if she wanted. But she sits with her shoulders hunched, like she's trying to take up as little space as possible. A bear who doesn't know she's been let out of her cage.

I lean forward and blow gently on her nails. I'll do it for her. Summonings aren't difficult, and Will never asks for much. At least she has someone to summon. My only family is Mom; I don't have any aunts or cousins or dead grandmas. Will has a whole host of dead people to talk to. Sometimes I wonder which is better— dead family or no family at all.

I lean back on my hands and study Will's face. She's looking down, her eyebrows scrunched, her hands clenched tight around her knees. The wet polish glimmers in the lamplight. I can't let Clara, her grandma, see her wound up like this. Ghosts can be mean when they want to be, and I don't need Clara haunting me for a week because she thinks I upset Will. Time to ease the tension. "I feel like the only reason you keep me around is 'cause I can talk to your granny."

Will rolls her eyes and her shoulders relax, just a little. "Whatever. You know that's not true."

"Then it's because I make your nails look like hot shit." I smile as she laughs. Her shoulders relax even more.

"Emphasis on the shit part." Will shakes her hand delicately, still giggling. "Conrad's look better than this."

My dog lifts his head from his massive paws and his thick tail thumps on the carpet. We're in Will's room, so Conrad had been sleeping on the dog bed her parents bought him. We're always in Will's room. The cream-colored walls, canvases of Will's spray paint art, and the soft carpet feel like a second home. Way better than my leaky bathroom and secondhand mattress without a bed frame. Conrad yawns and stretches, favoring his right back leg, and then makes a beeline for Will.

"Don't," Will warns, leaning backward, but it's too late—Conrad swipes his tongue over her nails, leaving streaks of pink polish up her hand.

I laugh as Will jumps up, swearing under her breath, and Conrad turns to me. He pants and licks my face, a trail of drool stretching from my chin to my temple. "God, Conrad! You're so gross. Go away." I wipe my face with the sleeve of my sweater, giggling.

He doesn't listen; instead, he sits beside me and puts his heavy head on my shoulder, his dog breath wafting into my nose. Conrad is a mastiff mix, with tawny fur, floppy ears and jowls, and deep brown eyes. He's getting older, and longer walks make him limp. I hug his neck tight, and he tries to lick my chin again. This giant, goofy mutt is one of the only things I have that's all mine. I'll take him, drool and all.

Will grimaces as she rubs her hand on her pajama pants. "I thought you trained him not to do that."

I release Conrad from the hug and kiss his wet nose. "He can't help it. He loves his Aunt Will." Will looks unimpressed, so I continue. "Don't be mad at him. I'll fix your nails before Monday, promise. Can't have them looking bad at school."

Will shifts a little, not looking me in the eye. Her shoulders are tight again. "About school . . . Why were you late yesterday? Was Gerald—"

"No." I cut her off, the smile vanishing from my face in an instant. I don't even want to think about my mom's boyfriend, with his bloodshot eyes and rancid breath. I dig my fingers into the plush carpet. "Just overslept. And I wasn't late for work, which is what really matters."

"They're gonna kick you out of school, you know."

"Good." I turned sixteen a few weeks ago, so I just have one more year until I can drop out. The only thing holding me back is Will; I'd miss seeing her every day at lunch. That, and most jobs won't give a full-time schedule to minors. I can't even lie about my age—I have a round, pudgy baby face that's ruined every fake ID I've ever tried to make.

Will's got her disapproving *I know you're full of shit, Katrell* face on, so I change the subject. "Why do you want to talk to Clara, again? About the contest?"

Will starts to answer, but we're cut off by my phone ringing. When I pull it out of my jacket pocket, my stomach sours. Gerald.

Will and I stare at the phone until it stops buzzing. It immediately starts again. When it stops for the second time, there's a lull . . . and it starts up again.

I silence the ringer, my fist clutching the phone so tight my knuckles hurt. Will watches me with a pitiful expression, somewhere between anxiety and fear.

The phone stops vibrating in my hand. A voice mail notification pops up.

Will shakes her head. "Just leave it," she says. She's practically begging.

I can't leave it. Call it morbid fascination or self-loathing, but I always listen to his voice mails. I play it out loud.

"Damn girl never—where are you? Huh? You ain't been back in days." He's drunk; his words are slurred and his voice thick. "You gon' stop ignoring me, Katrell. When you get back, we're getting your disrespect problem straightened out." There's a loud crash, like he slammed his hand against the table, and the voice mail ends.

Will meets my eyes like she wants to say something, so I grab my backpack. I don't want to think about Gerald. I come to Will's to get away from him, but he's always hanging over me like a shadow. He's like a living ghost—gaunt face and form at the edge of my vision, glaring at me. Except, ghosts can't hurt you. Gerald can do a lot worse than watch me from the corner of my room. "Let's talk to granny, yeah?"

"Trell—"

I grab my notebook, a battered spiral one I took from the lost and found at school. "I'm sure she misses you. It's been a while."

"Trell, I don't think you should go home tomorrow—"

"Here, I'll start. The usual?" I don't wait for her reply. I open the notebook and start writing the letter that'll allow us to communicate with Clara, who died when Will was five.

I don't know much about my powers. Mom doesn't have any special abilities and no one knows who my dad is, so I've been winging it for years. At first, I could just see ghosts out of the corner of my eye. At night, shadow figures without faces would hover at the edge of my bed and in the corners of the room. Sometimes they'd touch my arm or shoulder—their touch was heavy and warm, like a real hand. Then Will helped me discover the letter-writing skill. Will's social worker wanted her to write a letter to her grandma to help her "let go," but she couldn't do it. I volunteered and that was it—Clara's first appearance. After that, I didn't see ghosts anymore, but I could talk to whoever I wanted through letters.

Communicating with the dead isn't a big deal. Not anymore. When I first discovered the skill four years ago, it was horrible; I'd get the shakes, like I had the flu, and I'd be so exhausted I couldn't move. But it was worth it. I don't charge Will, but I quickly figured out that people like to talk to their dead relatives and they'll pay me to help them do so. It's easy work—I write a letter, a simple one that says why the client wants to speak with the dead subjects and asks them to appear. I sign my name at the bottom, and bam! We can talk to a ghost.

I start with my usual opening: *I, Katrell Davis, compel you to answer my call.* Will says I'm too dramatic, but hey, it works. I scrawl a quick message mentioning Will and the art contest and sign my name. The ink turns orange, as usual, and then the letter bursts into flame. I drop it and the paper burns up before it hits the carpet. The ghostly image of Will's grandma floats out of the smoke. Full size, barely translucent. It's like she's really standing here. The ghosts were just disembodied voices when I first started, but I've improved over the years. Practice makes perfect and all that, I guess.

Will's grandma, Clara, blinks in surprise. She's tall, like Will, but her frame is thin and wiry. Will told me once that Clara used to be round and plump, but cancer ate at her until there was nothing left. Despite the cancer, now her head is full of loose white curls. I don't know what she was buried in, but she always appears in a summery green dress and red lipstick. She breaks into a brilliant smile when she sees her granddaughter. "Wilhelmina! Come here, baby. How are you?"

"I'm good, Nana," Will says, smiling up at Clara. This is the only time when Will's shoulders fully release from their tight knot.

I sit back while they talk. Will tells Clara about the art

competition she entered, and Clara asks about school and Will's adoptive parents. I stay quiet because I can only call Clara for about ten minutes before a splitting headache forces me to sever the connection. I've had several unhappy ghosts cut off mid-sentence because the pain got to be too much.

I try not to listen when Will and my other clients talk, but I can't help overhearing their conversations when they're this close. I frown when Will says she's been avoiding driving lessons with her adoptive dad, Allen. Why won't she let him teach her? I get that it's weird because he's not her real dad, but it's been four years since her adoption. I'd kill for a dad to teach me stuff. All I've got is Gerald and his slurred screaming. But if my mom's track record with men has anything to say about it, I won't have to deal with him for long.

When my head begins to throb with pain, Clara turns to me. Usually her kind face is peaceful and calm, but today it's scrunched in concern. "Katrell, listen. I have something important to say."

"Yeah?" I sit up a little straighter. Ghosts hardly ever talk to me.

Clara's eyes are dark with seriousness. "Do not contact me again."

I exchange a stunned look with Will. "What?"

"You are at a crossroads." Clara wrings her hands, her eyes darting to Will and then back to me. "You've been burning for a long while. It's consuming you, but you haven't noticed yet. But soon, it will be obvious to everyone."

I stare at Clara, at a loss. Why is she being so cryptic? She was clear about telling Will to wash behind her ears because she knows Will is lazy.

"What do you—"

"I'm not explaining this well," Clara groans. Her form flickers as the pain in my head ratchets up.

I hold one hand to my temple, gritting my teeth. "Hurry, Clara."

"There's no time," Clara urges. She flickers again, like the flame on a candle, the edges of her body turning transparent. "Don't contact me until the burning is over. This is important—don't write any more letters at all. Be careful, Katrell. If you're not, you'll burn down not only yourself, but everyone and everything around you."

With that, Clara disappears.

Will and I sit in silence for a few shocked seconds as my headache fades. Conrad whines and nudges my shoulder.

"Well," I say slowly, still staring at the place where Clara disappeared, "that sounds like something we shouldn't worry about."

"That *definitely* sounds like something to worry about," Will counters. Her eyes are stretched wide, like a startled deer's. "What did she mean? How long is this supposed to last? Wait, was this the last time I ever got to talk to her?"

"Relax," I say, careful to sound disinterested despite my thudding heart. I don't want Will to worry about this; she'll work herself into a panic attack. I'll handle it myself, like I always do. "It's probably a temporary thing, whatever she was talking about. It's fine."

"But—"

"Let's go to bed," I suggest, grabbing the sleeping bag I always use from under Will's bed. She watches as I spread it out and lie down. Her mouth is a tight line.

"Fine," she says eventually. I grin up at her—I've won. "But we're talking about this tomorrow."

"Deal." I have no intention of talking about this with Will ever again.

We say good night and I settle into my usual place, the space beside Will's bed. I lay my head on the pillow, my headache gone already, and Conrad snuggles under one arm.

Even though it's dark, even though I normally sleep like a rock, I toss and turn for hours, my stomach churning with dread. Clara's image burns behind my eyelids. What does it mean to burn everything down?

2

Conrad and I walk home the next day, thinking about what Clara meant by burning. Well, I'm thinking about burning. Conrad doesn't think about anything except food and belly scratches.

Ghosts usually don't talk in riddles; this is something new. They talk about the future sometimes, but it's always straightforward. "Take an umbrella tomorrow" or "don't eat the food at Tony's because you'll get food poisoning." It's never been something like this. How long will this "burning" last? Are all ghosts really off-limits now?

I cross my arms, shuddering against the unusual Alabama cold. Will looked so panicked last night when she asked if she would ever talk to Clara again. My letters are the last connection she has with her former family. I need to figure this out, and quick; I have three clients depending on me to summon ghosts for them this week, but Clara said not to contact anyone. I need that letter money. Someone has to pay the light bill soon or we'll be in the dark.

Conrad tugs at my backpack, whining. I roll my eyes and reach for his stuffed lamb, his favorite toy. Its wool is permanently gray and both eyes were chewed off years ago. Conrad charges ahead, tail a blur, and waits for me to throw it. I toss the toy into the air and he leaps, catching it in his massive jaws. He spins in the air once before landing on his feet with a whump. This is the only trick he knows. I love Conrad, but he's not the sharpest dog I've ever met. Sometimes he's scared of his own tail. I laugh as he runs back to me and nudges my hand, begging for more.

"No, no more. I gotta think about this ghost stuff and you're distracting me."

Conrad huffs. He falls into step beside me again, but he's slower this time. His hip is bothering him; he holds his back leg high above the ground. I pet his head, frowning. His old injury has been getting worse lately, and a trip to the vet is impossible. I'll have to give him some baby aspirin when we get home. And figure out what this "burning" thing is. And deal with Gerald eventually. Jesus, it's always something.

"What do you think she meant by burning, boy?" I ask Conrad. He wags his tail in response, his jaws clamped around the lamb, and I scratch behind his ears.

Conrad and I hop over the railroad tracks, the unofficial divide between my neighborhood and the rest of Mire. It takes ten minutes to get from Will's house to mine on foot. Manicured bushes and perfectly mowed lawns slowly melt into barred liquor stores and abandoned houses. Men smoking on their stoops watch me pass, uninterested. No one messes with me. They know I have nothing to give them.

One house is nothing but rubble. Rumor has it, Marquis burned it down last year because the owner, Mrs. Jean, couldn't settle her debts. Well, it's not really a rumor—everyone knows the price of getting on the bad side of Marquis, Mire's biggest drug dealer. Mrs. Jean is lucky she's still alive.

I rub the top of my head, remembering the scent of hot combs running through hair. Mrs. Jean's house was a makeshift hair salon, a place where kids crowded into her living room on hot Saturday afternoons. Mom used to take me there to get my hair pressed and to gossip with the other parents. I liked Mrs. Jean, but I got sick of Mom wasting forty dollars every two weeks, so I shaved all my hair off. Now it's short and curly, but manageable. And every month, we're eighty bucks richer.

By the time I get home—a tiny two-bedroom town house with faded brick facade, crumbling steps, and a leaky bathroom I haven't managed to fix yet—I'm winded and wishing I could go back to Will's. I stayed at her house all day today, Sunday, dodging her questions about Clara and helping her start a new art project so I could avoid Gerald. He should be working his shift at Wendy's by now. Should.

I pet Conrad and he licks my arm in support. "All right, Con. Here we go."

Conrad tips his head to one side, his brown eyes searching mine. He nudges my leg with his wet nose. Dread swirls in my stomach. I'm right in front of the door, but I don't go in.

I sit on the porch instead, careful to avoid the patch of loose concrete, and grab my phone. I ignore Will's *are we going to talk about Nana?* text and pull up a picture of my baby. The $4,100 Honda Civic I found on Craigslist three weeks ago jumps on-screen. Bright blue, a hundred thousand miles, ready for me to take it. Cash only, which is kind of a problem, but I can get there. That's why I work a shitty hamburger job after school.

Will laughs at me for being obsessed with this car, but she doesn't get it. Will has been sixteen for five months and she doesn't care about driving. Not interested in learning or anything. It blows my mind because I've known how to drive since I was eleven. Will says driving "makes her anxious."

Maybe, but she's missing the bigger picture. A car is freedom. A car is getting to work thirty minutes early and making three dollars and sixty-three cents more per day, which is eighteen extra dollars a week. I can maybe get another job and just lie about my other one so I can work full-time after I drop out of school. A car will change my life.

If I had a car, I could drive away from here.

"Okay," I say aloud, standing. Conrad looks up at me and yawns. I can't sit here and mope forever. I need to at least check on Mom. I put Conrad's lamb into my backpack. "If he starts any shit, we'll leave. Okay?"

Conrad doesn't say anything, so I pat his head and unlock the door.

All the tension in my body melts away as the smell of sweets hits my nose. Mom is baking. She never bakes when Gerald's around. Safe for now.

"Is that you, baby?" Mom calls from the kitchen, her back to me.

"Yeah." I open my bedroom door to dump my backpack, and

Conrad darts inside. He flops onto my mattress and stretches out for a nap. I smile and head to the kitchen.

Mom is washing dishes, soap floating in tiny bubbles around her. Her hair is tied in a messy bun, feathery loose tendrils framing her gaunt face, and she's wearing her favorite pink bathrobe. Though the bathrobe is starting to fade, it complements her skin tone. Mom didn't give me her warm, medium-brown complexion; I'm light-skinned, or "high yellow," as Gerald often sneers. Like he's too far off.

Mom looks at me while she works, smiling. "How was Will's house?"

"Good." I think fleetingly of Clara's message, but put it out of my mind. "She's gonna enter an art competition soon. Which she should, since she—"

"Good for her," Mom cuts me off, which is an annoying habit of hers. She concentrates on scrubbing cookie dough from a glass dish. "Why don't you try entering something like that?"

I shrug. "No time. Gotta work."

"Well," Mom says, rinsing the last dish and turning to face me. "Work *is* more important. You can draw on your day off."

I fidget a little, my gaze wandering to the cookies cooling on the stove. Mom knows I can't draw. I've always been good at writing letters. Writing has always been my thing. Not stories really, but poetry. Always nonfiction. Though since I started working thirty-hour weeks, I haven't had time to practice. "Yeah, I guess so." I reach for a cookie, but Mom smacks my hand.

"No ma'am," she says, still smiling. "Those aren't for you."

I rub my stinging hand, resisting the urge to roll my eyes. She didn't have to hit me that hard. "Fine. Who're they for?"

"Nosy, aren't you?" Mom laughs and pulls a Tupperware bowl from a shelf. "If you bring me some ingredients, I'll make you some."

"I get paid next week, so you better not be bluffing."

I'm kidding, but Mom gets an excited look on her face. "I'm glad you get paid so soon!"

Unease coils in my gut. When Mom is excited about money, it's not a good thing. "Why are you glad?"

"Doesn't matter. More importantly, when Gerald gets home, we need to have a family meeting."

I can't suppress a groan. "Come on, Mom—"

"You can talk to him for a few minutes, it won't kill you." When I don't answer, her expression softens. She touches my face, her hands still damp from the dishes. "I know. Just trust me. It's you and me, like always. But sometimes we have to do things we don't want to do to survive. You understand."

I do. Gerald isn't the first boyfriend, and he certainly won't be the last.

Mom grabs a cookie from the tray and gives it to me. She arches her eyebrows, an amused grin on her face. "Now, are we gonna behave?"

I sigh, push the questions from my mind, and take the cookie. "Yeah."

"Good. Now go on, I got something to do." Mom starts packing up the cookies, her back to me again. "We'll talk more later, okay?"

I stand there for a few uncertain seconds, but when she doesn't turn around, I sigh and go to my room. Conrad lifts his head when I enter, tongue lolling. I sit next to him on my mattress without a bed frame and he covers me in kisses and dog drool.

"At least you're happy to see me." I give him the cookie and he wolfs it down in one bite.

I pick up the notebook I use to write letters in. It's thin—I've used almost all of the pages. I try to write a poem, like I used to, but my brain is whirring. Clara's words run through my mind, but they're quickly replaced by Mom's. *It's you and me.* But Gerald is here too. Isn't she tired of this? They only stay a few months at most, and Gerald's on month three, so he should be on the way out. And yet here we are, having "family meetings." My only family is Mom and Conrad. I doodle on a blank page, something similar to hurt curling in my chest. Can't it just be me and her, just for a while? Why isn't that enough?

I don't have time to think about it. I hear the sound I've been dreading—the front door opening and heavy footfalls. Mom calls out a greeting and a man's voice responds.

Gerald's home.

3

Conrad whines and nudges my side. I pet him unhappily, the pen clenched in my right hand.

"It's okay, boy," I tell him, but I'm really talking to myself. "Maybe he'll forget about it."

"Katrell," Gerald's muffled voice calls. "Get in here. Now."

So much for that.

I scratch behind Conrad's ears. He licks my chin, his brown eyes sympathetic. I shake my head. Might as well get it over with.

"Come on, boy. Let's go."

Gerald is standing in the kitchen, arms folded. Mom's at the table, the Tupperware of cookies open and half empty. I match Gerald's posture and glare at him, Conrad's pressure against my legs comforting me.

"What do you want?"

Gerald's eyes narrow. He's tall, so he thinks he's intimidating, but he's got the lanky body of an overgrown twelve-year-old and a face like a boar, so he makes me laugh more than anything else. "I want you to watch your mouth."

Mom jumps up from the table, smiling. "Okay, you two, let's talk this out. Calmly, please?"

I shrug, my nails digging into my forearms. Just get through this, and I can go back to my room. I can do this. "I'm listening."

Gerald stands straighter, glaring at me. "First, we gon' talk about you disrespecting me. Why you don't answer when I call?"

I roll my eyes before I can help it. "Maybe I'm busy?" Maybe I don't have time to listen to his shit?

Gerald grits his teeth. "It was important."

"Oh yeah?" I can't keep the scoff out of my voice. "What was so important, then?"

"Gerald." Mom's voice carries a warning. "Now isn't the time——"

"We needed to know when you got paid last," Gerald says. "Something came up."

All the disgust and annoyance turns into fear. I turn to Mom, panic rising in my chest. "What does he mean? What happened?"

Mom sighs, still smiling, like this is somehow funny. "I told him I'd talk to you myself. . . . It's not a big deal. A little setback. We're short this month, but I'll pay you back."

"What?" The panic creeps into my throat. "What do you mean? How short?"

"Don't worry about it, adult problems," Mom says, laughing. "I just need a bit more than usual this month, then we'll be fine. And you can just do some extra letters, right?"

Shit. Mom doesn't know about Clara's ominous warning. She knows about my power (how could she not? Parents notice when their kids start seeing ghosts), and the letters I do, but I try not to talk about it much with her. She's never told me, but I think it freaks her out. That's irrelevant now, though. I can't do letters, and now doesn't seem like the best time to tell her that.

"Mom, you have to tell me how much. What happened? Is it the lights again?"

"Hey," Gerald says, startling me. He's glaring still, his fists clenched at his sides. "She said it's grown folks' business."

"I'm not talking to you," I snap. I turn back to Mom. "How much? We have enough for rent, right?"

"Hey." Gerald takes a step toward me. "You talking to me now."

I turn, hoping my face expresses every bit of disgust I feel.

His eyes, bloodshot and dilated, look me up and down. He seems disgusted with me too. "You got a disrespect problem, Katrell. You ain't gon' talk to your mom like that, or me. And you still ain't answered my question. Why didn't you answer when I called?"

"'Cause I don't have to answer to you, Gerald."

Gerald's eyes narrow. He rounds on Mom, his nostrils flaring like an angry horse's. "You hear this? You hear the way she talk to me? And to you?"

"Katrell," Mom says, the corners of her mouth upturned. "You mind him, all right? You know he don't mean any harm."

Frustration builds in my chest. Gerald's been here for three months, eating our food, screwing up our bathroom, and I have to listen to him? For what?

"I'm going to my room," I say through clenched teeth. I'll text Mom so he can't interfere. I nudge Conrad with my knee, but Gerald steps closer, uncomfortably close.

"We ain't done talking," he growls. "You need to tell me and your mom where you go at all times of night—"

"What do you care?" The frustration's in my throat now, bubbling out of my mouth. "I don't have to answer my phone if I don't want. Do you pay for it? Do you pay for anything? Why aren't you covering us if we're short this month?"

"Katrell." Mom's voice carries a warning. She's no longer smiling.

The frustration's at the top of my head. Used to, I'd listen to Mom and back off. But if I've learned anything from Mom's boyfriends, it's that this is how men are. You can tell pretty much in the first week what kind of man they'll be. Some are nice and want to bribe you with jewelry or headphones or school supplies. I like those, but I haven't seen one in a long time. Gerald's the other type. The type that wants to grab you by the neck and break you down if you let them. He's going to hit me—I know that. I can see him tensing, hear the anger in his voice. But I know it doesn't matter what I do. I've tried everything—getting low so they don't see me, running away, trying to please them—but the result is always the same. If someone wants to hit you, that's what they'll do. So now I don't run away or cower or beg. Now, if they're going to give me hell anyway, I do my best to give them hell back.

Gerald clenches his jaw so hard, tiny veins in his forehead bulge. "Listen, you got an attitude problem. And you gon' fix it, or I'll fix it for you."

I cross my arms, my chin inclined. The last time he hit me, his punch was pathetic. It barely left a bruise. Gerald doesn't scare me. He isn't even the worst in Mom's long streak of loser boyfriends. Might be the ugliest, though.

"Fuck off, Gerald."

Gerald reaches for the waistband of his pants so fast I barely register what's happening. Conrad whimpers and presses his belly to the floor. Mom gasps and reaches for my arm. Gerald grins, his eyes dull and narrowed, and holds something up to the light.

It's a gun.

Gerald says something, but fear chokes all sound out of my ears. A gun. Someone gave this idiot a gun. He's holding it casually at his side while he gloats. A threat. Some of the panic fades and slow-churning rage fills my gut. What right does he have to threaten me with a gun in my own home? In the house where *I* pay bills? And he's talking about me respecting him? I get an urge to spit on him so strong, I have to grit my teeth.

"What are you doing?" Mom's voice is a whisper. Her eyes are stretched wide in alarm. She's half in front of me, shielding part of me with her body. "Baby, she's a kid. Just put that away, okay? We'll talk about this."

"Don't worry," I growl. "He won't shoot me. He ain't got the balls."

Gerald's smile disappears in an instant and his eyes get a hard glint. He steps toward me, but I don't move, my chest swelling with a mix of defiance and cold anticipation. Metal's going to hurt a lot worse than his fist. He takes another step, the gun pointed at the floor, and another, until he's right in my face. Mom shifts slightly, so she's standing next to me, not in front of me, and lets go of my arm.

"Don't touch me, Gerald." My voice doesn't sound like my own; it's a high-pitched, girlish whine. Almost pleading.

I can't stand it.

"You're the most disrespectful kid I've ever seen." Gerald's so close, his foul breath washes over me. It smells like alcohol and stale Wendy's. "Normal stuff don't work on you. Thought we could try something else."

I take a shaky breath and steel myself. I can't let him win this. If I do, it'll only get worse. "I respect people who deserve it. That ain't you." My voice comes out calm, steady, but my hands are trembling so hard I'm holding on to my jeans for support. "You wanna try something else? Go ahead. I'm waiting."

Gerald's face twists as he raises the butt of the gun. Without thinking, I shove him as hard as I can. He stumbles backward, into the counter, and swears. It's dead silent. Mom looks back and forth between me and Gerald, her hands clasped nervously in front of her. Conrad presses against my calves, his body trembling. Gerald straightens, glares at me, and charges, the gun raised high over his head.

It's chaos in the kitchen. Mom starts screaming and Conrad's barking and Gerald is trying his best to hit me with that gun, but I'm so sick of Mom's boyfriends hitting me that I ball my hands into fists and hit him first. Pain jumps into my knuckles as my fist connects with Gerald's chin. A savage pleasure warms my chest when his head whips backward. Mom screams my name, but Gerald recovers and levels the gun at me—

The gunshot is so sudden, I'm paralyzed by the sound. He shot me. He shot me? No, there's no pain, I'm not hurt. Ears ringing, confusion clouding my vision, I follow the gun's trajectory to my

22

right, where a big red stain blossoms from the middle of Conrad's chest.

For a long time, there's silence. Conrad sinks to his stomach without a sound. I watch the blood leak out of his chest in a lazy ooze onto the dirty floor, spreading in a dark pool under him. Glassy brown eyes wide with surprise. Pink tongue slightly visible against his open jowls.

Conrad is dead.

There was silence, but now there's screaming, my screaming, as Conrad's blood seeps into my shoes.

Gerald says something, his dumb eyes wide like a cow's, but I don't hear it. Sharp grief hits my chest, my arms, my whole body. I'm hot and cold all at once. But right after, a burning boils in my chest, filling me with rage and shoving the sadness down to my toes. He killed him. He killed Conrad. My hands ball into fists. Gerald's still holding the gun, but I lunge at him. I hit him, as hard as I can, over and over. I can't see—my vision is blurred with fury and tears. He shoves me away, swearing, and the butt of the gun connects with my left temple.

The blow snaps me back to reality. I'm on my ass, Gerald standing above me with a gun, my palms slick with Conrad's blood. Gerald looks mad as hell, probably because there's a quickly forming bruise on his cheek and scratches on his throat. The gun is trained on me.

I look to Mom for help, but Mom doesn't say a word.

"Stop, just stop." Gerald's breathing hard, wheezing. His eyes are wide as if in shock, but then they harden like shit-stained diamonds. "You get it now, don't you? You got me all worked up and I had to kill the dog. This is on you, you hear me? All you had to do was respect me. This is what happens when a child think they're bad enough to disrespect adults. You got it?"

I don't answer. I'd rather die than give him an inch of satisfaction.

Gerald grunts and puts his gun back into the waistband of his jeans. He goes to the front door, still breathing hard. He puts his hand on the doorknob, but then looks back and smiles at me, a victorious yellow-toothed grimace.

"I bet you'll mind me now, Katrell."

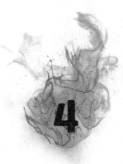

4

Will reaches for the knot on my temple, but her hand falls away before she can touch it. "You need ice for this," she says, her voice a familiar whisper.

I don't say anything. I'm sitting on my bedroom floor, shivering, wrapped in a blanket. I called Will a few minutes after Gerald left, a blubbering mess. I don't know how she got here so fast—she showed up alone, panting. She must have snuck out. She couldn't have told her parents; Will's not usually allowed at my house at night. For good reason, huh? No one even called the police when the gun went off. Everyone knows better.

I must have cried for an hour. Right there on my porch, sobbing like a baby. Then we buried Conrad in my backyard. Two hours, two shovels, two silent girls covered in my best friend's blood. When it was over, Will made me change clothes, but my arms are still covered in flecks of red. It's cold in here, it always is, so Will took off her hoodie and gave it to me, and then brought me a blanket. I can't move. I can't think. I can't even cry anymore.

Conrad is dead.

"Your lip is bleeding," Will says.

I got Conrad when he was just a puppy. Got caught in a trap I set for raccoons, the big idiot. I took him everywhere. He's lived in three different apartments in three different cities. Once, in a burned-out crack house. Once, in a small car with no heat and no air, perpetually parked in a supermarket parking lot.

"Trell, can you hear me?"

He was seven years old. He wouldn't bite a biscuit. He slept next to me all night, every night, for seven years.

I lean my head on my knees, closing my eyes. Pain, raw physical pain, tears at my chest. Conrad's gone. Gerald killed him to get back at me. No, he killed him to break me.

"We have to do something."

I look up at Will, but her face is a dark brown blur. I blink and she swims into focus.

Will's frowning fiercely at her hands. A few flecks of blood stain her painted nails, though we washed our hands a hundred times. "I can't leave you like this. We have to call someone—the police?"

"No." The police won't help. They don't even do patrols around here because they don't care. If I called, I bet they wouldn't even come. And if they do come, then what? I say Gerald killed my dog and they laugh at me? Or worse, they call DHR and take me and leave Mom with Gerald? This isn't a problem for the shitty police force of Mire to solve. It's on me. It always is. "No cops."

"Then who?" Will's voice is still that aggravating whisper. She never speaks up. Not even now. "Maybe Mike?"

I snort. What's our school guidance counselor going to do? "He'll call the cops, you know it."

"Then you can come and live with me."

I look at Will, and for one second, I desperately want to say yes. Yes, I want to get out of this hell I'm in and have clean clothes and parents who will take me driving and not kill my dog. But I think of Mom, how it's always been just me and her, and I shake my head. "No. It's okay. I'm not scared."

"I am," Will urges. Her eyes are big and sad, like they get when she talks about her past. "I'm worried, Trell. He's got a gun, he killed—"

"I'm fine." My voice comes out sharper than I intended. I take a deep breath. "I'm fine. Go home."

Will's eyebrows knit together in concern, but I look away from her, to my trembling hands. Will's mom calls a few minutes later; I can hear her desperate "where are you?" from here. And so Will goes. Of course she goes, because Will is a good kid who listens to her adoptive mother. Will is a good kid who has been where I am, who has felt the butts of guns on her face and seen lives torn apart, and she leaves because she's scared to come back down to my level.

After Will's gone, I press my forehead to my knees and wish I was dead.

That doesn't last long. I can't sit here and mope forever. I have to get up. Do something. Conrad was just a dog, right? Just a dog.

I mop up water from the leaky toilet in my bathroom, take a cold shower, look at my Craigslist car. I stare at the wall and listen to the TV blaring in the living room. I listen to Gerald come home from who knows where, stumble into the table, and shatter something in the kitchen.

I miss Conrad so much.

I can't take it anymore, so I slide my red headphones over my ears and everything goes quiet. I put on a rap song, an aggressive one, and pull out my notebook. Will's grandma said not to write any more letters, but honestly, fuck that. I need to tell Conrad I'm sorry my big mouth got him killed. I need to tell him I hope he's in dog heaven or whatever. I need to see him again.

I start Conrad's letter with the usual fanfare, *I, Katrell Davis, compel you to answer my call,* blah blah, but I crumple that up and throw it away. The music's blaring in my ears. Tears run down my cheeks. He wasn't just a dog. He was part of the only family I had left.

Conrad,

Please come home.

—Katrell

The ink ignites and burns hot, hotter than it ever has before. I jump to my feet as a vicious inferno consumes the entire notebook, then the dirty carpet around it. The fire suddenly goes out, leaving a perfect circle of black on my floor. And then . . . nothing. Nothing happens. For the first time since seventh grade, there's no ghost. No image to talk to. I wait, hope dwindling in my chest as the minutes tick on. The music throbs in my ears. He's not coming.

This has never happened before. I've always been able to

conjure something, whether it's a disembodied voice or a realistic figure like Will's grandma. Even a lizard once. But nothing?

I take off my headphones. It's quiet, except for the TV's canned laughter and Gerald's snores. Tears build in my eyes. I've lost Conrad and now my power too? What else can disappear? Despair settles in my chest and my hands start to tremble. What else do I have left?

I can't sit still. I can't sit here and think about my powers and stare at the circle on my floor and Conrad's favorite stuffed lamb next to my mattress. I need to leave this house. There's an abandoned apartment building a few minutes' walk away, and I go there sometimes to avoid Mom's boyfriends. I've collected junk in one of the apartments for years, and it's almost as good as my room. It's either that or Will's, or somewhere. Anywhere besides the place where Conrad died.

I open my bedroom door and tiptoe to the kitchen. The counter is filthy, covered with empty beer cans and snuffed-out cigarettes. No food. I didn't go to work today, so there won't be any until Monday afternoon. Gerald's sleeping on the couch, just a few feet away.

My hand closes around a knife on the counter. It's dirty, crusted with food. I bet he would get an infection. It's dull too, hasn't been sharpened in years. I bet it would really hurt.

I close my eyes and dump the knife into the sink. Gerald sleeps on, oblivious. Hatred boils in my gut, but shame too. How can I even think about killing him? Or even just stabbing him? If I go to juvie, Mom'll starve to death. Or worse, stay with this sack of shit forever. I'll have to get back at him some other way. Maybe I can piss in his beer. He's so stupid he won't notice, though, so it won't be satisfying.

I grab the doorknob, looking back at the kitchen one more time. Mom cleaned up the blood, so the floor is smooth and shining, like Gerald didn't murder my dog. Like nothing happened at all.

I swallow the regret, disgust, and powerlessness, and open the front door.

My heart jumps into my throat. There's a dark shape at the end of the driveway, just out of reach of the porch light. A man? A robber? I grab the baseball bat we keep by the door, my hands slick against the cold metal.

"What do you want?" I bark, trying to sound tough. It's probably someone who's been drinking and stopped to throw up on our front lawn. Drunks usually go away if you yell at them enough.

The shape turns and moves toward me. It's on all fours—are they crawling? I take a step back, my heart stuttering in my chest. The shape gets closer, then steps into the light.

The air rushes out of my chest all at once. The bat slips from my fingers.

It's Conrad.

Conrad, his chest stained red, his ears smeared with dirt, cocks his head to one side. He's not a ghost. He's solid, real, alive. He wags his tail and trots into the house, his nose in the air.

5

"All right, don't panic."

So Will says, but she looks like she's about to have a panic attack.

It's almost midnight and I snuck into Will's house through her bedroom window. I brought Conrad too, and we're both sitting on her floor. I'm numb with shock, but Conrad's quiet, staring at the wall.

"He was dead," Will mutters, pacing from the bed to the bathroom and back again. "I saw him. I helped bury him. How are you so calm?"

I don't know. I wasn't calm, not at first. I let out a strangled squeal and hugged Conrad, and he licked my face. It was really him, drooly and warm and just like he was before. But then Gerald started to wake up, so I booked it to Will's. I haven't had time to process anything. Or plan. How am I going to hide him from Mom and Gerald?

"I'm just kind of . . . numb," I admit. "I can't believe it. Maybe we're just dreaming."

Will shakes her head. "Okay, start from the beginning. What did you do after I left?"

I tell Will about the letter and the burn mark on the carpet.

"What did you write?" Will asks. "The usual?"

"No, it was a lot shorter. I asked him to come home."

Will's quiet. I can practically see the gears turning in her head. "Did you know you could do this?"

I shake my head. First seeing ghosts, then talking with them, and now this. None of it makes sense. My powers are a confusing jumble of messing around with the dead.

"Wait, do you think this is what Nana meant?" Will leans closer, her eyes wide. "Is this the 'burning'?"

"I mean, the letter burned up, but they all do that. Conrad's was hotter, though. It left a mark on my floor."

Will is deep in thought for a moment, then she takes a shallow breath. "We'll deal with that later. First, Conrad. Is he okay?"

I look at him and he meets my eyes. His chest is still caked with blood and dirt. Grass sticks to his jowls, but he's not drooling like usual. He looks the same, just dirty. "Looks good to me."

Will frowns at him. "I don't think he's breathing."

"What? Of course he is." I crawl to him on my hands and knees and put my palm under his chest. Conrad licks my chin. I hold my hand there for a long time, but . . . there's nothing. No gentle rise and fall. No heartbeat. "Oh. That's not good."

"I don't know, Trell, this is . . ." Will looks at Conrad uneasily. "This is too much. He's not really alive, he's—"

"He *is* alive." My voice is forceful, determined. I'm trembling, mostly with excitement. My powers aren't gone, just changed. He's back, with me. I can make things up to him. "He's alive, he knows me and you. He's not breathing, but so what? He's here."

Will doesn't say anything. She tiptoes to Conrad's side and cautiously pets his head. He wags his tail. Will runs her hand over his wound, a dark patch of fur on his chest, but Conrad doesn't flinch.

"The bullet hole is gone," Will says.

So he's not breathing, he has no heartbeat, and his wound has healed? And he's warm. I pet Conrad's head and he closes his eyes.

"What should I do?" I ask Will.

She picks at the skin around her nails. "I don't know. But I don't think you should write any more letters."

I stroke Conrad's massive head, uncertainty eating at me. I'll have to stop my letter business for real. I accidentally resurrected my dog, and I have no idea what else I can do. Unless . . .

"Do you think I can bring people back to life too?" My head's pounding, half with fear, half with excitement.

"Wait, Trell." Will's voice carries a warning. "Don't get all excited yet. We don't know if your powers have really changed or if this is a fluke."

I'm barely listening. "How much do you think people would pay for a person's resurrection?"

"No," Will says. "No, Trell, no way."

"Why not? I mean, I can resurrect dogs, and I'm assuming humans, now." My mind goes through the possibilities at a rapid rate.

Resurrecting people for money. Way more valuable than letter writing, surely. How much would my clients pay to see their loved ones again? Not just see but touch? Hold?

"It's wrong," Will says. She brings her fingernails to her mouth, then back to her lap. She's already ruined my paint job on her right hand. "It's not right. I don't blame you for bringing Conrad back—it was an accident—but no more. You can't just bring people back from the dead, Trell. They're dead for a reason."

"You wouldn't want me to bring back your parents?"

Will's eyes go flat and I curse myself for going too far. Will's parents died when she was only a baby, and then her grandma five years later. No one to take care of Will, so she went into foster care. For a long time.

"No," she says, her voice calm and distant. "I wouldn't want you to resurrect my parents. A little too late for that."

"Sorry," I say quickly, barely stifling the urge to wince. "I promise I won't. And not anyone else, at least not right now. I don't know if it would even work on someone else, you know? Conrad . . . he's different. I know him. So it probably won't even work on other people."

Will's eyes soften. "Okay, good. No more letters. Promise?"

"Promise."

Will and I give Conrad a bath and talk about school and her nails and everything except my split lip and potentially resurrecting her parents. She convinces me to spend the night, so I curl up on her floor, the sleeping bag softer than I could ever hope of my ratty secondhand mattress. She turns the lights out, but I stay awake for a long time, thinking about how much money a resurrection is worth.

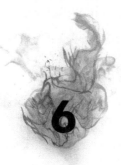

6

oday is a school day.

Not every day is. Sometimes it's a "sleep till noon" day. Or an "I'm sick of school" day. School's not important, not really. The most important thing is I'm always on time to my part-time job at Benny's, a mom-and-pop burger joint that serves mediocre hamburgers. They pay me to mop grease off their kitchen floor. No one pays me to listen to teachers ramble about shit I don't care about.

But today I'm at school. Will's mom, Cheryl, caught me snoring on her daughter's floor, and she gently bullied me into getting ready. She always makes me go to school when I stay over. I'm not complaining, though; she bribes me with homemade pancakes. I don't get breakfast usually. I'm good at sleeping through hunger pangs.

It's the end of third period, history, and I get up from my

creaky desk in the back to wander out of the classroom. I have no idea what Mrs. Wary said. I never do. Kids from my class eye me warily as I pass. I'm wearing Will's clothes, which dwarf my body despite me being pretty chubby, and I have a split lip and an aching bruise on my temple from Gerald's attack, but that's not why they're staring. It's not a secret I can talk to the dead, not really. It's like a rumor—Frieda got pregnant by Jabari, Demarcus is in alternative school because he knifed a kid last week, Katrell can talk to ghosts. I only have a few clients, and somehow the whole school knows. But what do I care? They can try to snitch on me. I'd like to see them prove it.

I have PE fourth period, so I just don't go. School is pointless. Write your silly essays, do your dumb science experiments, sit slack-jawed and listen to bullshit for eight hours so your parents can go to work. Trouble is, Mom doesn't go to work anymore, I do. And it's real hard to think about writing an essay on the American Revolution when I get home from Benny's at ten-thirty at night and Gerald has eaten all the groceries I bought for the week.

They don't care about that. It's always "Katrell, you have to apply yourself." Or, "Katrell, you're not even trying." It makes me sick the way they pretend to care. As if they give a shit about my Fs and zeros; they'll pass me along to the next grade so they don't have to deal with me. All their whining is just because they're required to say something or they'll get in trouble with the higher-ups. They don't care about anything but themselves.

Instead of PE, I go outside, to the basketball court, where the other kids who don't give a damn about school hang out. I walk past the stoners, the wannabe players, the kids who trade drugs in the shadows next to the building. I sit in my favorite spot, a shady hideaway under the bleachers, and close my eyes.

Conrad. What am I going to do? He's in Will's room while we're at school—safe for now. But he can't stay there forever. I told Will's mom we were bug bombing our house and the chemicals aren't good for him, but she'll eventually wonder when he's going home. And Will is nervous; she doesn't like that Conrad doesn't breathe. Neither do I, but I can't tell her that. I'm hoping she'll keep him until I can figure something out. Or Gerald drops dead. We should be so lucky.

I run my thumbnail over a crack on my headphones. Gerald. Talk about a headache. This isn't the first time I've had a gun aimed at me, but it is the first time someone actually used it. I'll have to talk to Mom. My eyes pop open and my heart rate increases. I forgot because of Conrad, but Mom said we were short this month. She never told me how much. I pull out my phone to text her.

How short are we

I have to wait for a few minutes, but the text comes. *Rent and lights. Something came up. But you get paid soon right? And you can do a letter or two.*

I bury my face in my hands, nausea swirling in my gut. Numbers run through my head in quick succession. Rent is five hundred thirty-five dollars. Water and lights combined is a hundred ninety-five, when it's not summer. That's seven hundred thirty dollars of "have to" money. I have to pay the rent. I have to pay water and lights. I used to include food in our "have to" budget, but totaled up, it's four hundred dollars because Gerald eats like a fucking horse. So food is out. We can survive for a month without

37

it. I'll eat my shift meal, Gerald can eat at Wendy's, and I can sneak some food home for Mom after work. It'll be tight, but we'll make it on weekdays. Weekends, we'll have to drink a lot of water.

The check I'll pick up today after school should be two hundred fifteen dollars. Next week's should be the same. Four hundred thirty dollars isn't enough. Normally I would supplement the money with letters, but I can't do letters. . . . I dig my nails into my scalp, the beginnings of a headache pounding behind my eyes. I'll have to dip into my car savings. Again. But after this time, what are we going to do? I don't have much left. What's this "something" that ate up our rent money? If it's Gerald, I swear to God I'll kill him.

I put my phone away—I don't have the energy to text Mom back. I take a shaky breath, peeking out of the gap in my hands at the cold gravel below. My minimum-wage hamburger job isn't cutting it anymore, not without the letters to help. What am I going to do?

"Yo, Katrell."

I jump, but relax when I see Justin. Justin's a stoner kid from my neighborhood, short, stocky, dumb as a bag of hammers. He's also one of my first and most consistent clients.

Justin frowns down at me, his hands in his pockets. "You okay?"

"Yeah. What's up? Wanna talk to Kenny?"

Justin nods. He pulls a crumpled wad of bills from his pocket. I don't get too excited; it's no more than thirty dollars. Justin is cheap and only talks to his uncle for a minute, so I don't charge him as much. Still, it'll help with the rent. Just need five-oh-five now.

I reach for the money, but then remember Conrad. "Oh shit, sorry. Can't do it."

"What? Why?"

"I, uh . . ." For a split second, I debate about lying to him. But what's the point? "I'm having a power malfunction. I can't communicate with ghosts right now."

Justin raises an eyebrow. "Thought you were a witch? What, you get rained on or something?"

Justin spends an annoying amount of time laughing at his own joke. When he's done, I decide to tell him the truth. Who'd believe him? "No, but I accidentally resurrected my dog last night."

Justin's eyes widen. "You're shitting me."

"No shit, my man. But you see why I can't write letters now. Gotta figure this out."

"Damn." Justin puts his money away and my chest aches. "You know, I bet people would pay a ton for that."

"Oh yeah?" I don't want to seem too eager, but I'm listening closely. "How much would you pay for me to resurrect your uncle?"

"Nothing 'cause that's creepy as hell. But I bet some white people would go for that shit. They'd pay you a thousand bucks."

A thousand dollars? I'd only have to do four resurrections to pay for the car. Then I could get a better job that's farther away. . . . Wait, if I just did resurrections, I wouldn't have to work at all. I could be self-employed. An entrepreneur.

"I wouldn't, though," Justin says, reaching into his pocket for a pack of cigarettes. He lights one with a cheap Bic lighter. "That's weird as hell, Katrell. Talking to them is one thing, but bringing them back . . ." He shudders. "Look, let me know when you've figured it out. I got thirty dollars with your name on it."

"Oh, and what's that thirty dollars for?"

Justin and I jump, but I relax almost immediately. It's Mike, the new guidance counselor at Mire High. He's a tall, thin guy with high cheekbones and a soft voice, and he's always wearing an ill-fitting suit. He walks like a cat; lithe, slow, silent. Some kids call him Slenderman. But I like Mike. He's always sticking his nose in other people's business, like now, but he means well. Plus, he never snitches on me when he finds me skipping PE.

"Smoking? At fourteen? Classy, Mr. Wiggins." Mike tugs Justin's cigarette from his lips and flicks it to the ground.

Justin rolls his eyes. "Later, Katrell."

I nod and Justin leaves. He lights another cigarette as soon as he's out of grabbing distance from Mike.

Mike looks at me, his funny half grin on his face. "Skipping PE again, are we, Miss Davis?"

"Always." I get to my feet. "What're you doing? Ruining teenage lives?"

"Always." Mike's grin fades. "What happened to your lip?"

Uh-oh. I like Mike, but like I said, he's nosy. "Nothing. I mean, I fell. Not a big deal."

Mike's got these sharp, light brown eyes that can cut through any kind of bullshit. He stares me down, his mouth a thin line of disapproval. Sweat beads along my hairline.

"Anyway, I should go to class. I'm really late." I try to ease away, but Mike's still staring me down.

"Is everything okay at home, Katrell?"

Here we go. Mike and I have had this conversation a lot in the past few months, since Mom met Gerald. Each time he gets pushier about it. He's just doing his job, and he's annoyingly good at it, but I'm sixteen now. I don't need some guidance counselor who has "follow your dreams" posters in his office to call DHR on Gerald. Because then what? I go to a group home and get tortured for two years like Will? I'd rather handle the Gerald problem myself. I just need to talk to Mom.

"I'm fine," I tell Mike, stepping backward to escape his piercing gaze. "I mean it. I'm gonna go to class now, promise."

Mike is quiet, but finally nods. "See to it that you stay there, okay?"

"Oh yeah. You got it." I turn to leave, but Mike calls my name one more time.

"Katrell? You can talk to me whenever you want. About whatever you want. My door is always open."

I nod and hurry back to the gym. I shiver and pull Will's hoodie closer around me, wondering if Mike heard me talking about bringing people back from the dead.

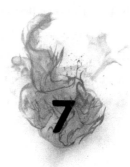

I wipe grease and sweat from my forehead with my sleeve. I'm mopping the kitchen—I always mop—while the waitresses laugh up front.

It's almost eleven o'clock; we had a hard night. Usually takes thirty minutes to close, and today it took forty-five. But I'm almost free, and I can stop by Will's on my way home to check on Conrad. She texted me earlier, but I haven't gotten a chance to read it.

Julio, my manager, pops his head into the kitchen. "Katrell? When you're done, come to the office."

I frown, but Julio disappears as quickly as he appeared.

Maybe . . . I'm getting a raise? My heart soars with hope. That'll help cover the money we're missing this month. I know I'm not in trouble—not to brag, but I'm the best employee they have. Not so good with the customers, but if they need food out fast, I'll get it to them. My coworker Sharon told me she got a raise last month, from $7.25 to $8 an hour, so maybe it's my turn.

I finish mopping and dump the bucket of filthy water down the drain in the mop closet. If I do get a raise, things will be a lot easier. I won't have to worry as much about us being short, and I can save more for the car. No, wait, I'll buy a safe so I can lock some emergency food away. And maybe I'll have enough at the end of the month to fix the leak in the bathroom. It's getting ridiculous.

I wipe my hands on my work pants and take a deep breath. Don't look too eager, play it cool. I open the door to the office.

Julio looks up when I enter. He has long hair he keeps in a low ponytail and he always wears a serious expression. Julio is a great manager—chill, doesn't work too hard. He's always telling me I work too much. He hired me six months ago, when I was still fifteen and desperately needed a job. I lied on my application about age and experience, and he could have fired me on the spot. But he didn't. We've gotten along great ever since. By that, I mean I keep my head down, answer questions with "yes sir" or "no sir," and don't get in any trouble.

"Sit down," he says, gesturing at the chair in front of his desk. I do and fold my hands in my lap. Don't freak out when he gives me the raise. Act natural.

Julio rubs the back of his neck. "Katrell, there's no easy way to say this, but . . . they're cutting your hours."

I stare at him, speechless.

"I know it's probably a shock. You're the best employee we have." Julio shakes his head, his eyes focused on something high above my head. "They told me to say it's from downsizing, but

43

here's the truth: the boss's son was whining that he wanted a job and they're giving him some of your hours." Julio grimaces. "Part of some others' too."

I try to swallow the lump in my throat, but it won't go down. Julio's words are muffled by a shrill ringing in my ears. A pay cut. I'm getting a pay cut.

"How much?" I manage to croak out.

"I put you on Mondays, Tuesdays, and Wednesdays. That's all I could do."

I was working five days a week. Monday through Friday, four to ten. Now I'm down to three days a week. From thirty hours to eighteen.

I'm going to be sick.

"I can't . . ." I clear my throat. "I can't get my hours cut that much. I need the money, Julio."

"I know, Katrell. So do I." Julio shakes his head. "I got a few of mine cut, and Roger got ten of his shaved off. All for a spoiled college kid who's too lazy to get a job in his field. Sucks, don't it?"

"Sucks" isn't the half of it. How am I going to pay rent? How am I going to keep the lights on? Mom hasn't found a job yet. Gerald doesn't share his money from Wendy's, and he works part-time anyway. We're going to be on the streets again.

"The plus side is that you'll get a four-day weekend." Julio's trying to be optimistic, but he's grimacing. "You can take some time to just be a kid. You work too hard, you know?"

"Yeah." I stand up robotically, my head fuzzy with the realization I'm going to be homeless if I don't figure something out. "I'm gonna go home."

"Okay," Julio says. "Sorry. I really am. Good night, Katrell."

After work, I tap on Will's window. When it's late like this, I don't use the front door. It would freak Cheryl and Allen out.

Will opens the window. Normally she'd be smiling, but she looks sort of frazzled. She's dressed for bed, so her hair's wrapped in a pink silk scarf, and she's breathing hard.

"I'm glad you're here," she says. "Something's up with Conrad."

Air squeezes out of my lungs in an instant. "What? What happened? Is he okay?"

"He is, but—"

I climb through Will's window and tumble into her room, heart in my throat. Conrad's sitting beside Will's bed, staring calmly at me. No blood or broken bones or anything else my brain imagined. Some of the panic dies. "He looks fine. What happened?"

Will chews at the sides of her fingers. Her nails are already short and bloody. "When I got home from school, he was fine. I tried to play with him, but he wouldn't, so I figured he was tired. But then about thirty minutes ago, he jumped up and started whining and pacing for no reason. I tried to calm him down, but he ignored me."

I frown at Conrad. Normally he'd have run to me when I came through the window, but he's still, silent. I go to his side and kneel in front of him. "What's the matter, boy?" I rub his face with my thumbs; his fur is warm and soft. His eyes stare into mine, but he doesn't move.

"He wasn't limping," Will says.

"What?"

"When he was pacing earlier." Will's still over by the window, far away from me and Conrad. "He wasn't limping at all."

I hug Conrad and get to my feet. "Maybe his leg healed when he came back? And don't worry about the pacing, sometimes dogs do that. It's not a big deal."

Will looks at Conrad uneasily. "I don't know, Trell, he's acting so weird. He won't play with his toys, and he just sits and stares at the wall all day—"

"It's fine," I snap at her. I rub my temples, trying to coax away a headache. "Sorry, I just—he's fine. He has to be. He's still getting adjusted to being, uh, alive again."

"Yeah . . . ," Will says, still looking at Conrad. "Are you staying over tonight?"

"Can't." I think of my cut hours and bite my lip. "I've got some stuff to figure out."

"What kind of stuff?"

I tell Will what happened and her face falls. "Oh no, Trell. I mean, it's sort of good though, right? You were killing yourself working that hard."

"Good?" My voice creeps up in pitch. "How am I gonna pay rent? I can't do letters anymore, so that money's out. I have some savings, but after that's gone, then what?"

"Has your mom found a job yet?"

I glare at her until she looks away. Will knows Mom has been looking for a job since she lost hers at Walmart in April. I started working at Benny's full-time to help out, but I don't mind. We have to survive somehow. Mom'll find something, she just needs more time. Will's never been a fan of Mom, but I don't take her too seriously on that. Her relationship with Cheryl is far from perfect.

"Okay, okay," Will says, sighing. "It's just that it's been six months and she hasn't even looked—"

"I'm going home," I grunt. I pat Conrad's head and go to the window. He doesn't move. "I'll see you at school tomorrow."

"Trell, I—"

I don't wait for her to finish. I clamber out her window, wave goodbye, and head home.

I rub my face with my hands, barely holding in a scream. I have to figure out what to do about Conrad. He's weirding Will out, but I can't bring him home. And what do I do about my hours? I can't give up my savings for the car—that'll help me get a better job. The thoughts cycle in my head over and over, in an endless loop. I need more hours. I need a better car. I need more money.

When I get home and unlock the door, my most annoying problem is sitting on the couch and staring me in the face.

Gerald.

He looks at me, his eyes bleary and unfocused. "Heads up, I ate the last three Pop-Tarts. Couldn't find anything else."

Rage bubbles up in my chest and my hand curls into a fist. I go to school for eight hours, work for six, come home at 11:30, and a goddamn freeloader has eaten my Pop-Tarts. After screaming at me and killing my dog. After getting Mike on my ass because of the split lip he gave me.

I'm going to kill him.

Gerald wobbles to his feet and saunters toward me. He towers over me, so I'd have to look up to meet his eyes. I stare stubbornly at his chest instead.

"You look like you got something to say, Katrell."

Don't say anything. Let him talk his talk, pass out on the couch, then go to bed. I can do this.

"Looks like my lesson sunk in." He laughs, short and cruel.

"Who knew all it took was killing the dog? Shoulda done that weeks ago."

I grit my teeth, but don't answer.

"Since you gon' mind me now . . ." Gerald leans closer, his nasty breath washing over my face. "I need some money. Like I said, we're out of Pop-Tarts."

I ball my hand into a fist to punch him in the mouth.

Gerald sees me tensing and steps back. He rests one hand at his hip, his eyebrows raised. He's still grinning. "You sure?"

First fear stalls my heart, then rage. I'm scared, scared of this filthy idiot who eats all our food and lazes around all day. I'm scared in my own home.

"I think this was good for you," Gerald says, smirking at me. "What'd you say earlier? You only respect people who earn it?"

"That's still not you." My voice is quiet and calm, but my heart's jackhammering in my chest. But I can't give in. When you give in, you lose for good, and they'll have their boot on your neck until Mom decides to move on to someone else. "I'm just not stupid, unlike you. Good luck earning anything, you freeloading meth head."

Gerald's eyes harden. "Fine, Katrell. But if you spare the rod, you spoil the child." His voice is heavy with promise. "Remember that."

I go to my room without answering and lock the door. He bangs on it, talking about respect and other bullshit, but I put on my headphones. Soon, all I can hear is heavy bass and quickly spoken words.

I close my eyes. Count to ten. Think about the car. Think about turning seventeen and dropping out and getting a better job.

Think about asking Will if I can stay at her house on the nights I don't work. Don't think about Gerald or Conrad's pacing or getting the pay cut. It's going to be okay.

I open my eyes, a little calmer. Anger seethes under the surface of my skin, itching to get out, but I ignore it and reach for my phone. Will texted me twice, one thirty minutes ago, one ten minutes ago. The first says, *Sorry about what I said about your mom. I didn't mean to hurt your feelings.*

The second says, *Conrad's upset again. He ripped up his bed.*

My heart sinks to my toes. Conrad's acting up—it must be because I'm not with him. I have to figure out what to do. He doesn't sleep, breathe, or have a heartbeat, but he's warm. He licked my hand. He knew me.

I send Will a text—*it's okay, I'm sorry too*—but she doesn't text me back. She's probably asleep. I open Twitter, then Instagram. I Google "how to hide bruises" and watch a makeup tutorial. Finally, I land on my car's page, the four-thousand-dollar car that will change my life if I can just save up enough money. It's still there, still not sold, probably because it's a piece of junk. I rub my thumb over the picture, the sudden sting of tears building in my eyes. I've been saving for years, and after dipping into the shoebox in my closet over and over, all I have is two hundred dollars. I've been spinning my wheels this whole time, desperately trying to get ahead, and what do I have to show for it? A split lip and my final two hundred dollars going to pay for rent this month. I'm never getting a car.

I'm never escaping this.

Tears blur my vision and I'm crying and I can't stop. Benny's cut my hours, we're going to be on the streets again, and we don't even have a plan B. Mom sold our car a year ago when we got behind on bills. We have no safety net. Next month, if we're short, it's over. Everything I've worked for will crumble to dust.

I cry for a long time, my hand over my mouth so Mom won't hear. When I'm spent, I close my eyes. I take a deep breath, a strange calm washing over me. There is something I can do. There's something I can try—I've known it since Conrad appeared on my doorstep, covered in dirt and his own blood. Will won't like it, Clara certainly won't like it, but it's time to see if Justin's bet pays off.

I'm resurrecting people for money.

8

I hide my face with Will's hoodie while I search for obituaries on the school computer. We're supposed to be doing research for an upcoming essay on *The Great Gatsby*, but I couldn't care less about that. Rich white men pining to death over a girl? Spare me. I need to make money, and dead grannies is the way to get there.

I've been wired since last night. I've thought about it—I should do a test run first. If Conrad truly is a fluke, I can't get people's hopes up and have it not work. I'll get my teeth kicked in if I'm not careful. So I figure I'll pick someone who just died, preferably with no family, and see if I can write a letter to resurrect them. It might work, it might not, but I have to know. I've got to do something, and soon. It's rent and lights today, but maybe food tomorrow, something else the next day. I have to know if I can do this, because if it doesn't pan out, I don't know what else to do.

A woman named Rose Theodore catches my attention. Old as dirt, glazed brown eyes. Eighty-eight, died two days ago, no living family. Hasty service yesterday, in the ground today. Perfect.

"Miss Davis, is that research for your paper?" Mrs. Harnell asks. I look over my shoulder and glare at her. I don't have to say a word; soon she gets uncomfortable and walks away to babysit the Goody Two-shoes who give a shit about Gatsby and his stalker crush. I return my attention to Rose, my chest tight with nerves and excitement. Tonight, after work, I'm going to attempt to bring her back to life.

I stand outside the local graveyard, shivering. Rose was buried at the back of an old, run-down church—no security. No people for miles. I step into the gravel parking lot, trying to ignore the looming building to my right. Churches always attract a ton of ghosts; I'm glad I can't see them without writing a letter anymore. They used to hover around me, silent, still, their heavy hands on my arms and shoulders. No sense of personal space.

I search for Rose's grave with my phone's flashlight, blowing into my hands to keep warm. It's not too cold—Octobers in Alabama are usually mild—but I don't have gloves or a thick jacket. Will's hoodie is comfortable, but thin. I find an unmarked mound of earth between two wilted, cracked gravestones marked THEODORE. I crouch beside her grave and touch the ground. It's still soft.

So, how does this work? Do I have to dig her up? Conrad just appeared at my door, covered in dirt. Maybe he dug himself up, but this lady's probably in a pine box. Will she be able to get out by herself? I walk around the grave twice, doubt eating at me. If this doesn't work, I'm going to have to do something else. But what else can I do? Will anyone hire a sixteen-year-old dropout? And if I do drop out now, won't Mom get in trouble with the school because I'm not seventeen? This has to work. It has to.

I sit cross-legged in front of Rose's grave. I prop my phone against my backpack and set it to record. If I'm successful, I'll need something to show prospective clients. Then I pull out a notebook and pen to start the letter.

I hesitate, my pen hovering over the notebook. How do I *really* know I can't do letters now? Clara could be wrong, or maybe I can do letters *and* resurrections. That would help a lot. Double source of income. I twirl the pen in my fingers. Usually my letters are long, eloquent pleas for the dead to come and see their family members who miss them . . . I can try it. Worst-case scenario, Rose comes out of the ground, and that's what I want anyway.

I spend a few minutes scratching a long letter to Rose, begging her to appear so I can ask her questions. But when I'm done signing my name, nothing happens. No fire, no smoke, no ghost. I grimace at my notebook in disappointment. Clara: 1, me: 0.

I rip out the first letter and think back to Conrad's letter. His was short, direct. I'll try that again.

Rose,

It's time to get up. Please return to the land of the living.

I debate for a while, then scratch that out. Instead, I write:

Rose,

   Wake up.

—*Katrell*

The ink ignites as soon as I'm finished with the final *l* in my name. The letter burns up and there's silence in the graveyard. My heart thumps in my ears. Ten seconds, twenty, thirty . . . nothing. Is it not working at all . . . ? Maybe Conrad really was a fluke. Maybe I've truly lost my powers and it's all over—

The ground rumbles beneath me, ceasing all thoughts. I watch in horrified fascination as the ground turns a bright red, like molten lava. First one hand, then another pushes out of the dirt, and the corpse of Rose Theodore claws her way out of the ground. She stays on all fours for a heartbeat, then rises to her full height. Like a letter, her body's engulfed in bright red fire.

The flames fade and the old woman stands before me, frowning down at me in confusion. She's painfully thin, but she's standing tall, her shoulders back. Deep wrinkles crease the dark brown skin around her eyes. We stare at each other, speechless. I did it. I resurrected someone.

I scramble to my feet. A sharp pain hits me between my eyes, but quickly disappears. Side effect? No, worry about that later— I have an honest-to-God dead person right here. Conrad can't talk, but maybe I can gauge her "aliveness" from her responses.

"Hello," I say cautiously.

She'd been looking around her, frowning at the open grave, but when I speak, she looks at me. She doesn't reply. Her eyes are dull, uninterested. But at least she can hear me.

"Do you know where you are?"

No answer.

"Do you know your name?"

No answer. She's staring at me intently now, her eyes a bit brighter. Goose bumps race up my arms and neck. I thought she'd at least talk. She's wearing a long, pretty blue dress. No shoes. Is she cold?

"Do you want to leave?" I'm trying hard to be suggestive. I have an idea of where we should go, but we'll have to walk. . . . I didn't think to bring her shoes. Next time.

The woman nods, still staring at me. Okay, progress. Gently, I take her hand in mine. She's warm, like Conrad.

We walk away from the graveyard in silence. I've got a slight headache, but it's probably normal. When I first started doing the letters, I would feel sick for days. But the more I practiced, the less bad I felt. I'll be a pro at this soon.

The woman says nothing the whole trip. I try to ask her about her shoes, if she's cold, if she's hungry, but she won't answer me. Finally, I give up and we walk in silence until we get to my master plan—the abandoned apartment building on my street. Apparently, it used to be a hub for block parties, cookouts, occasionally drugs. The health department shut the place down due to unsafe living conditions and it's been sitting empty ever since. They half-assed locking it up too, so I come here to relax sometimes. It's perfect for hiding people who shouldn't be seen.

I climb the chain-link fence, panting with the effort, and land hard on the other side. I start to open the gate for her, but the woman clambers over the fence with ease and lands beside me. Pretty athletic for someone who's eighty-eight years old.

We climb the steps to my favorite apartment, 6C. No one

bothers me here, and it's even got an old mattress. Probably better than mine at home. I open the door and the woman follows me in, looking at the room with disinterest.

"Are you okay with staying here?" I ask her.

She turns her sharp eyes to me. She's quiet for a while, then says, "Have you seen my husband, Charlie?" Her voice is soft and brittle, like dry leaves. She looks around, frowning. "He was just here."

The obituary said she had no family. Was there a husband I missed? Uh-oh. I push down the sudden panic and swallow hard. "No, I haven't. Sorry."

The woman nods absently and wanders to the mattress. She sits on it, then lies on her side. Tired, maybe? "Do you need anything? Are you cold? Maybe I could start a fire or something—"

"No." Her voice is strong, forceful. She glares at me over her shoulder. "No fire."

"Uh, okay . . ." Not a fire fan, got it. But she has to be cold. She's just wearing a dress.

I bring her the blanket I always use, but she swats it away. "Stop, Katrell," she says, her eyes staring into mine. "I don't need that."

I hold the blanket, slack-jawed. I never told her my name.

9

After school, I peek into apartment 6C. The woman lies on her side on the mattress, still. Her chest doesn't move up and down. I take a hesitant step into the room and she rolls over to look at me, her eyes dull and unreadable.

It's Wednesday, the first Wednesday I've had off work in six months, and I'm checking on the old lady I resurrected last night. I decided not to tell Will . . . yet. When I have more information, maybe she won't be so mad I went back on my promise.

"Hi, Rose. How are you doing?"

Rose doesn't answer. She sits up on the mattress, ignoring her crumpled blue dress, and folds her wizened hands in her lap. She stares at me intently.

"Um, so, how was your day?"

No answer.

This is going to be harder than I thought. I ease closer, so I won't scare her, and sit cross-legged in front of her. She continues to stare at me.

"Can you answer some questions for me?" I'm trying hard to sound gentle, but I'm starting to get annoyed. I can't sell resurrections if they just stare at me. Maybe Will was right and this was a bad idea.

Rose stares at me for a long time and then opens her mouth. "Yes."

Now we're cooking with grease. "Great! Hang on a second." I prop my phone against my backpack and set it to record. Hopefully I can get some proof that she's fully functional for future clients. And to ease Will's fears. "Do you know your name?"

She nods. "Yes. Rose Theodore."

"How old are you?"

"Eighty-eight."

"Where did you live before I brought you back?"

She hesitates, seemingly stumped. She shrugs.

I'll cut that out of the video. "That's okay. Did you sleep okay last night? And while I was at school?"

Again, she shrugs. Well, at least she's responding a little. I'll take it.

Cautiously, I move closer and touch her hand. It's warm, like it was last night. Her skin isn't leathery or cold or brittle. It's real skin, like a living person's. I'm not good at science, but I have vague memories of the scientific method. Form a hypothesis, conduct an experiment, draw a conclusion, blah blah. I'm in the experiment step and I need to get to a conclusion. I need to find out as much as possible about her so I can show my clients this is the real deal.

"Can you feel my hand?"

She doesn't answer. She's staring into my eyes.

"I'm going to pinch you," I say. "Just a little. Tell me if it hurts, okay?" I take a bit of her wrinkled skin between two of my nails and pinch slightly. She doesn't react.

"It doesn't hurt, Katrell," she says. "I don't feel anything."

Goose bumps race up my arms and I move my hand away. Does that mean Conrad can't feel my touch either? I'm glad he can't feel pain, but to feel nothing . . .

I shake my head, trying to clear it. This is about Rose, not Conrad. I'll worry about him later. "Um, were you okay while I was at school? What did you do?"

She's silent again. I'll have to cut that out of the video too.

I get up and go to my backpack, careful not to move my phone. I grab a deck of cards, a worn set a local church gave me last year. Sometimes they give out free food, sometimes they give out cards and toys. I much prefer the food donations, but at least the cards are coming in handy now. I bring the deck back to Rose.

"Can you play a game with me?"

Rose studies my face for several seconds. "Are you lonely, Katrell?"

I stare at her, openmouthed. "What?"

"I'll play with you," she says, ignoring my disbelief. She palms the cards in one hand. "What do you want to play?"

"Uh . . ." I don't know what to say. But I need to get it together for the recording's sake. "Okay. Do you know how to play—" I cut myself off. The card game that jumps into my head first is Bullshit. Is it wrong to ask a woman this old if she knows the rules?

She stares at me with dull eyes, so I blurt out, "Do you know how to play Go Fish?"

"Yes," she says.

I breathe a sigh of relief. Go Fish is pretty simple, so it shouldn't confuse her. I shuffle the deck and deal us seven cards each. I resume the recording and we start the game.

"Can I have all your sevens?" I ask.

Slowly, moving like she's stuck in molasses, she gives me two sevens. I add them to my deck.

"Can I . . ." She trails off, studying her hand. "Can I have all your fives?"

I part with two of my fives and draw two more cards, a five of hearts and a six of diamonds. "Okay, do you have any eights?"

"No," she says. "I need the final five."

I give it to her, frowning. I just drew that card. How did she guess? Maybe grandmas are good at kids' card games.

The game continues and she kicks my ass. She has six books in no time, compared to my one.

"Can I have your twos?" she asks.

I glance at my single two. She's got three twos, I know it, so I'll be handing her the game. "Go fish."

Rose stares at me for a long time. "No," she says. "You're lying."

How did she know? Is my poker face that bad? But I've always been good at hiding my emotions; I kill Will in any game that involves deception. Speechless, I give her my two.

She tucks it with her other twos. "Your turn, Katrell," she says.

We finish the game (3-10) and I pack up the cards. The sky outside is starting to gather a pink hue. I should go home. Now I have enough for a video proving I can bring people back to life.

I stop the recording while Rose watches me. It was kind of fun, hanging out with her. She doesn't say much, but that's okay, isn't it?

I could come here every day I don't have work, play a card game, then hang out with Will. Rose and I could talk. Maybe she'd have good grandma advice about Gerald. I meet her eyes, uncertainty weighing on my chest.

"Hey, do you mind being . . . back?"

She doesn't say anything.

"Do you miss your family?"

Again, no answer.

Maybe I shouldn't get attached. She's not related to me, and this is just business. I brought her back as an experiment, not to play cards with after school. "What do you think about a nickname?"

"You may call me whatever you wish, Katrell."

"How about Two? Because you're the second one I brought back."

She nods. Two it is.

I shoulder my backpack and put my phone in my pocket. "Okay, Two. I'll come back tomorrow and check on you. Do you need anything?"

Two shakes her head and lies down on the mattress. She turns away from me and looks out the single window. "No. Goodbye."

"Bye." I go to the door, hesitating. When she doesn't turn around, I leave the apartment and close the door. Time to edit my video for some prospective clients.

10

"**W**ill, don't be mad." I push open the door to 6C and reveal Two, who's sitting calmly on the mattress and staring into space. Will stares at her for a moment, then looks at me. Her eyes are huge and livid.

"You didn't."

I shrug, smiling sheepishly, and Will groans and covers her face. "Trell, what have you done?"

It's Friday afternoon, and me, Will, and Conrad are at the apartment. I considered keeping Two a secret from Will, but I caved. Will knows everything about me, and she's keeping Conrad for me too. I couldn't hide it from her. Even though she's clearly pissed off.

"Don't worry, Two's harmless," I say. "And she has no family, so it's a victimless crime."

"Two?"

"Oh, that's what I call her." I wave a hand in her direction and she glances at me. "She's experiment number two, you know? Conrad's number one."

Will shakes her head slowly, her eyes on Two. "Trell, this is crazy. This is actually crazy. You resurrected someone, on purpose!"

"That was the point." I enter the apartment and stand beside Two, my arms folded. "Listen, I spent the day with her yesterday, and I think I understand better. She doesn't eat or breathe, and no sleeping so far. But she can talk, and she's warm. She can play cards and hold a conversation. That's enough for someone who misses their family, don't you think?"

"Trell, this is madness." Will stays in the doorway, as far from Two as possible. Conrad trots into the room and sniffs Two's hand. Two pats Conrad's head. "You can't possibly think that's enough. You don't know anything about these people. Or Conrad. You don't know what you can and can't do."

"I know I can bring people back to life. What, you want me to just sit on this?"

Will nods and I snort. Fat chance.

"Okay, fine," Will says. "You said she can talk. Show me."

Uh-oh. I told Will she can hold a conversation, but that doesn't mean she will. Two barely said a word to me right after her resurrection, but she was fairly chatty yesterday. What will it be today? And there's no guarantee that what she says will make sense. I researched her husband, Charlie, at school; he's been dead for fourteen years.

"She doesn't talk much."

Will narrows her eyes at me. "Won't, or can't?"

"Won't," I say, a little force behind my words. "She can, she's just shy."

Will takes a step into the room and Two's head snaps in Will's direction. Will and I both freeze. Two studies Will and then, for the first time since being resurrected, she smiles.

"Hello, Will," she says.

Will looks at me, panic all over her face. "Why does she know my name? Did you tell her?"

"Uh, yeah." I definitely didn't. I thought Two might have known my name because I signed it on the letter, but I never even mentioned Will. . . . Well, maybe I told her I would bring Will by yesterday? I can't remember, but that has to be it.

"Did you have a good day at school?" Two is smiling at Will gently, like she's known her for years.

Will backs out of the apartment again. "Trell, I don't like this. I don't like this at all."

"Two's being friendly and you're being rude." I join her in the hallway and pat my leg for Conrad to follow. He stares at me for a few seconds before obeying. I pet his ears, and his tail wags. "But that answers your question. You see she can talk, right? Nothing preventing me from making some cash off this."

"This is wrong, Trell. It's immoral—"

"So?"

Will and I stare at each other for a long moment, our shoulders tense. We never fight, never. But Will doesn't look like she's going to back down. An unfamiliar sick feeling swirls in my gut. I want Will on my side. I need her on my side.

"Will, I'm in some trouble." My voice is soft.

"Enough to do this? To bring people back to life?"

I hesitate, looking away. "We're short on rent this month. Again."

Will's anger softens. Most of the tension leaves her shoulders. "How much? I can spot you. I don't mind."

"No, it's fine."

"Are you sure? I won't ask Cheryl. I could probably get a job after school."

At first, gratitude swells in my chest, but it's quickly replaced by anger and misery. I'm happy Will wants to help me, but I can't have her bailing me out every month. It's embarrassing, not being able to stand by myself. I have to be able to fix this on my own. "You don't get it—we're always short, Will. Always. I've used up my car savings, and Gerald eats like a pig, so our food bill is huge, and we just . . . we can't get ahead. I just want to be able to pay rent and not have to worry about being homeless."

"You shouldn't have to worry about that," Will says, a bitter edge to her words. "This is something your mom should be thinking about. She should be helping—"

"Well she can't," I snap. "Not right now. But I can help myself, you know? I can do this, and we can get a little ahead, and everything will be fine. So . . . will you help me?"

A number of emotions cross Will's face. Pain, torment, regret. I catch her staring at my healing split lip and then at my torn shoes. They're too small, ratty, dirty.

"Okay."

I look up at Will, hope in my heart. "You'll help me?"

Will sighs heavily. "Yeah. But only until you get back your savings, and then we stop. Okay?"

"Deal," I say, grinning at her. "Let's pick out who will be lucky number Three."

I check my phone for the hundredth time. It's 11:30 on Saturday night, and in thirty minutes I'll have my first resurrection client.

Well, hopefully. I picked an old letter client, a couple who lost their son, Daniel, to gang violence two months ago. They heard about me from Justin—he and Daniel were on the football team—and have been slinking nervously into alleys to meet with me ever since. I texted them and they jumped at the chance to hear my new deal. They're my best shot because they're always sobbing by the end of our sessions, begging for one more minute. They miss Daniel, bad. Bad enough to bring him back, I hope.

I put on Will's hoodie and the cleanest jeans I can find, and leave my room. Will's meeting me at the location, the alley beside the apartment building, and she'll probably get there early. She has Conrad with her, but I know she'll be scared shitless. She hates sneaking out this late, and my neighborhood isn't the safest place to be.

When I'm almost at the front door, Gerald calls me.

"Where you think you're going?"

I flip him off without turning around. I tense when I hear the couch squeak as he gets up. I could run, but I don't. I stay still, frozen, one hand on the doorknob.

"I said, where you going?"

"Out."

"Did I say you could go out?"

I finally turn around. He's close to me, within striking distance. I ball my hands into fists. Close enough for me to strike too. I open my mouth to speak, but Mom pushes between us, laughing.

"Calm down, you two," she says. Her shoulders are relaxed

and her lips are upturned in amusement. "Let me talk to her, babe. She's in her little rebellious stage, you know how teenagers are."

Gerald glares at me, but turns and goes back to the couch. A modern miracle.

Mom heads toward her room and crooks one finger at me. "Come on, don't just stand there."

I roll my eyes, but follow. At least we'll be away from Gerald's listening ears. Mom pushes the door open to her room and I'm hit with the warm smell of apples and cinnamon. Mom has several candles burning at all times. Her room, whatever house we lived in, has always been spotless. Clean carpet, immaculate bed, everything in its place. It's almost like a hospital room—clean and sterile. Mom told me once that a clean room signifies a clean mind. Whatever that's supposed to mean.

Mom rummages in the drawers of her vanity. The vanity is the only thing that's not pristine—it's full of glass trinkets and shot glasses and other junk she can't bear to part with. Mom grabs an old brush with a silver back, an alleged family heirloom despite her never telling me who it belonged to, and a small tub of hair grease. She points at the foot of her bed. "Sit down."

"Mom, I have somewhere to go," I say, sighing, but sit cross-legged on the floor beside her bed anyway. I need to meet Will, but the urgency slips to the back of my mind. How long has it been since Mom touched my hair? Probably years. Probably not since I shaved it all off.

"It won't take long," Mom coos. She sits behind me on the bed, and soon the smooth bristles of the brush run gently over my scalp. As she brushes my hair, I lean against her legs. Memories surge to the front of my mind: Mom combing my hair in front of a fireplace, twisting it into long plaits. Scolding me for getting it wet and frizzy. Kissing the top of my head when she was done and running me off to play outside with the neighborhood kids. "You oughta be shame for cutting all your hair off," Mom says now, clicking her tongue. "You had some pretty hair, you know."

I don't answer. I close my eyes instead, savoring her soft touch and the memories of when life wasn't so damn hard.

"Even if you don't have much anymore, you gotta take better care of your hair. It's dry as a bone up here."

Who has the time, honestly? My hair's lucky if I remember to scrub it a few times in the shower. I have to hold in a laugh. "Okay, Mom."

Mom pauses, just for a second. "Now, Katrell, you know you can't be talking reckless to Gerald. He just wants you to mind him, that's all. Can you do that for me?"

My shoulders stiffen and I open my eyes again. The light of the ceiling fan reflects in the glass figurine of a wolf, blinding me for a moment.

"Don't get all stiff on me," Mom says, laughing. "We're just talking."

I look at her out of the corner of my eye. She's smiling down at me, softly, and my stomach fills with lead. Mom has always been carefree, easygoing, but she was right here when Gerald shot Conrad. And I'm not wearing the makeup I use for school, so I know she can see the split lip and yellowing bruise on my face.

"Mom, I—"

"I keep trying to tell you, you can't be so disagreeable," she says. "All you gotta do is listen, say 'yes sir' and 'no sir.' It's all about ego, honey. I keep telling you that, but you never listen."

She's right, in her case. I've never seen Gerald say so much as an unkind word to her, and Mom definitely doesn't have bruises on her face. Seems like he's content taking out his aggression on me. Doesn't matter who you're punching as long as you have someone to hit, I guess.

"Now, what have we learned?" Mom runs her fingers over my scalp, soft and slow. "You're gonna go in there and apologize, and then you can go hang out with your friends however long you want. Okay?"

I struggle for words for a few seconds. I want to agree with her. I want it all to be as simple as an "I'm sorry, Gerald, can I please go out and play?" But Mom doesn't get it. It's not about apologies or being nice. It's about power. And if I give him what I have left, it'll all be over.

"Mom, I think you should leave Gerald."

The words are hard to say, words I've been chewing on for weeks, but Mom doesn't bat an eyelash. She keeps massaging my temples, her touch comforting. "Oh, honey, this is about Conrad, isn't it? It was an accident. He didn't mean to."

"But the gun—"

"He was never gonna use it on you!" Mom laughs, as if my suggestion is the funniest thing she's ever heard. "Listen, Conrad was barking, there was a lot of confusion. He was a big dog, you know? Gerald panicked. You'd have done the same thing. And you weren't making it easy on him, you know."

Heat creeps up my neck—I can't tell if it's anger or confusion or shame. She's saying Conrad's death was an accident? Or is she blaming me for it?

Mom wraps her arms around me from behind, her forearms

pressing into my neck. Her mouth is right next to my ear. "Katrell, I know you're upset, but listen to me. It's you and me, it always has been. You know I love you, you know I always make it work, so trust me and mind Gerald for a while. Okay?"

The heat dissipates and the tension leaves my shoulders. All I'm left with is shame, weakness, and the desperate wish to believe her.

"Okay."

"Good!" Mom lets me go and rises to her feet. She puts the grease away and places the brush on her vanity, next to a shot glass she got at a casino. "Now, go ahead and go out. I'll talk to him for you this time, but try to rein it in a little bit, okay? Oh, and I borrowed some money so me and Gerald can go out tomorrow night."

I stare at her, my head throbbing with her touch and thoughts of money and Conrad dying and Gerald's ego. "What? How much? Mom, what about rent—"

"With your check and letters, we have enough! You always worry so much. And this is good for you, you know? It'll get him out of your hair for a bit." Mom tips her head and kisses my forehead, right next to the bruise Gerald gave me. "Go on, have fun. Remember what I said, okay? It's me and you, like always. Hang on a little longer." Mom gives me one last smile and leaves her room.

I sit on the floor, my back pressed against her bed, for a few seconds, trying to pick apart the tangle of rage and confusion and sadness coursing through me. Then I take a deep breath, lift Will's hood onto my head, and leave the house to meet my clients.

11

Will's already waiting in the alley when I arrive. She's wrapped in a coat, a new one I haven't seen before. Dark gray, black around the collar and cuffs, six large buttons down the middle. It's nice, way nicer than any coat I've ever owned. Even Conrad has something new—he's got a dog-sized plaid sweater. How'd she get him to sit still? He hates wearing clothes. And where'd she get a sweater for him anyway? His ears perk up as I approach, but he doesn't run to meet me.

"Hey." I lean on the brick wall beside Will. I pet Conrad, and as he presses his heavy head against my thigh, I notice a splash of white paint on the sleeve of Will's jacket. "Nice coat. You've been painting?"

"Yeah," Will says, sighing heavily. "This whole thing's got me stressed to hell. I've been painting all night."

"What'd you paint? You gotta show me after you're done."

"Yeah, sure," Will says. She hesitates, just for a second. "You okay?"

I bite my bottom lip. "Tried to get Mom to talk about Gerald. Didn't go so well."

Will's eyebrows bunch. "I knew it. She's not gonna listen to you. She never does."

I rub my forearms, trying to ignore the sting of truth brought by Will's words. "I don't wanna talk about it. Have you seen the Joneses yet?"

Will shakes her head. "Not yet. But I was thinking, we don't have to do this. I can sell some of my art, maybe."

I sigh, a white cloud dissipating into the air. "You can go home if you want, Will."

"Trell . . ." Will is uncommonly close to me, shivering in the chilly night air. Conrad sits next to my feet and stares calmly ahead, as if deep in thought. "We can back out. We can still go home. There has to be another way."

"No." I breathe into my hands as footsteps approach, thinking of when I was nine and sleeping in the frigid backseat of Mom's car. "You can leave if you want, but I have to do this. I don't have any other choice."

Will is quiet and Mrs. Jones rounds the corner with her husband. Showtime.

The Joneses approach us, looking over their shoulders several times. Mrs. Jones clutches her bag with white knuckles. The Joneses have constant bags under their eyes and every week they seem smaller, like a strong gust of wind will blow them away. The first day they approached me, Mrs. Jones couldn't stop crying. Even now, they remind me of nervous rabbits, ready to bolt at a moment's notice. I guess white people would be nervous in my neighborhood, regardless of what business we're doing.

"Hello," Mr. Jones says. He glances at Will, wringing his hands. "Are we, um, ready to get started?"

I nod in response, stand up straighter, and clear my throat. Here goes nothing.

"Mr. and Mrs. Jones, I know you're anxious to see Daniel again. But do you really want to see him? In the real world?"

Mr. and Mrs. Jones exchange a confused look. Will gives me a judging glance from the corner of her eye. She's practically screaming, *Tone it down.* Okay, okay.

"My power has changed, and I can do more than talk to the dead." I put a hand on Conrad's huge head. "I can bring people back to life."

Mr. and Mrs. Jones still look confused, so I continue. "My dog, tragically, lost his life last week. But as you can see, he's back."

Mrs. Jones's face twists into a mix of horror and disbelief. "This is cruel."

"No, no," I say quickly, "it's true. Look, Conrad died and I brought him back. He's here, alive, happy. And I can do the same for Daniel, if you'll let me."

Mr. and Mrs. Jones's confusion turns into scowls. "I don't know why you're doing this, but it's not funny. If you don't want to summon Daniel for us—" Mr. Jones's voice hitches and he goes quiet.

"Trell," Will whispers. Her voice is as heartbroken as Mr. Jones's face. "Don't."

Don't. Don't do this. But what choice do I have? Benny's cut my hours. I need to pay rent and keep the lights on. I need more money. I clench my hand around Conrad's collar and his body

73

stiffens. Will can afford to be hesitant, to feel sorry for the Joneses. I can't.

I step forward and pull out my phone. "I can, and I can prove it."

I show them the video and stay silent. They gasp when Two emerges from the ground and their eyes widen when she looks at me for the first time. When it's over, I show them the videos I took during my day with Two. I made sure to focus on the moments when she acted normal and on our card game, and cut out the weird, silent-staring-at-me-creepily bits. Will looks like she's going to throw up the whole time.

Mr. and Mrs. Jones are quiet when the videos are over, so I clear my throat and speak. "As you can see, she's doing well. My dog is too. You can see your son again, Mr. and Mrs. Jones, and not just see him but talk to him for more than ten minutes. Touch him. Hug him. Have him be part of your family again. I can do that for you, if you'd like."

The couple look like I'm holding them at gunpoint; faces ashen, eyes wide and frightened. I really expected them to be happier about this. . . . Maybe this was a mistake. I exchange an uncertain glance with Will. Her mouth is a thin grimace and her eyes are sharp. *I told you so.*

"Can we . . ." Mrs. Jones's voice fails, and she tries again. "Can we have some time to think about it?"

"Of course." That's not a no, so maybe this will work out after all. I put my phone in my pocket. "You have my number. Text me when you're ready."

I jerk my head at Will and she unsticks herself from the brick wall. I nod at Mr. and Mrs. Jones and leave them in the alley to think about whether they want me to resurrect their son.

12

Mr. Thomas touches my shoulder, waking me up.

"Lunchtime, Miss Davis," he says. He nods his head to the door. "Go on, go to the cafeteria. I don't want to hear your snoring during my free time."

I wipe drool from my mouth with my sleeve. The classroom is empty except for me and Mr. Thomas. I check my phone—two minutes late for lunch already. He could have woken me up earlier, the jerk.

I get to my feet and leave the room, headed to the cafeteria. I'm starving. I slept at home last night, so there were no homemade pancakes waiting for me. But I do have a sandwich with my name on it.

When I get to the cafeteria, Will's not at our usual table. I stand by it, uncertain, then head for Will's fifth-period class. Her teacher always lets them out early, so if she's not here, something's wrong.

I don't have to go far. The hallway is empty, except for two people. Will's one of them, pinned against the lockers. The other is Chelsea, a girl from our grade. I narrow my eyes and start walking faster. Chelsea's bad news. Will and I haven't had to deal with her since middle school, but she's notorious for kicking around the freshmen any chance she gets.

As I get closer, Chelsea's low purr reaches my ears. "Come on, don't you think it's a good idea?"

"What's a good idea?" I say, startling Chelsea. Will meets my eyes and relief crosses her face.

"Oh, not you." Chelsea scrunches up her nose like she's stepped in something unpleasant. "Come to save your girlfriend?"

"Depends." I squeeze between her and Will, making both of them back away from me. "Does she need saving? What's a good idea?"

Chelsea scowls at me, her shoulders tense. "None of your business. I was talking to the mute, not her pet bulldog."

"Watch it," I warn.

Chelsea laughs, cold and cruel. "You think you scare me, Katrell? We're not kids anymore. My dad'll call the cops on you if you try anything. But based on those bruises, it doesn't look like you've been winning your fights."

I grit my teeth. "Watch your mouth, Chelsea."

Chelsea shrugs, still laughing. "I just wanted to talk to your gorilla friend, but I guess you'll butt into anything. Maybe it's for the best. She's probably too stupid to understand me, anyway."

The rage is usually slow, creeping, but I'm on fire immediately. I curl my trembling hands into fists and take a step forward.

"Chelsea." My voice is quiet. I'm looking dead in her eyes, so she knows I'm serious. "If you don't shut up, I'm going to punch you in the mouth."

I'm not kidding; I've done it before. I was suspended two years ago over Will and I'll do it again. People pick on Will because she's tall and quiet and shy. They know she won't fight back. But I will. I always have. It's all I know how to do.

"Oh, I'm so scared," Chelsea says, rolling her eyes.

So be it. I hope I wreck her thousand-dollar smile. I hope it hurts.

"Hey," Mr. Thomas barks, his head poking out from his classroom. "Stop whatever you're doing, go to the cafeteria. I mean it."

Chelsea and I don't move.

"Girls," Mr. Thomas warns. "Go. Now."

"Trell," Will whispers in my ear. "Let's go."

"I knew it," Chelsea says, laughing. She flips her long black hair over one shoulder. "All bark and no bite. Ghetto trash through and through."

I don't move until Chelsea finally breaks eye contact and flounces down the hall. The fire's at the top of my head now, smoldering, burning. I hate that girl so much. Because she's pretty and lives in a nice house on the other side of the tracks, she thinks she's better than everyone else. I hate her because even though she's rich, she always has to take and take and take. From Will, from everyone around her. I wish I'd punched her in the mouth, felt her teeth splintering against my fist. It would have been worth the punishment to see her eyes widen in pain and fear, and realize ghetto trash and silver spoons bleed the same.

"Thanks," Will says as we sit at our usual table. She's staring at her lap. "I was coming out of English and she cornered me—"

"Will, you can't let her push you around." I'm still mad, still on fire. My hand opens and closes over and over. "People will take everything from you if you let them. If she's being a bitch to you, speak up. Say something. Don't let her walk all over you."

Will says nothing. She's completely still, frozen, like a statue.

"And if she doesn't listen, you make her listen. I can't be there all the time, you know? One day someone's gonna hurt you and I won't be around. What then?"

Will nods, her eyes still on her lap. Most of the fire is gone now and I'm just tired. I sigh.

"Just tell me if she messes with you again, I'll take care of it. Anyway, I'm done. What's for lunch?"

Will looks up at me and relaxes a little when she meets my eyes. Regret fills my chest. I need to be more careful. Will is sensitive, and I just yelled at her because I missed my opportunity to punch Chelsea. I shouldn't take things out on her.

Will pushes a brown paper bag toward me. Will's mom always packs two lunches, one for me, one for Will. "Cheryl said she ran out of ham, so she hopes turkey is okay."

"Perfect." I'd eat crumbs from her mom's floor if I had nothing else. I'm always starving.

We eat in awkward silence for a few minutes. Will's still looking down at the table. Maybe I should apologize. Maybe I should find Chelsea after school and finish what she started. I know where she lives. I've been there, just once, in middle school. I left when I realized the birthday party was an excuse to make fun of my old clothes and cheap gift.

"Did you hear from the Joneses?" Will asks.

I shake my head. I obsessively checked my phone every hour

last night, but nothing. "Not yet. But it's just been two days. Maybe they need more time? It's a big decision."

Will grimaces at her sandwich. It's honey, peanut butter, and peach jelly, always. She's been eating the same thing for four years. "I'll say. You can still call it off, you know."

"Not a chance."

Will heaves a sigh. "I wish you'd listen to me, but I know you won't. 'Bullheaded,' Cheryl calls it."

"You and her talk shit about me when I'm not there? I'm flattered."

Will finally smiles, a small upturn at the corner of her mouth. "She asks me about you a lot. She was asking me if she should increase your lunch to two sandwiches."

"Yes. Please do."

Will laughs. "Okay, I'll tell her. Oh, I forgot—I have to show you something."

I wait while Will pulls out her phone.

"Remember the competition I entered? For my paintings?"

"Yeah?"

Will shows me an email. "They got back to me yesterday and said I'm in the final four."

"What? No way!" I'm grinning, warmth filling my chest. Will is an excellent artist. She's always been good, but recently she's really leveled up her skills. She works mostly with spray paint, and I've had several shirts ruined because Will wanted me to hold cardboard at a certain angle. Will hardly ever relaxes, but when she's shaking a paint can, eyes focused on a blank canvas, she seems truly happy.

Will's embarrassed now. She won't meet my eyes, but she's

smiling too. "Yep. They said I have to pick more of my stuff to show them. A portfolio."

"This is awesome! What do you get if you win?"

"An art showing at Kennings. And a scholarship."

"Holy shit." Kennings is a fancy museum, the kind where people read pretentious poetry and coffee costs ten bucks a cup. I've never been, but it's famous for being the only nice building in Mire. I've always wanted to go and hear a poetry reading, but the admission fee is thirty dollars. "You have to win. You have pictures of your stuff on your phone, right? Let me help you pick."

"I don't have them all," Will admits. Her face falls. "But I don't know if I should send my portfolio in. Chelsea's in the final four too."

Understanding dawns on me, and a surge of leftover fire flows through me. "She was trying to get you to drop out?"

Will nods, her head bowed. "She's really good. I don't know, I—"

"You're not dropping out." I lean forward, staring into Will's eyes. "I won't let you. Chelsea wouldn't have bothered talking to you if she wasn't scared. You're gonna win, okay? I'll help you. I can come over today and help you pick out paintings, and then you can rub your scholarship money in her face."

Will's expression softens and she smiles. "Okay. Deal."

The bell signaling the end of lunch rings and I scramble to shove the rest of the food in my mouth. Will and I go back to class, talking about which paintings to pick for the art contest. But I keep glancing at my phone, hoping for a text from the Joneses.

13

Will grabs a bag of chips from her backpack, opens it, and stuffs a handful in her mouth. "I hate that Rose talks to me like she knows me. Doesn't it freak you out?"

I shrug. "Maybe Two likes you. Who am I to judge the love between an eighty-eight-year-old corpse and a stunning young beauty?"

Will's lip curls in disgust and I laugh.

We're sitting on the stoop of the apartment building, waiting for Will's mom to pick her up. We went to Will's house first and picked out paintings for her portfolio. Around five, Will's mom dropped me off at home, but Will asked to stay until dark so we could hang out. We visited Two and played Go Fish, Nines, and Bullshit. Two's really good at Bullshit.

"Any news?" Will asks.

I shake my head. I've been looking at my phone every few

minutes, but nothing yet. I know Will's hoping the Joneses won't call me, but this is important. Will has a home and a family and three meals a day. She has new coats she can spill paint on and doesn't have to worry about the water getting shut off. I've got an empty shoebox and Gerald's fist that won't stop meeting my face. I don't even have my dog anymore; he's still staying with Will.

"So, say they go for it," Will says. "How much will you charge?"

"A million."

Will snorts out a laugh and I grin. "No one's going to pay you that much," she says. "And you want cash for sure, right? It's gotta be something reasonable."

True. The Joneses aren't rich, so there's no way they'd have too much cash laying around. Maybe I can feel this one out, test the waters, and then charge whatever they give. "Fine. But Justin says at least a thousand."

Will raises an eyebrow. "That's a lot for a shell."

"Excuse me?" Anxious heat floods my face. "What're you talking about?"

Will takes a chip from the bag, but doesn't eat it. She holds it delicately between two fingers for a while, then offers it to Conrad. He just stares at her. "Conrad won't eat or sleep. He barely comes when he's called. Do you really think he's the same as before? Don't you think something's off?"

I don't know what to say. Of course he's the same. He has to be. Conrad looks at me, silent, his mouth closed tight. Normally, he'd be panting, white clouds pouring from his mouth like a steam vent. Now, there's nothing but silence.

"Are you saying this isn't Conrad?"

"Not exactly, but—"

"When's your mom coming?" I don't want to talk about this anymore. Conrad's fine.

Will glares at me reproachfully. She hates it when I call her adoptive parents her mom and dad. "*Cheryl* said she'll be here in five minutes."

"So now," I say, standing, "let's go to my house before she catches us here." Will's mom is notorious for being on time.

We walk in silence. Just as we get to my yard, Will's mom pulls up next to us in her white Camry. She waves at me cheerfully from the driver's seat. "Hey, Katrell! How are you?"

"Fine, Mrs. T." I smile back. I don't know what's with Will; her mom is awesome. She's short and dark-skinned, slightly over-weight. She wears her hair in a braid and smells like lavender. Al-ways grinning, always carrying snacks. Always making sandwiches for my lunch and asking me and Will if we've brushed our teeth or whatever. Will doesn't like it, or so she says, but I think it's kind of nice.

"Did you have fun?" Will's mom asks her.

Will takes a shaky breath. She's already picking at her nails. "Y-yes."

Will's mom smiles at her, a warm one that reaches her eyes. "I'm glad! What'd you girls do?"

Will struggles for words, then looks down at her shoes. I have to hold in a sigh. Will's gotten better at talking to her mom and dad, but sometimes she'll get tongue-tied and won't say anything at all. When I first met her, I thought she was mute. It took three solid weeks of me chatting aimlessly at her during lunch for her to crack a smile. Two more for her to say a sentence to me. And when we got closer, I found out she hadn't talked to her adoptive parents in three months! That changed pretty soon after we met, but it made me realize Will is stubborn. And really scared that people will leave her. We're alike in that way, I think. Stubborn, I mean.

Will looks at me for help and I nod slightly. Katrell to the rescue.

"We just hung out," I tell her mom. "Talking about the art show. Will's gonna win for sure."

"Oh, definitely!" Will's mom laughs and Will shoots me a grateful look. I give her a grin and she smiles, rolling her eyes. "Hey, you sleeping at our house tonight? I can pick up pizza."

"No, that's okay." As much as I want to say yes, I can't wear out my welcome at Will's. If they get tired of me, I'm done for. "Maybe next time."

Will opens the back door and Conrad jumps in. I miss him, but I'm glad he's safe with them. Will's mom loves Conrad; she's always trying (fruitlessly) to teach him tricks. And she bought him a dog coat. I haven't gotten a new coat in two years. Will looks at me, just once, and climbs into the passenger seat without a word to her mom.

"All right, then, Katrell. See you next time!"

I wave as Will, Conrad, and Mrs. Tapscott disappear down the street. I turn to go inside my house, my stomach full of lead. At least Conrad doesn't have to be around Gerald.

When I open the door, Mom stands up from the couch. She comes to me, smiling, and I look at my dirty shoes. "Hey, baby. You been out with Will?"

"Yeah." I fidget, itching to get to my room.

"Well, that's good! When I was your age, I was always running around with my friends, getting into all sorts of stuff." Mom winks at me. "With lots of boys too."

I press my lips together. I haven't had a crush on anyone since I was seven years old.

"Anyway," Mom chatters, not waiting for my response, "I'm glad you're home. We gotta talk. I know you been down since Conrad, and I get it, I do, so me and Gerald are gonna take a trip for a while, to give you a break."

I frown. "Where? For how long?"

"You know that little casino up in Mississippi? I've always wanted to go." Mom smiles and strokes my left cheek with her thumb, where the bruise is slowly fading. "Give you a bit of a break, like I said."

I look at my feet again. I know what's coming next. "I can't give you any money, Mom."

"Oh, baby, just a little!" Mom coos. She moves her hand to my arm and squeezes it gently. "Just a little to get gas on the way and back. It's not for gambling, promise. Gerald has some contacts we have to meet, so it'll be perfect. And when I get back, I'm gonna really start looking for some work so I can help you out with the bills, don't worry."

My stomach sinks. I've heard this excuse before. "What kind of 'contacts'?"

Mom looks away for a split second. "Just some business. Don't worry about it."

Yeah, I'm sure. Everyone knows that Gerald runs with Marquis, Mire's most dangerous drug dealer. I don't care if Gerald goes down for dealing, but I don't want Mom going down with him. "Mom, I don't think you should—"

"I said don't worry about it." Mom's still smiling, but her eyes are sharp now, daring me to argue. Anxiety swirls in my gut, but

Mom's smart; she won't get caught. Surely. Mom's eyes soften and she strokes my arm with her thumb. "Just a little for gas, Katrell. After this, our troubles will be over. You'll see."

I bite my bottom lip. It's time. I can't hide it from her anymore. "Mom, Benny's cut my hours. I'm down to eighteen a week. And I can't do letters anymore. We have to keep the lights on."

Mom frowns. "What happened with the letters?"

I can't look her in the eye. No letters, no hours from Benny's, no call from the Joneses. It's so pathetic, I want to be sick. "I don't know. They won't work anymore. I don't know what happened."

Mom's frown deepens. "Are you sure? You can't summon anyone at all?"

When I nod, a dark expression crosses her face. But only for a second; it's gone as soon as it appears.

"Okay. That's okay, we'll figure it out." Mom's grip on my arm tightens slightly. "This is even more important now. Just a bit for gas, okay?"

"Mom—"

"You and me, remember? We always make it. We always have. And you know, this helps you too. Gerald's so angry with you right now. This is a good thing, I promise."

Slowly, as I've done a ton of times before, I dig in my backpack for two twenties and a ten and give them to her. It's my last fifty before I have to dip into my car savings. I was going to use it for a school notebook. And some more Pop-Tarts. Mom's eyes brighten immediately.

"Thank you, baby. You're so sweet. Don't worry, let me fix things." She leans close and places a wet kiss on my cheek. Then she releases my arm and disappears into her room. I can still feel the imprint of her hand on my skin.

I go to my room and shut the door. Every time. This happens every time. Twenty dollars here. Thirty dollars there. "I'll pay you back." "This'll be the last time." She didn't even bother with her usual lines this time. Just took it to waste at a casino.

I stare at the wall, a fierce burning building in my chest as the sound of zippers and Mom talking to Gerald on the phone floats to my ears. My stomach churns with shame. Why do I always give in? She's just going to blow it, I know, but every time I give in. She's my mom, that's what I tell myself, but it's sort of disgusting. Her for her shameless begging and me for being weak enough to give in.

I put my headphones on and blast music to drown out the sound of my mother getting ready for her joyride with my money. My phone vibrates twice, but I ignore it. I can't stand it if it's Will, asking me if I'm all right. I will be once I get some real cash. I will be once money is one less thing to worry about.

My phone vibrates repeatedly, like someone keeps calling me. I wait until the vibrating stops to pull out my phone. Two texts from Will, predictably asking if I'm okay . . . and one missed call from Mrs. Jones.

I sit straight up and yank off my headphones. I call her back, my heart in my throat.

"Mrs. Jones? Hello?"

"H-hello." Mrs. Jones takes a deep breath. "We talked about it, and we're in. We want you to bring Danny back tomorrow night."

14

"**S**hould we dig him up?" Mr. Jones looks at me, fear and something else in his eyes. He can't stay still; he shifts from foot to foot. For some reason, he and Mrs. Jones are dressed like they're going to church. It *is* a special occasion, I guess.

"No." I stare down at their son's grave, my heart fluttering with excitement and dread. "This will do just fine."

Will, Conrad, and I are at the grave of Mr. and Mrs. Jones's son, Daniel. Will didn't want to come, but I begged her to. Truthfully, now that I'm here, I'm nervous as hell. It worked on Two, sure, but what if it doesn't work on Daniel? I didn't account for time. Two had just died, but Daniel's been dead for two months. And I'm going to have to make up a bunch of rules about being discreet so this doesn't get out too fast. . . . A dull headache pounds behind my left eye. I massage my temples and step away from the grave. Take a deep breath, talk to the family, resurrect the kid. Easy.

"Okay, Mr. and Mrs. Jones. When he first gets up here, he might be confused. Don't crowd him."

Mr. and Mrs. Jones nod, their eyes wide. They have no idea I'm talking out of my ass. Who knows what's going to happen.

"Remember, he won't be exactly the same. But he's fully capable of talking and he'll definitely remember you."

Hopefully.

"And you need to keep Daniel away from anyone who might recognize him. Okay? You tell anyone about this, and the deal is off and he'll drop dead."

Like I actually know how to return them to being dead.

"Got it?"

"Yes," Mrs. Jones says. She trembles against the cold, clutching her purse and adjusting her green scarf. "Please, go ahead. I want to see my son again."

Okay, here we go. I take a deep breath and pull out my pen and notebook, and rip a sheet from the back. Conrad's and Two's letters were short, to the point. I touch the pen to the paper.

Daniel,

 It's time to wake up.

—Katrell

The letter burns up in my hands and a tremor runs from my feet to the grave in front of me.

Will looks around like a scared cat. Conrad stares calmly at the grave. Mr. and Mrs. Jones are dead silent. We wait ten seconds, twenty. And then the earth splits open and a disoriented seventeen-year-old boy climbs out, surrounded by fire.

Mrs. Jones gasps as Daniel looks around, seemingly confused. He's wearing a red letterman jacket, probably what they buried him in two months ago. No holes in his face from worms or whatever, thank God. He looks completely normal, human, alive. I knew Daniel. Knew *of* him anyway. He was a junior and I'm a sophomore, but I saw him in the hallways and the cafeteria. He looks exactly the same as he did before he died—short blond hair, square jaw, mean, beady eyes. His eyes meet mine and pain shoots from my temples to my teeth.

"Danny?" Mrs. Jones's voice is a trembling whisper. She moves forward, her steps hesitant. "Danny? Can you hear me?"

Daniel tears his gaze from me and focuses on his mother. A painful few seconds pass while he studies her. Then he parts lips that have been closed for months and says, "Mom?"

I step back while Mr. and Mrs. Jones weep and embrace their son. Will comes to my side, shaking her head silently, but I can't help grinning. I did it. It went off without a hitch. Daniel's talking, laughing, crying—all like a normal person. Two was just old and senile; I've got nothing to worry about. And that means I can do this again.

"I can't believe it worked," Will says, her voice shaking. With cold or horror, I'm not sure. "You okay? You look kinda pale."

I massage my temples, willing my headache to go away. "Headache. Come on, they gotta pay."

Will looks like she wants to protest, but I hurry away from her and approach the Joneses. Daniel—Three from now on—looks at me as I approach. Mr. Jones separates himself from his wife and son, his cheeks shining with tears.

"Thank you, thank you so much. I can't . . . I don't even know what to say."

I shrug, smiling. "No problem. Just remember the rules and we'll be good."

"Yes, of course. And I know this isn't much, but it's all we had. . . ." Mr. Jones puts a large envelope into my palm. The sharp edges of stacked bills jut through the paper and cut into my skin.

"How much is it?" I didn't negotiate a price, just in case I screwed it up. And I wanted to see how much two desperate parents think their son is worth.

"Thirty-five hundred dollars."

I stare at him, speechless. 3.5K. Three thousand five hundred dollars. In cash.

I'm rich.

"Bless you," Mrs. Jones says, but I can barely hear her. I open the envelope and stare at the stacks of twenties bound with thick rubber bands. Mom could go on a hundred trips to Tunica with this. Hell, I could go, if I wanted. And I can finally buy those damn Pop-Tarts and avoid Gerald threatening to shoot me.

"We should go," Will whispers, tugging on my sleeve. I snap back to reality. It's cold and we're in a graveyard with a recently raised-from-the-dead person. I gotta get out of here.

"Bye," I say hastily, shoving the money into my hoodie pocket. "Remember what I said, okay? Text me if you have any problems."

"We will," Mr. Jones says as Mrs. Jones lovingly brushes dirt out of Three's hair. I wave goodbye and back away from them. Three stares at me, his eyes boring into mine.

"Goodbye, Katrell," he says.

A cold shiver snakes up my spine. I tug on Conrad's collar and turn to go home to count my money.

15

I straighten my new jacket and wait for Will to arrive at the nicest restaurant in town.

I scratch under one sleeve absently, looking at my phone. Three texts from Mr. Jones: pictures of Three and his family eating dinner, playing a board game, and watching a movie. A text from Mrs. Jones, simply saying *thank you*. One from Four's family: a resurrected husband and his wife sitting on a porch and smiling. I scroll past them all to get to Will's number so I can call her.

"Sorry, I know I'm late."

I look up as Will slips into the seat across from me, out of breath. She's wearing a pretty green dress, silver earrings, and a thin necklace. Her hair, normally straightened, is wrapped in a neat bun. "You better be sorry. Had all these white people eyeballing me," I say.

Will looks over her shoulder nervously. "I feel like they're watching me too."

It's been a little over a week since I resurrected Three, and I decided to treat me and Will to the first nice dinner we've ever had. With this much money, one nice dinner can't hurt, right? I also bought a new jacket. I needed a warmer one with the right length sleeves, but it's nowhere near as nice as Will's new coat. Mine is stiff and itchy and I kinda wish I could just wear Will's hoodie. But you can't wear hoodies to a fancy restaurant. I'm already pushing it with my ancient bright red headphones wrapped around my neck.

Will smooths her dress. "Did you already order?"

"Nah, I was waiting for you." I push a menu in her direction. It's heavy and thick and made of real leather. "Look at this. Twenty bucks for hyped-up mac and cheese."

"No way."

"I'm not kidding. Wish I was."

Will and I shit-talk the rich-people menu for a while, giggling nervously at the prices. Will's adoptive parents aren't rich by any means, and most of her life she's lived the slum life like me. We don't belong here. It's apparent from the judgmental stares of our neighbors, crystals dangling from their earlobes and diamond necklaces laced around their throats. But I'm not leaving. I refuse. I deserve something nice, for once, and I'm going to get it.

"How's Conrad?" Will asks me after we decide on our entrées.

"Good." Conrad's been staying with me this past week. After I resurrected Three, I came home to an empty house and a hastily scribbled note from Mom on the kitchen table. For once, I have the house to myself. Not having to see Gerald's ugly face and snuggling with Conrad's warm body at night have been so peaceful. "It's been nice, because it's just us."

"Your mom's *still* not home?"

I shrug.

"Trell." Disappointment drips from Will's tone.

"It's fine, really. It's like a mini vacation."

"But it's been a week. Aren't you worried?"

I bite my bottom lip. I want to say yes, I am worried, she's been gone for too long with that violent dog-killer and every time I text her, she doesn't answer. I want to say I'm getting scared that she got caught dealing drugs with Gerald. But I don't. Instead, I smile at Will and offer her some complimentary bread.

"Okay, okay." Will takes a dinner roll and one of the butter cups. She carefully paints the surface of her roll with a thin layer of butter. I've already finished eating mine by the time she starts a coat on the inside. "We don't have to talk about it."

"Good," I say, giving her an exaggerated smile. The less I have to think about it, the better. She'll come back. I'm sure she's just lying low for a bit.

Will finally takes a bite of bread. "Anyway. How are the Revenants doing?"

"The what?"

"I named them. The"—Will glances behind her and whispers—"the people you resurrect. They're not like zombies, because they can talk and don't eat people. So let's call them Revenants."

"Sure, okay." Will reads a lot and loves research; better her do it than me. Revenants has a good ring to it. "They're good. Clients keep sending me pictures and thanking me, and I guess that's weird. But I'm happy for them."

"You haven't resurrected any without me, right?"

"No, I'm still at four. Including Conrad."

"How much . . ." Will trails off, but I know what she means.

I lean closer. "Seven thousand two hundred and thirty-six dollars."

"Holy shit," Will breathes. "You have enough for the car now, right? And extra for savings!"

"Yep." I can get the car and . . . then what? I sit back, arms crossed, frowning. Every night before bed, I count the money and store it in hollowed-out books and under the floorboards. It's comforting to know I have a little savings now, but still . . . there's no guarantee an emergency won't happen. What if Mom gets in trouble at the casino and we have to pay someone back? What if Gerald breaks my arm and I have to pay for a cast? That money is a security blanket. I can sleep easy knowing it's there. But if I spend it on a car, it'll be gone and I'll be right back where I started.

"Trell?" Will's watching me, her eyes slightly narrowed. "What's wrong?"

"Nothing," I say quickly, my mind on coats I can't afford and my mattress without a bed frame. "Just thinking."

She starts to say something, but our waiter finally shows up and we order a meal worth over a hundred dollars. As he walks away, my skin crawls and I pull my new jacket closer to my body. I've been really cold lately, and spending this much money on food . . . I shudder. Spending money and not hoarding it will take some getting used to.

"What were you thinking about?" Will asks.

I draw a small circle on the white tablecloth with my finger. "I was thinking that this dinner is expensive."

Will's expression melts into an anxious one. "I brought money, I can pay for mine—"

"No, no, I'll pay for us tonight. That's not what I meant." I watch the waiter stop by our neighbor's table and refill their wineglasses. "I was thinking that maybe we could . . . live like this all the time."

Will stares at me for a few seconds, and then understanding dawns on her. "Trell, you're not thinking about continuing the resurrections, are you?"

"I was just thinking about it." My voice has a defensive edge. "Haven't you thought about how it feels to have money? Real money, like them?" I nod at a white woman to our right, whose bag probably costs more than a month's rent.

Will puts her elbows on the table and leans forward. Her face is calm but alert and her shoulders are tense. "Okay, say you continue resurrections. You make thirty-five hundred a resurrection, right? What'd you do with the money?"

"I'd save up, to pay bills," I say, shivering slightly. It's freezing in here. I guess heat is for poor people.

"You have seven thousand dollars. That's more than enough for bills."

"So you'd think. But it's not, not even close. Seven hundred and thirty is what I have to have each month. If I add food, it goes up. Here's reality, Will: Every month, I have to come up with one thousand one hundred and thirty dollars. That's rent, utilities, food. Food, water, shelter. Basic necessities." I type the number into the calculator app on my phone and multiply it by twelve. "That's thirteen thousand five hundred and sixty dollars a year. Every year. And that's not including clothes, and school stuff, and anything else. I have to have almost fourteen grand just to keep breathing."

Will bites her lip, her eyes downcast. I know she's been where I am, but now that she has Cheryl and Allen, she hasn't had to think in numbers like this for a while. How soon we forget. "But, Trell, what are you gonna do? Resurrect everyone you can find? You'd have to have a whole town full of dead people to actually turn this into a full-time job."

"Yeah," I say, thinking of turning Mire into an aboveground graveyard. "But maybe I could charge more. Thirty-five hundred is a steal, honestly."

"Trell, come on." Will hates that I charge as much as I do. But I really am undercharging. I should double my prices, at least.

"I was just thinking," I say, trying to ease the tension. "Just wondering, you know? I'd like to sleep easy sometimes. And I'd like to give some to Mom so she can work at getting a new job."

Will's expression melts into one of anger. "That woman doesn't deserve a cent of your money, Trell."

"Hey, that's my mom," I warn. But Will's hands are clenched and she's glaring at the bread basket.

"I know. And she's run off for a week with the guy who beats you. Sorry I don't have a high opinion of her."

My mouth is as dry as cotton. I knew Will didn't like Mom, but she's never said anything like this. I look down at my lap, confused. I really thought this night was going to be more fun.

"Anyway," Will says after a moment. Her voice is shaky; I don't think she meant to say what she did. "Fine, fourteen thousand. That's enough for a year, right? Then we can stop. Honestly, I can't wait for this to be over. I hate watching them come out of the ground."

"But—" I'm interrupted by a violent sneeze. When I look up from wiping my nose on the expensive tablecloth, Will's frowning at me.

"Are you all right? You look kinda sick."

I look away. "Yeah. I'm fine. Allergies."

"In October?"

Will's relentless when she knows I'm lying. "Okay, fine. There is a problem."

"Yeah?"

"I'm having side effects after resurrections." I touch my temple, which is sore from my constant massaging. "Headaches. And I'm kind of cold?"

Will's frown deepens. "Does it get worse every time you do it?"

I consider lying, but she's staring right at me, through me. "Yeah."

"You have to stop." Will shakes her head uneasily. "We can come up with the rest of the money some other way, okay? We're already doing something we shouldn't, and now you're sick—"

"I'm fine," I snap. Will thinks the resurrections are creepy, but they're my ticket out of homelessness. Maybe my ticket out of a lot of things. I couldn't care less about a cold. "I'm doing more resurrections. It's easy money, and I can finally start saving some. And spending some."

"Can't spend your money if you're dead."

"Don't be dramatic. It's just a headache. Hell, maybe I'm getting sick and it has nothing to do with the Rev-whatever."

"Revenants. And listen, Trell, I'm worried—"

"I'll handle it." A familiar, slow rage is building in my gut. "I'll handle it like I handle everything else."

Will doesn't say anything for a full minute. She looks a little angry, a little sad. Finally, she sighs.

"Okay. Fine."

The anger disappears and I'm left empty and sorry for snapping at her. Will means well. She always lets me sleep at her house on bad days. She brings me lunch every day because she knows I can't afford it. It's not her fault we live very different lives. I shouldn't take anything out on her. "Hey, sorry. I'm okay, I promise. If it gets worse, I'll think about quitting."

"Just think about it, huh?" Will puts a hand under her chin. "I'll hold you to it."

Will and I finish dinner, talking about the art contest and school and not Revenants. When I get the bill, it's one hundred fifty-three dollars. I swallow hard, and it feels like I'm eating acid. I painfully part with nine twenties and stand. I'm never coming here again, rich or not. Lobster isn't even that good. Will and I walk out of the restaurant and into the cool night. I look for the familiar white Camry, but Will's mom isn't here yet.

"I'll admit, a car would come in handy right about now," Will says, looking up at the overcast sky.

"Oh, shut up, you won't even drive." I move closer to her, so I can mooch off her warmth. I'm careful not to touch her. "When I get a car, I'll teach you."

A ghost of a smile crosses Will's face. "I'll hold you to that too."

We wait in comfortable silence, our hands millimeters apart, for her mom to pick us up and take us home.

16

Mike leans down, smiling, and peeks into my hiding place under the bleachers. "Skipping physical education again, Miss Davis?"

"Piss off," I say, but I'm smiling too. Today is a school day, and it's been a pretty good one. I've secured another resurrection client, and they've agreed to meet me in the graveyard beside Waffle House. The best part is that they agreed on my newly upped prices—five thousand dollars. Last night, I dreamed about getting a new bed frame, so I'm in a fantastic mood. Good enough to humor Mike.

"It's good for you," Mike says. "Gets your blood pumping, socialization, camaraderie."

I pat my not-so-flat belly. That's one bad thing about eating one meal a day; your metabolism goes haywire. I'm a comfortable size 14, with no signs of getting thinner. Which is a good thing, because I'd have to buy a whole new wardrobe if I gained or lost anything. I maintain my size 14 at all costs. "Do I look like I want to go to PE?"

Mike rolls his eyes, still grinning. "Why don't you come to my office for a bit? If you do, I'll write you an excuse."

Tempting. "Why? What do you want?"

"Just to talk. Give me ten minutes, tops."

I sigh, but pick myself up off the ground and dust off my jeans. They're not new like my jacket—I haven't been able to buy clothes yet. Or anything else. I've only spent money on one overpriced dinner and one itchy jacket. "All right, lead the way."

I follow Mike to his office, a glorified closet near the principal's office. The huge desk and stacks of beige filing cabinets make it seem even smaller. His desk is a mess of loose papers, manila folders, and coffee-stained documents. The only trinket on his desk is a photo of his husband, a short, heavy man with a brilliant smile. I sit in the wooden chair across from Mike's, and I'm reminded of my meeting with Julio. Suddenly, unease fills the pit of my stomach. Seems like I only get bad news when I'm sitting on this side of a desk.

"Okay, first, how are you?" Mike smiles at me kindly. "How are you feeling?"

"I'm good." I stare at Mike, daring him to push me.

Mike's smile only gets wider. "Okay. I believe you. We've established mutual trust, yes?"

"Yeah, yeah, get to the point, Mike." I lean back against the chair. "Which old fart snitched on me?"

"Let's call them something else," Mike says, chuckling. He pulls out a file from the mess on his desk and opens it. "I'll get to the point, though. Your history teacher, Mrs. Wary, is concerned about you. She says you've been sleeping in class."

"So?"

"So, if you're asleep, you're not learning." Mike leans his elbows on his desk. "Why're you sleeping in class, Katrell?"

"Maybe because I'm bored and don't care what Mrs. Wary says."

Mike nods, seemingly deep in thought. "Okay, let's pivot: Have you thought about what you're going to do after high school?"

I shrug. The answer is no. I assumed I'd work at Benny's for a while, or maybe somewhere similar for better pay. I'm not really thinking about the future. I'm worried about right now.

"Based on your transcripts last year, I noticed you're good at math and English. Very good grades in creative writing. Biology and history could use some help, but you're a hard worker. Maybe we can brainstorm based on your interests."

"No thanks." I sigh, weary of this conversation already. "Are we done, Mike? I appreciate your concern, but I'm not going to college. This is it."

"Wait, wait." Mike rummages in his desk and pulls out a folded glossy pamphlet. He gives it to me and I scan the cover. *Trade school*. "College isn't the only option, you know. Just think about it."

I roll my eyes, but put the pamphlet in the front pocket of my backpack. "All right. Can I go?"

"Not yet." Mike's grin returns. "We need to talk about truancy, Katrell."

"Oh boy."

"Don't act surprised. Are you aware you've been late to school eleven times this semester?"

I didn't know it was that many. I shrug, not looking him in the eye.

"Each tardy counts as one-third of an absence. So, you have three and two-thirds of an absence. You get up to seven unexcused absences and you're in trouble, Katrell."

I've been careless. If I get in trouble for truancy, they'll make Mom go to court. Everything really will fall apart then. I grip my knees and nod. Mike's annoying, but he saved me this time. Got to be more careful.

"Okay, good." Mike closes the file. "We'll take things one day at a time. First, try coming to school on time. Once we've mastered that, we'll address sleeping in history. Maybe we'll even get to your failing grade in PE!"

"Hilarious."

"I was also thinking we could talk about why you've been late." It's phrased as a statement, but there's a question in his voice, asking how much information I'm willing to give up. "Is it transportation? Or perhaps something else?"

I weigh my options. I'm not going to tell Mike about Gerald, but he brings up a good point. If I got a car, I wouldn't be late for school. But if I do get a car, that eats into my "have to" money. Maybe fourteen thousand isn't enough.

"I have to walk to school," I tell Mike, my mind on the Craigslist blue Honda. "And I wake up late sometimes. So I'll just have to leave earlier in the morning."

"Tired?"

"I work a lot." As soon as I say it, I curse my carelessness. Mike's sharp eyes are looking right at me.

"How many hours do you work each week?"

"Thirty." Mike's eyebrows shoot up to where his hairline would be if he had one. "Calm down, it's not that bad," I say. "And I don't work thirty hours anymore, so it's fine. My hours got cut two weeks ago."

Mike seems like he's struggling to find something to say. After a few long seconds, he leans back in his chair, no longer smiling. "Again, Katrell, are you okay? Is your situation at home safe and healthy?"

"I'll leave right now, Mike."

Mike holds his hands up, palms facing me. "Okay, hang on. I'm only asking because I'm worried. Please, just be honest. Are you safe and healthy in your current environment?"

I look at my ratty shoes, at the three-week-old stain at the bottom of my jeans. "I'm fine."

Mike pauses, then nods. "I'm going to believe you, because I trust you. So if that changes, if something happens, you can come to me. Okay?"

"Okay." I fidget in the hard chair. "Are we done?"

Mike's eyes soften. "We can be done." I stand and Mike opens the door for me. "My door's always open, Katrell."

"I know." I walk out of Mike's office, a strange mix of anxiety and peace churning in my chest. But I can't think about Mike anymore—it's time to think about my next resurrection.

17

I pace outside the cemetery, my eyes on my phone. The glow of the Waffle House sign next door illuminates the graves with an eerie yellow. Conrad follows me with his eyes, his body still. Will's supposed to meet me here, but she's fifteen minutes late. I've called twice—no answer. I chew on my lip, tasting a bit of blood. I start to call the client and cancel so I can go to Will's, but her picture pops up on my phone. I answer immediately, my stomach flooding with relief.

"Where are you? Are you all right?"

"I'm okay." Will's whispering, even lower than normal. "Sorry, I—I'm trying not to get caught with my phone. Cheryl caught me sneaking out."

"Holy shit." Will and I have always snuck out since I started my letter clients, but she's never been caught before. Her mom and dad are in bed by ten o'clock. "What happened? What'd she say?"

"This is the second time, so she was pissed," Will says. "She kept asking me where I was going and why I was going out so late. But I didn't tell her, don't worry."

"What do you mean 'second time'?"

"Remember? I came to your house when Conrad died."

Guilt surges through me. I barely remember that night, except that I was rude to Will and she left. I didn't know she got caught by Cheryl. "What'd she do?"

"I thought she was gonna beat my ass," Will says, huffing a little laugh. "But she didn't. I'm grounded, apparently. But she forgot to take my phone, so I called you before she remembers."

"Grounded? I thought only white kids got grounded."

"I know!" Wonder touches the edge of her words. "I really thought she was gonna hit me. But she didn't. She even called Allen, and he didn't hit me either. He just lectured me about how dangerous it is to go out at night by yourself."

Warmth spreads through my body. I keep telling Will her mom is awesome, so maybe she's starting to believe me. "Good for you. What's grounding like?"

"So far, a slap on the wrist," Will says. "She took my laptop and said no TV for a week. But I can't come to resurrections anymore. Not for a while, anyway."

Unease jumps into my chest, but I beat it down. This is good for Will. She's always been creeped out by the resurrections. I'll miss her, but I don't want her to get in trouble with her parents. Not over me. "It's okay. I have Conrad, so I'll be fine."

"You sure?" Will asks. "I can maybe—"

"It's fine, I swear," I reassure her. Conrad's ears perk and I turn around—my clients are pulling up in the parking lot. "I'll text you later, they're here."

"Okay, be careful. Text me if something happens and I'll be right there." We say goodbye and I hang up.

I smile at the approaching clients, shoving the mix of sadness and warmth to my toes. "Welcome. Who would you like to bring back tonight?"

I pull my new jacket around me, shivering, as I walk home from the cemetery. Five, a young mother who died in a car accident, has been successfully resurrected and reunited with her family. And, with the five thousand dollars her husband gave me, my problems are one step closer to being over. Despite my good mood, my head is pounding with a dull headache. I pinch the bridge of my nose and hope the pain goes away.

Conrad's nails click on the pavement as he walks beside me. What does he think about resurrections? He's always so calm, almost disinterested. He's been calm since he came back to life.

"Conrad, what're you thinking?"

Conrad looks up in response to his name. I pet him and his tail wags, just once.

"Do you think I should quit my job?" I adjust my backpack, reaching into the front pocket for his stuffed lamb. We haven't played fetch in a while. "Yeah, wouldn't that be nice. Gotta work to eat, bud." I stop walking and Conrad turns, meeting my eyes. I hold my arm like I'm going to throw the lamb, but he doesn't move. "Ready? Catch!"

When I toss the toy, he doesn't leap for it. He stays still, paws firmly on the ground, and the lamb bounces off his head. He looks at me for a long moment, then turns around and trots toward home.

Well. Not in a playful mood, I guess.

I scoop the lamb from the ground, wiping dirt and gravel from its worn fur. I stare at the toy, struck with a pang of sadness. What's wrong with me? He's probably just tired of this one. It's old and dirty, and it doesn't even have eyes anymore. I'll get him a new one.

I massage my temples as I round the corner to my house. I reach into my backpack, trading the lamb for my keys. "God, my head's killing me. Do dogs get headaches?"

Conrad stares at the house as we approach, his muscles stiff.

"Do you feel any pain?" I pet Conrad's head and scratch behind his ears, unease in my chest again. He doesn't react. Does he feel anything at all?

I unlock the door and Conrad shoots inside as soon as I open it. Someone gasps and a light flicks on, and I'm staring right at Mom and Gerald.

Shit.

"What the—" Gerald leaps to his feet as Conrad enters the living room. Gerald's eyes are bulging and red and he pulls the gun from the waistband of his pants. Conrad's body tenses and the fur along his spine stands straight up. "I killed this mutt! I killed it!"

"Leave him alone!" I shove myself between Gerald and

Conrad, backing up so Conrad has to back up too, putting distance between him and Gerald. Conrad's nose is hot against my back.

"You better explain yourself." Gerald's voice is a commanding growl, but he looks wild and panicked. He's high as hell, one hand clutching the pistol. My heart pounds in my chest.

"This is a new dog," I blurt out. "A stray I found. He just looks like Conrad."

"You must think I'm a goddamn idiot. It's got a mark where I shot it!"

Fuck.

"You explain, Katrell, right now." Gerald grabs my arm in a tight grip, his too-long nails digging into my skin. He shakes me once, hard. "Why is that dog alive and in my house?"

"Your house?" My temper flares and I jerk my arm free. "This is my house, you shit-stain. What I do is none of your business. What dog I bring into the place where I pay rent is none of your business either—"

Gerald punches me in the mouth.

Blood spurts from my split lip and I yelp in pain. He hits me again, and adrenaline takes over. I shove him away, my teeth gritted, and Gerald aims the gun at me.

Mom looks fearfully back and forth between us. "Please, please stop. Calm down, she's just a kid—"

"She gon' learn to watch that mouth," Gerald spits. He's so furious, he's shaking. "I'm off trying to fix everything and I come back to this shit? Explain this damn dog, Katrell, or I'll kill it for sure this time."

I start to say something, fear and fury making me light-headed, but Conrad lifts his lips and snarls at Gerald. He's never growled at anyone before in his life. Not even before Gerald killed him.

"Shoot, then," I grunt, my heart pounding raggedly against my ribs. "Shoot, if you think you're bad enough. You wanna see him come back again? What makes you think he'll stay dead?" I jerk my head at my snarling dog. "If you shoot me, he'll rip your throat out. If you shoot him again, I'll do it."

Gerald's chest is heaving. "You're a witch," he says. "You're not normal."

"What're you gonna do, Gerald?" My head is pounding; it's like Conrad's growling is coming from inside my skull.

Gerald puts the gun back into his waistband and my knees almost collapse with relief. "Keep it away from me," Gerald warns, and lurches toward the door.

"Gladly." When he's in the yard, I lean out the door and yell, "If you hit me again, I'll kill you! You hear me? I'll fucking kill you!"

I slam the door and lock the dead bolt so he can't get back in. Conrad stops growling and looks up at me, his eyes dull. I pet his head and point to my room. He follows my instruction without me having to say anything.

There's a long silence while Mom and I stare at each other. She looks exasperated, like I've ruined her peaceful night. "Oh, baby. Hang on, let me get you some ice."

Some of my fury fades while she wraps a dish towel around loose ice cubes. She presses the makeshift ice pack to my bloody lip and I wince. I look at the floor, trying not to cry. My lip throbs in time with my heartbeat—fast and painful. I get a sudden, fierce longing for Mom to brush my hair.

"A new power, I see," Mom says, running her thumb over my quickly forming bruises. "One you should've kept hidden."

"Mom, I didn't—"

"Katrell, I told you, *told* you, not to do anything except letters around anyone. It scares people." She sighs and shakes her head. "And now look what happened."

My hands curl into fists. Mom made me promise to hide my powers when I started scaring her boyfriends off by talking to people they couldn't see. And I did; I have for so long. But how am I supposed to hide this? Wait, why should I have to hide it? Why is this my fault? "Why are you taking his side? He punched me for no reason, just 'cause he could. He's such an asshole—"

"Katrell," Mom warns. She's dabbing at my lip, but her eyes are narrowed and focused.

Pain and leftover anger give me strength. "Mom, you can't just ignore this." I fight back frustrated tears. "You can't ignore him hitting me."

"I told you not to bring that weird stuff here." Mom's voice is hard, venomous. "Now you've gone and made Gerald upset, and you paid for it. This fat lip is your fault. All you have to do is listen to me, and you can't even do that. I took him away to give you a break and this is how you act when I get home? Screamin' and carryin' on like you're a child?"

Anger rushes into me so fast, it scares me. "Maybe if you weren't dating a lunatic who killed my dog, this wouldn't have happened."

"Katrell." Mom's voice is a lethal whisper. "You better think hard about what you say next."

I don't answer. It's shameful, but I'm cowed by her anger. I'm not scared of Gerald. I am scared of her when she's mad. Boy-friends come and go. Mom will always be here.

Mom takes a deep breath. She keeps her eyes closed for a few seconds and her expression smooths. She opens her eyes again, smiling. "I'm sorry, it's been a stressful day. For Gerald too, you know? You can't be pushing his buttons, you know that. I'll tell him what's going on, then it'll be fine. Just keep Conrad in your room, okay?"

I nod, trembling, blood from my lip oozing into the corner of my mouth. I pull my face from her hands, go to my room, and close the door. I hear the front door open and close.

As soon as I'm alone, I burst into tears.

My lip throbs and my head hurts, but the pain in my chest hurts worse. I'm crying and I can't stop. It's all hitting me at once—Gerald is a jackass and Will can't come to resurrections anymore and I'm so tired all the time, and everything was going so well and they just had to come back. Everything was going okay without them. Why did they have to come back?

Why am I even thinking this? I wanted Mom to come back. I did. I have to. She's my mother. She's been here from the beginning, before Will, before Conrad. We're family. I have to hold us together. Even if that means resurrecting people so we can pay the bills. Even if that means swallowing the fact that Mom loves Gerald more than she cares about my bruised cheek and bloody lip.

I sink to the floor, sobbing, and cover my eyes. Conrad sits on my mattress, calm, distant. He used to be so lovable. He would have kissed my tears away before. But he's just sitting there, staring at me. That's all he does now. Stares at walls, at Will, at me. He won't even play with his stuffed lamb anymore.

I have a headache.

I curl up beside Conrad and bury my face in his fur. My head throbs with the beat of my heart.

Eventually, the front door opens and Gerald and Mom return. They're arguing. The words "freak" and "witch" float to my ears. Their muffled voices aggravate my headache until it's almost unbearable. Even after their voices subside, the pain doesn't go away.

I toss and turn on my creaky mattress for hours, sweating, burning. My headache has evolved from a dull ache to a sharp, piercing pain between my eyes. It moves from side to side—it's like there's a bug in my head. I grind the heels of my hands into my eyes, groaning, then sit up. I can't sleep like this. There must be some Advil in my backpack.

A soft scratching sound pulls my attention to the window . . . where the shadow of a person waits.

I scream, but quickly stifle it with my hands. The shadow stands still, like a statue. Oh shit. Who is it? Gerald? I look to Conrad in disbelief. He always used to bark when someone stepped foot in the yard. Now? Silence. He stares at me calmly, unmoving.

Okay, think. Conrad isn't barking or growling, so it's probably not Gerald. Maybe someone is playing a prank on me and left a mannequin outside my window. I take a deep breath and move the curtain out of the way.

And look straight into the eyes of Two.

18

snatch my window open, half furious, half relieved. "What the hell are you doing here? Are you all right?"

Two stares at me. She doesn't answer.

I reach for my new jacket, then grab Will's hoodie from my desk. "Stay there. I'm coming outside."

I pull on the hoodie and shoes and join Two outside, Conrad close behind me. Two turns to me, frowning, but stays silent.

"Okay, what's going on? Are you hurt?"

Two shakes her head slowly.

"Okay, good. Why are you outside my window in the middle of the night?"

Two seems confused. She looks into my room for a while, then at me. "Have you seen my husband, Charlie?"

Oh boy. I really don't need this right now—my head's still killing me. The pain is ebbing, though, thank God. "Let's go back to the apartment, okay?" I grab her hand gently and she lets me take it. I lead her back to the apartment building and up to room 6C. I tell her to lie down and she does, facing the wall. I put a hand on her shoulder, hesitant. I resurrected Two as a test, but what am I going to do with her? She doesn't have a family like the rest of them. Am I going to take care of her for the rest of my life? How long do Revenants live?

"Stay here, okay? Just rest."

Two stares at the wall, her eyes dull and unfocused. She doesn't respond.

I stand and back out of the abandoned room, then call Will. My hands are shaking.

"Hello?" Will's voice is soft and sleepy.

"I'm coming over." I put my hood on my head and Conrad stares at me blankly. "Open your window."

In the half-light of sleep, everything is blunt, muted. I'm curled up on soft ground, has to be Will's floor, and noises are all around me. The quiet squeak of a mattress. Running water. A stifled yawn. Someone pulls a blanket up to my chin and I bury myself further into sleep.

"Trell." Will's familiar voice floats into my ears. "Trell, wake up. We gotta go to school."

I open my eyes, light flooding my senses. Will's cream walls and the stuffed panda she keeps by her desk swim into focus. I close my burning eyes again. My face throbs faintly and exhaustion threatens to drag me back to sleep. At least my headache is gone.

"You okay? You look awful."

I look up at Will groggily, my mouth cotton. "I'm so tired. You'll never believe what Two—"

"Holy shit, what happened to your face?" Will reaches for my cheek, but her hand falls away before she can touch me. I touch my right cheek instead; a shooting pain jerks through my face and I flinch. "Oh my God, your eye . . . Trell, what happened? Gerald?"

I'm wide awake now. I sit up and grab my phone, and turn on the front-facing camera. I wince at the image. My face is swollen and dark, and my right eye won't open all the way. Fucking Gerald—I can't go to school like this. Mike will call DHR in a heartbeat and then I'll be sent to foster care. Who knows what'll happen to Mom. This will have to be absence number four.

"Hey, look at me." Will's eyes are huge, like a startled deer's. "This looks bad. Do you need to go to the doctor?"

"And let them call the cops on me?" My mouth is dry and sour. "It doesn't matter. Listen, something wild happened last night." I tell Will about Two showing up at my house. Her eyes get even wider.

"What're you gonna do?" She puts her fingertips to her mouth, already about to chew on her nails. "This is bad, Trell. What if someone had seen her? She just died, so people are gonna remember."

"I know." I bite my bottom lip, wincing at its tenderness. "I'll figure it out. Just keep an eye out for her, okay?"

Will nods, picking at her bloody cuticles. All the polish is gone. "I don't like this. It feels bad. Maybe you should call the families? To check on the Revenants?"

"Not yet. Two's just old, and I don't want to scare them." I stand and stretch. "Anyway, I gotta find a place to crash for a while. Till Gerald calms down."

"You can stay here."

Will is staring at me, her eyebrows scrunched with determination.

"You can stay here," she repeats. "I don't like Gerald hitting you. When I was little—" She cuts herself off, then shakes her head. "You know."

I do know. Will's history with foster parents has been horrific. One locked her in a closet for three days. One burned her with cigarettes and made bets with his wife if she would cry. Plenty were just indifferent, neglectful. She's dealt with her fair share of Geralds. But she's forgetting that I have too.

"All I'm saying is I care about you, Trell. And I don't want you to get hurt. I'm scared he's gonna kill you."

A part of me softens and I want to hug Will. Instead, I shake my head. "Don't worry about it. I'm fine."

"You're not," Will presses. "You look sick, Trell. And tired. Just come and live here."

I hold my breath so I won't say something unkind. It's easy for her to say I should live with her, but it's not realistic. She can say it all she wants, but she won't ask Cheryl or Allen if I could for real. She's too scared they'll hurt her. Which is ridiculous, but I get it. Will doesn't want shit-stain parents again. She's got it made and doesn't want to mess it up. But I can take care of myself. I can handle this. I always have.

Pain crosses Will's face when I don't answer, but it's quickly replaced by determination. "Okay, fine. Can you at least stay a few nights? We can do whatever you want. I just want to make sure you're safe."

All the bitterness whooshes out of me at once. I give her a smile, one that reopens my split lip. "Yeah, okay. I'll come over this weekend."

Some of the tension eases from Will's shoulders. She starts to say something else, but her bedroom door swings open and her mom walks in.

"Will, it's time for— Oh my God, Katrell, what happened?"

Shit. "Nothing, Mrs. T. A fight at school, no big deal." I grab Conrad's collar and tug him toward the door.

Will's mom blocks me, her hands on her hips. "No, uh-uh, let me see your face." She touches my face gently, running one thumb over my sensitive skin. "Oh, honey. What happened? Who did this?"

The lies usually come so easy, but it's like my mouth is full of sand. Tears well up in my eyes, a remnant from my crying fit last night. I'm so tired. I am, but if I tell her what really happened, Mom will be in trouble. I swallow the sand and pull my face from her hands. "A fight at school, like I said."

"I don't believe you." Will's mom says, her tone matter-of-fact. "Who did this? I'm calling the police."

I struggle for words, but Will rescues me.

"It was a fight," Will says. She meets my eyes and I hope she can see the gratitude in them. "She and Chelsea got into it."

Doubt crosses Will's mom's face and I pounce. "She was being a dick to Will, so I beat her up. Don't worry, she won't bother Will again."

Will's mom frowns. "Katrell, you shouldn't be fighting. I appreciate you looking out for Will, but—"

"I know, won't happen again," I say. "I have to go. See you later."

I push past Will's mom and practically run from the house. I pull my hood up to hide the bruises and check my phone. I text Will, *Thank you*, then turn my attention to the other texts. A picture of a happy Four and his wife; two of Five holding a toddler. My thumb hovers over Mrs. Jones's name, but I put my phone in my pocket instead. It's fine—Two is probably just lonely and wanted to see me, that's all. I chew my sore lip, trying to ignore a fact that sends chills up my spine—

Two shouldn't know where I live.

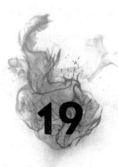

19

fiddle with my headphones and stare at rows of peanut butter, mentally calculating the best deal.

It's been two days since Two surprised me at my bedroom window, and she's been calm and docile since. After I resurrected Six, a college kid who died of an overdose, I spent the day with Two. We played cards, although she kept spacing out. It was nice. I still have no idea what I'm going to do with her, but keeping her in the apartment is good enough for right now. I'll cross that bridge when it comes or whatever the saying is.

Two aside, I've met my goal—Six's resurrection netted me five thousand dollars, bringing my total to seventeen. A year's worth of "have to" money covered, plus a little extra in case of emergency. I expected to feel relieved, but I'm sort of disappointed. It's not like I can touch that money. I've rationed it out for twelve months, and

I've already spent this month's money on rent and utilities. Like I thought, back to the same old same old.

Now my priority is food. Gerald came back to the house and is ignoring me. That's fine, but he's eaten us out of house and home again. I have to find food that's cheap, and preferably something he doesn't like. Peanut butter is good because you can eat two spoonfuls with crackers for a meal and really make it last. I'll keep it in my room so Gerald can't get to it. I can also get a lot of ramen noodles for cheap, but they start tasting like nothing after the fifth day in a row. I pace between the milk and eggs, torn. Eggs just don't last. Gerald can eat six at a time. But if I buy milk and cereal, Gerald will get high and eat the whole box in one go.

I decide on the essentials—ramen, peanut butter, crackers, several cans of Vienna sausages. I go to the front to check out.

"That'll be thirteen forty-five."

I stare at the cashier, a twenty in my hand. I look down at the money in my palm, my brain buzzing behind my ears. I have seventeen thousand dollars in my house. I have three hundred in my backpack. Why am I buying peanut butter and crackers? Vienna sausages?

I can buy whatever I want.

I tell the cashier to wait, and I run to the back of the store. I chuck whatever I see into the buggy: chips, cake, pizza rolls. Whatever I see goes into the basket. I race to the front again, giddy with excitement. When it's all said and done, I spend two hundred forty-two dollars. I peel off the twenties and pay, a sense of pride filling my chest. I roll the full buggy outside, then pause.

I don't have a way to get all this home.

Well, shit. Will was right—I do need a car. Before I started the resurrections, I could fit my groceries in my backpack. And now I bought all this junk food and have to lug it a mile down the road. Will is gonna laugh her ass off when I tell her about this. I sigh and start pushing the buggy away from Walmart and toward home.

Huffing and puffing, I daydream about a car. I have seventeen thousand right now, minus two hundred forty-two. I can't go on a grocery shopping spree every day or anything, but maybe I can use that extra two thousand on stuff like this. I don't have to save all of it. Maybe I can use all my Benny's money for the blue Honda. Not that it's much—a little over a hundred every two weeks isn't going to get me a car anytime soon. Until then, it's hoofing it a mile to my house.

A car pulls up beside me and I turn, curious. A Mercedes, light gray, brand-new. Maybe I should save up for one like *that*. I keep pushing, wiping my sweaty forehead with the sleeve of Will's hoodie, and the car keeps pace with me.

"Hey!" a familiar voice yells. I follow the voice and see Marquis.

I hesitate, slowing my buggy to a stop. Marquis grins at me, his silver grill shining in the afternoon sunlight. Marquis is a well-known murderer and drug dealer, and also a letter client who asks me to talk to his dead daughter every three months or so. Will almost died of fright when I first started working with him, but he's really nice when it comes to his daughter. He also pays me two hundred dollars where everyone else pays thirty or forty, so I have no problem working with him. Trouble is, we talked to Taylor a month ago. Either he's missing her real bad, or I've done something wrong.

"Where're you going, sweetheart?" Marquis puts the Mercedes in park. "Who you steal those from?"

"I bought them. At Walmart." I fidget uncomfortably. "Nice car. New?"

"Brand-new." Marquis is grinning so much, his face looks like it'll split. "Heard you came into some money, sweetheart. Now where would you be getting that?"

My blood runs cold. Marquis is not a person I want to think I'm slinging drugs on his turf. "It's not like that, I swear. It's related to our, uh, business."

Marquis raises his eyebrows. "Oh? You can do better than letters now?"

I nod. "Better. Much better."

Marquis nods at the passenger seat. "Get in, bring your groceries. We got a lot to talk about."

I shift from foot to foot, unsure. Will would probably kill me for getting into his car. Conrad's at home, guarding my room from Gerald. Marquis is unstable, ruthless. A killer. But he also has money and that's what I need.

I load the groceries into the Mercedes, mentally rehearsing what the letter to resurrect Taylor will say.

"Tell me 'bout this business," Marquis says as we pull away from the curb.

I sit in the passenger seat, rigid, my hands clenched in my lap. The leather seat is warm against my thighs. Heated seats. A plastic bag full of stacked hundreds sits at my feet, right out in the open. Marquis doesn't care if anyone sees it. No cop in Mire would dare pull him over. This was a bad idea. If Marquis doesn't like resurrections, no one will ever see me again.

"It's, um . . ." I trail off as we pull into my neighborhood. The men who sit on their porches and smoke watch us pass with interest. "It's a step up from talking to the ghosts. A big step."

"I'm listening," Marquis says. His voice is a smooth coo, like he has all the time in the world.

I don't answer; instead, I watch Gerald pass us, leaving for work. He glares at me, but when he sees Marquis, he visibly starts and hurries away. Marquis's eyes follow him until he rounds the corner.

"Hmm." Marquis strokes his beard thoughtfully. "You got bruises you hiding, don't you?"

I watch Marquis from the corner of my eye. What's he getting at?

He laughs a little. "None of my business, though, is it? Come on, I'll help you with them groceries."

I help unload the car, my mind numb. I'm unloading a Mercedes full of groceries with the most dangerous drug dealer in Mire. He carries the bags to the doorstep, waits for me to unlock the door, and then strolls into my house like it's the most natural thing in the world. I look for Mom, hoping she'll say something, but her bedroom door is closed. Conrad eases from my room, tail tucked, ears flat against his head. His dull brown eyes look from me to Marquis. He looks exactly how I feel.

"Hi, pup," Marquis says to Conrad. He's worked with me enough to know Conrad would never bite anyone. He knows Conrad couldn't help me if something went down. Marquis looks at me, still smiling, his dark eyes intense and focused. A silent command for me to start talking.

"Well . . . I can bring people back to life."

Marquis's expression changes from cool confidence to confusion. "You gon' have to explain yourself, sweetheart."

"Gerald killed Conrad. He shot him. But I brought him back, and it's not perfect, but . . ."

Marquis is ignoring me. He leans in front of Conrad, studying him. Conrad looks up at me, and I pet his head for comfort. Marquis touches Conrad's chest, running his hand over where the bullet hole should be. "He was shot here?"

"Yeah."

Marquis presses his hand to Conrad's chest. "No heartbeat?"

"No. But they're warm and they remember who you are. I've resurrected five people so far, and Conrad. That's where I got the money."

Marquis is silent for a long time. He stares at Conrad and Conrad stares back. "You can do this for my little girl?"

I hesitate. I want to refuse, to make up some excuse, but Marquis really might end my life. So I nod, dread eating at my stomach.

Marquis stands. He's smiling again, his face giddy. "Come on, sweetheart, bring the dog. We're takin' a ride."

I watch him leave the living room, my mouth dry. Conrad looks up at me and I reach for my phone. My thumb hovers over Will's name, but instead I call Benny's.

"Hey, Julio? I'm not coming to work today. Something came up."

Marquis stands behind me, silent, as I prepare to resurrect his daughter. It's dark already, but it's still earlier than my midnight resurrections. I take several shaky breaths, more nervous than I've ever been. I know I can do it, but here's the tricky part—Taylor has been dead for five years. I haven't resurrected anyone who has been dead more than a year.

I look at Conrad, dread eating at me. I can't depend on him to help me if something goes wrong and the resurrection doesn't work. I wish Will were here. I tug at my collar, hot and cold at the same time. Do or die, Katrell. Here we go.

I write the letter and sign my name, and the ink ignites. We wait, and thirty seconds later, the ground rumbles. The grave glows red, like always, and a tiny hand pushes through the dirt. Marquis takes a step forward, his eyes glued to the grave. Another hand pops out, then a small head with hair in four plaits with white balls at the top. Taylor, Marquis's four-year-old daughter, crawls out of the grave, her body twisting and popping as she rises to her feet. She looks up at us with big brown eyes, blinking, her white dress stained with dirt.

Thank God it worked.

Marquis gasps. I turn to him, smiling, and point to a bewildered Taylor. "There she is. She'll be confused at first, but—"

Marquis doesn't wait for me to finish. He sprints to his daughter's side and scoops her into his arms. He's crying, really sobbing, and Taylor clings to his neck.

"Daddy," she says, her voice quiet. "I missed you."

I watch the reunion, overcome with relief. Thank God I get to keep all my teeth. As Marquis kisses her cheek and Taylor giggles, my chest fills with warmth. Marquis isn't such a bad guy. Intimidating as hell, but not so bad. Seeing him cry softens the fear.

After a few minutes, Marquis carries Taylor to me. He pulls

me into a rough hug, still sniffling. My nostrils are flooded with the smell of cigarettes.

"Katrell, thank you. I can't thank you enough. My little baby . . ." Marquis plants a kiss on Taylor's forehead. She doesn't react. She used to be talkative, telling Marquis about butterflies and birds in our letters. Now she's quiet, her expression dull. "How much?"

"It's okay," I say, some of the warmth in my chest fading. Could her personality have changed? Taylor meets my eyes and pain leaps into my temples.

Marquis studies me for a second, then puts Taylor down. She clings to the hem of his shirt. "No, it's not okay. Running a Business 101: customers always pay."

Yeah, with him it's either in cash or blood. I'm just happy he didn't kill me.

"I'm gonna help you. 'Cause I like you. You remind me of myself, when I was your age." Marquis pats Taylor's head. "You've got something people want. Something people want bad. How much do you normally charge?"

"I did thirty-five hundred, but my last two were five thousand."

"Five thousand." Marquis snorts. "Why you charging chump change for something this valuable?"

I look away, to the too-small shoes I've had since the seventh grade, my mind on my promise to Will. "I was just doing it to catch up on bills."

Marquis shakes his head. "Katrell, let me tell you somethin'—five grand ain't nothing. Nothing. This gift, and the money it gets you, belongs to you. No one else. This ain't the kind of money you use to pay bills."

What's he saying? That I shouldn't stop resurrections even

though I've met my goal? I fidget a little, uncomfortable that his words aren't sounding like a bad idea.

Marquis holds his hands up, shrugging. "Up to you. But I gotta pay you." He reaches for his back pocket, then pauses. His hand moves to the waistband of his jeans instead and withdraws a black pistol. I freeze, my heart stuttering, but he turns the gun around and offers the handle to me. With a sick headache pounding behind my eyes, I take it.

"Gerald's beatin' you, yeah? I ain't surprised. But it's inevitable. Someone's always gonna be beatin' on you, spittin' on you, holdin' you down. Unless you make them stop." Marquis shrugs his huge shoulders again, grinning. "If someone won't respect you, you make them respect you."

I nod, fear seizing my tongue. When I get home, this gun is going in the trash.

Marquis laughs, loud and long. "I had a feeling you wouldn't be too happy with that. I got something else. You ain't got a ride, do you?" He digs in his pocket and pulls out his car keys. He holds them out and I take them, speechless. "'Fore you ask, I'm serious. It's yours. You did something no one else could ever do: you brought my baby back to me." Marquis wipes his eyes. He's more like himself now—cold, serious, dangerous. "Anybody bothers you, including that piece of shit Gerald, they answer to me. From now until forever, you like family. Got it?"

"Yeah," I manage. He gave me his car. A Mercedes. I own a Mercedes.

"Good." Marquis gives me a wide, crooked smile. He scoops up Taylor, who's staring at the gun with dull eyes. "Enjoy the high life, Katrell. You've earned it."

20

I stare at a brown water stain on the ceiling, trying not to think about the gun in the glove box of my new Mercedes.

After I resurrected Taylor, Marquis made me drive him home, refusing to listen to my weak protests about the car. After that, I didn't know what to do. I own a Mercedes now, a $50,000 car that's brand-new. My little Craigslist Honda seems so far away. What's worse is that I keep turning Marquis's words over and over in my head. If I have a gift, shouldn't I use it as much as I want? But Will said it's wrong, and I have this cold. . . . I turn to my side, my back aching from the ancient mattress. If I had money, I could get a real bed. Like Will's.

My phone buzzes at my side. I pick it up—a text from a letter client.

Heard you're a real witch now.

I frown at my phone. It's Regina, an old woman who uses

my letters to talk to her mom. She's never called me a witch before.

Dont know what you mean.

I want to see my mom

Im not doing letters anymore

I know. I heard you can do better

Shit, so it has been getting out. I told them to keep quiet. . . . I scratch at a rhinestone on the back of my phone case. I expect to feel panic, but I'm sort of annoyed instead. You ask someone to do a few simple things—don't talk about what happened, keep them indoors, text me if you have any problems—and even that's too much. I swear to God, everyone except for me and Will are incompetent. I text a harsh warning to the four clients, and a much nicer warning to Marquis. Then I turn my attention back to Regina.

idk what you heard, but I'm not doing letters anymore. Or anything else. Sorry.

Text bubbles pop up on my phone, but I shut it off. I'll block Regina and everyone else. I can put this behind me. Everything can go back to normal. I pick at the rhinestones on the phone case, popping one of them off. I hold the fake stone between two fingers and squeeze, wincing a little at the pain. Too bad my normal is so shitty.

The door swings open and Mom walks into my room. She's not wearing her favorite pink bathrobe; she's in a frilly black top and tight jeans. She's even wearing earrings. "Katrell, I'm glad you're home! Bills are done for the month, so we can relax. I told you we'd figure it out. You always worry too much."

I paint a painful grin on my face. Oh, so it's *we* paid the bills now? Like she contributed at all. Not even a "thanks for saving my ass, Katrell"? No "I'm so happy you're here and can pay rent when I can't"? I try to cut Mom some slack, but today her casual attitude is grating on me. My headache from Taylor's resurrection is already worse.

"I'm heading out," Mom says, fastening a bracelet around her thin wrist. "Are you keeping ice on your eye? It still looks awful."

Some of the irritation fades. "Not really. I haven't had time."

"Well what do you do all day? Stare at the wall?" Mom says, laughing.

I find myself softening. Mom's trying. She's going to get a new job and then we'll be fine. It's always worked out before, like she said. Warmth fills my chest, but not the familiar white-hot rage. I should trust her more. "Mom, will you brush my hair again?"

She meets my eyes and smiles. "I baby you one time and now that's all you want, huh?" Her phone dings and she glances down at it. "Sorry, maybe next time. I gotta go, but I'll be back late tonight, promise."

The warm feeling in my chest subsides. "Where are you going?"

"Gerald and I are going out to celebrate catching up. Be good, I'll be back later!"

Before I can process what she said, she's gone.

I sit up on the mattress, moving slow, anger and my headache making it hard to think. All the warmth is gone. A date. She's going on a date, with Gerald, after I saved us from getting kicked out. She didn't even ask if I wanted her to bring food back. And how is she going on a date anyway? I know Gerald isn't paying. I pull the shoebox from my closet, where I decided to keep the money for bills, and count the cash, once, twice, three times.

One hundred and fifty dollars short.

I pick up a battered shoe and throw it at the wall, seething. Conrad looks up at me from his position under the window, his eyes dull but ears pricked. That could have been food money, or school stuff, or hell, gas for my new car. And she took it to waste on Gerald? On that asshole who makes me choke on my own blood?

I'm so mad, I'm trembling. My hands clench into fists over and over. She's my mother, but I think if she came back right now, I'd throw something at her. I pace back and forth in a tight circle because my room's so small. I need to do something to calm my nerves. I need to talk to Will. I ignore Regina's new text and press Will's name, the phone shaking in my hand.

Will answers on the second ring. "What's up?"

I swallow hard before answering. "Hey, what are you doing? Can you talk?"

"Sure," she says, and calm starts to replace the panic. "I can't talk long, though—I'm about to go to the movies."

The calm comes to a screeching halt. "A movie? Which one? With who?"

"It's a rom-com, I think?" Will doesn't sound too thrilled. "I'm going with Allen and Cheryl. They acted like they were sorry for grounding me, so I guess I better go."

I stare at the phone, struggling for words. Maybe I shouldn't tell Will about Mom. Or the gun for that matter. She'll see the car at school, so I can't hide that, but she's about to have fun with her foster parents for the first time in forever. I shouldn't ruin it. "Okay, well, have fun. If it sucks, we'll go to a different one later."

"What'd you want to talk about?" Will asks.

"Nothing."

She pauses for two seconds. Then, "Are you sure? You don't sound so good. You sound stuffy. Is your cold getting worse?"

"I'm okay," I say quickly. "I gotta go. Have fun at the movies."

"I'll call you after," Will says. Cheryl calls her from the background. "Promise."

We say goodbye and I hang up. I sit on the edge of the mattress, shivering. I can't tell if it's from cold or sickness or something else. Thoughts run rapid-fire through my head. Will's going to have fun with her family, while Mom's out partying with Gerald. Mom's taking my money, and she'll take it as long as I live here. I think about my mattress without a bed frame, my too-tight shoes, my slashed hours at Benny's. I think about my headaches, Two's appearance at my window. I think about Marquis's gun in the glove box of my brand-new car.

I turn over my phone and read Regina's message.

Please, it says. *I can pay you. I have eight thousand in cash.*

I take a deep breath, calmer than I've been in weeks, and send Regina a text.

Meet me in the graveyard by Waffle House.

21

I nod at number Eight, a middle-aged father, my head about to split open.

"Thank you," Regina says, her voice small. I wonder why she didn't ask me to resurrect her mom. That's who she asked me to summon in all the letters. She hands me a Ziploc bag. "It's eight thousand, plus a little extra. I hope that's enough."

My headache all but disappears as I grasp the bag with a tight fist. Eight thousand is the most I've ever received. And now that I think about it, I *should* charge more. Resurrections are priceless, right? I should be charging ten, twenty thousand. Maybe thirty.

I tell Regina the normal rules, then head to my car. Conrad follows behind, his head raised high. I unlock the Mercedes, but don't get in right away. I'm dreading going home. I bet Mom and Gerald are still partying, and I do not want to be there when they get back. Our walls are very thin. I want to go to Will's, but she's at the movies. I sneeze into my elbow, my sinuses aching. I should go home. Mom hasn't called or texted, but she'll probably wonder where I am if I get home after she does. I should go home.

My phone buzzes and I turn it over. It's Will.

"Hello?"

"I'm out of the movie," Will says. She sounds happy, actually happy, for once. "It was kind of good! Anyway, what was up earlier? You okay?"

I look at Conrad sitting in the front seat. He looks back at me, his head slightly cocked to one side. I take a deep breath. "Can I come over?"

"Yeah!" Will says. She sounds even happier. "Anytime."

Will shakes a can of spray paint over my head, her eyes sharp and focused. "Move it to the left."

"Here?" I move the stencil, a cardboard dove she traced herself, a few centimeters.

"Perfect. Hold still."

I hold my breath as Will sprays bright pink all over the stencil and my gloved hands. Some paint predictably stains my shirt, but I don't mind. This is normal, familiar. When Will is done, I carefully remove the stencil. The painting is beautiful: a dove the color of a starry sky, with swirling greens and blues and pinpricks of white, against a loud pink-and-white background. Will studies the painting for several seconds, then shrugs.

"Nah, that's not working. We'll start over."

"Will, come on," I groan, but she carries the painting to the trash, where three other dove-themed paintings rest. "That one was so good!"

Will shakes her head, already stowing the cans of spray paint on a shelf in the garage. "I can do better."

I lean back on my hands, watching her clean up the mess we made. It's after school, a Friday, and I decided not to go home. I texted Mom I was at Will's, and I got a thumbs-up emoji. So I guess I can stay here for a bit while I sort everything out. And it's been nice. I've missed Will's art and ridiculous standards. I've missed getting paint on my shirt.

"Okay, one more time," Will says, holding the dove stencil between two fingers.

"I'm tired," I whine. "Let's do something else."

Will frowns, but nods. "Okay. Want to watch a movie?"

"No, it's too early. . . . What about some food?"

Will smiles. "Deal."

We toss our gloves and leave the garage. Conrad follows us, his head low, like he's sleepy. I'm feeling sleepy too. My headache has eased up, but I'm exhausted. I'll have to ask Will if we can go to bed early.

When we get to the kitchen, I go straight to the bread and turkey. Will likes peanut butter and honey, but I eat enough peanut butter at home. Lunch meat is a luxury.

"You know, that last one was really good," I say, rummaging in the fridge for mustard and pickle slices. Will's mom must have just bought groceries—the fridge is brimming with food. "Let me have it. I'll hang it in my room."

"No," Will says. "It's not good enough."

"Everything doesn't have to be perfect!" I find my sandwich materials and dump them on the kitchen island.

Will doesn't answer for a few seconds. She's looking into a top cabinet thoughtfully. "I don't know. I was talking to Mike, and he was asking me about what I wanted to do after high school. And I think, maybe, I'd like to try art school."

"Oh, Mike got you too?" I finish making my sandwich and put everything back in the fridge. "But he's right, you should go to art school. I mean, you've already got a scholarship from Kennings."

"I don't have it yet," Will says as I sit down. "What do you mean 'got you too'?"

I think about the crumpled pamphlet in my backpack. "Something about trade school. Whatever. I haven't had time to think about it."

"That might be good, though, Trell." Will finally makes a selection from the cabinet and pulls down a ceramic bowl. "You like working with your hands and stuff. Better than Benny's forever."

Well, she's right about that. Slinging burgers is starting to get old. But if the resurrections go well, I can quit. I probably won't need trade school at all. My mind wanders as I bite into the sandwich, but the front of the fridge catches my attention. It's covered with appointment cards for Will's therapist, for her mom's dentist, her dad's doctor. There are also several sketches that Will made: a jeweled elephant, the cafeteria at school, one of Conrad. And, in the middle of the fridge, is a poem I wrote in April.

When Will sits down with a bowl of ramen noodles, I point to the poem, a feeling I can't quite name swimming in my stomach. "Why's that on your fridge?"

"What? Oh, your poem? Cheryl put it up. You gave it to her, remember?"

I do remember, but why is it on their fridge? Why is it next to Will's sketches and appointment reminders and report cards? I was sure her mom would just throw it away.

Will frowns at me, her fork halfway to her mouth. "You okay?"

"Yeah." I look down at my sandwich, no longer hungry. I haven't written a thing since that poem. Will's throwing away paintings like they're nothing, and I haven't done anything in almost six months. I used to like poetry. I used to be good at it. Good enough to hang on a fridge, anyway.

There's a noise from the back of the house and Will's parents enter the kitchen. They're dressed nice. Mr. Tapscott is even wearing a blue tie and khakis. Will tenses beside me as her mom comes to us, a brilliant smile on her face.

"Katrell! Nice to see you!" She hugs me, tight, and warmth spreads from my head to my toes. "What're you eating?"

"Snacks, looks like," Will's dad grunts. He straightens his tie, frowning at Will's noodles. "We can pick up something for y'all before we go. Something that's not junk."

"Where are you going?" I ask.

"Date," Mrs. Tapscott says, still smiling. "Gotta keep the love alive! Dating doesn't stop after you get married, you know. Remember that, girls."

Will grimaces into her noodles and I laugh. "Yes ma'am, we will."

"What do you want me to pick up for you?" Will's dad asks her. Her shoulders tense up again, but she takes a shaky breath.

"Nothing. I'm okay."

Will's mom and dad practically beam. It's painful to watch them get this excited over a normal response from their daughter. I know they're letting Will move at her own pace, but it's been four years. A strange, hollow feeling opens in my chest. I stuff it down as Will's mom leans over and kisses the top of my head.

"See you soon, Katrell. Try not to let Conrad tear the house down, hmm?"

I glance at Conrad, who's lying calmly by my feet. "He'll behave, promise."

Will's parents go to the door. I wave at them, but Will stares stubbornly at her bowl. "Bye, girls! Love you."

There's a tense, heartbreaking second as they wait for Will to answer. She clenches her fists and looks like she's about to say something, but the moment passes. Her parents, their expressions resigned but still smiling, wave at us and leave the house.

It takes Will a while to fully relax. A few minutes after their car leaves the driveway, she heaves a sigh and gives me a weak smile. "Let's try another painting."

The rest of the night passes quickly. We do two more dove stencils before Will is satisfied, we watch a dumb rom-com and some makeup tutorials. I attempt a poem while she's getting ready for bed, but I can't think of anything to write. After midnight, I crawl into my normal place by Will's bed, Conrad beside me. For a moment, everything feels normal, the way it did before. But I can't sleep, even after an hour, and I miss the familiar rise and fall of Conrad's chest against my arm.

"Are you still awake?" Will whispers.

I stare at the dark ceiling, too warm and too cold at the same time. "Yeah."

"What're you thinking about?"

Conrad. Marquis's gun in my new Mercedes. Trade school. Paintings that are good but not great. My fridge at home, which has no poems on it.

"I think you should be nicer to your parents."

The silence between us is heavy. I hear Will take a deep breath.

"I know."

I want to apologize, but I don't because I mean it. She's wasting such a good thing, day after day. She can't even tell them she loves them, even knowing they love her.

"You know," Will says, her voice soft, "I meant what I said the other day. You can live here, if you want."

I close my eyes, surprised at the prick of tears behind them. I pet Conrad's head and think about the car, and the Revenants, and all that money. I think about how me and Will aren't all that different after all.

"I know."

22

I watch Nine, a tall, serious-looking man in his fifties, leave the graveyard with his sniffling daughter. Another eight thousand to my name. Another blinding headache. I massage my temples and put the bag of money she gave me under my arm and head to my car.

It's Sunday night. I stayed with Will all weekend—it was nice. I had a good time. But tomorrow is Monday and I have school, and I can't just stay away from home forever. I hesitate as I get to the car, key ready to unlock it, but my hand unmoving. Time to go home. Time to face Gerald again. Dread and something disgustingly close to fear coils in my gut. I have to go home. I have to be strong.

Conrad nudges my hand and I look down. He turns and stares at something behind me—three guys my age. I recognize one: Demarcus, the guy in juvie who knifed his girlfriend. The other two are strangers. What're they doing at a graveyard in the middle of the night? New clients?

"How can I help you, boys?" I put the keys in my pocket and one hand on Conrad's back.

They don't say anything until they're a few feet away. The ringleader, Demarcus, grins at me. "Heard we had a witch in Mire. Wanted to check it out."

"Oh yeah?" I lean on my car, smiling. "I think you misheard. People usually call me 'bitch.'"

Demarcus and the other guys laugh. My grip on the money tightens.

"Maybe that's true too. You a witch for real, though?"

"Who's asking?"

"Me," Demarcus says. He steps closer and Conrad lets out a soft growl. "Word is, you got money now."

"So?" I'm trying to sound aloof, bored, but my heart is hammering against my ribs. There are three of them—what am I going to do? Should I give them the money? No, they'll always want a cut if I back down now.

"So, we wanna know where you gettin' all that dough." Demarcus steps even closer, within striking distance. His lackeys close in too. "We wanna know if witches share."

I try to take a step back, but the cold steel of the car presses into my back. Shit, what am I going to do now? I close my hand around the key in my pocket. Too late, I remember Marquis's gun locked in the glove box, safely out of reach.

Demarcus gets right in my face and my heart rate increases to an impossible speed. It's beating so hard, it hurts.

"You got money on you right now, don't you?" Demarcus's breath smells like trash mixed with alcohol. "So, do witches share? Or do we gotta take from them like everyone else?"

Demarcus reaches for the bag under my arm. I can't move; I'm frozen. He grins and grabs the bag, and Conrad jumps up and closes his mouth around Demarcus's arm.

I don't know who's more shocked, me or Demarcus. Conrad jerks his arm downward and Demarcus screams, an otherworldly wail that shakes me to my bones. Conrad lets go and charges at the other two guys. One pulls out a pocketknife, but Conrad tackles him anyway. All I can hear is the sound of clothes ripping, and screaming. The other lackey books it out of the graveyard and the one Conrad tackled struggles away and follows him. Conrad barks, snarling, his jaws covered in blood.

Holy shit.

I shake off my disbelief when Demarcus's whimpering reaches my ears. He's curled up in a ball on the ground, holding his arm. It's twisted at an unnatural angle.

"They told me the dog don't bite," he groans.

"Got that one wrong, huh?" I lean down to his level, grinning. "By the way, witches don't share."

I whistle for Conrad and he lopes to my side. I open the passenger door for him and close it after he jumps into the car. I hesitate for a moment, looking at Conrad through the side window. He's staring straight ahead, calm, blood staining his muzzle. He's never bitten anyone before. But he was protecting me; he must have been really scared for me. I'm sure it's fine—he'll only bite people who deserve it.

Satisfied, I grab my eight thousand dollars, crank up my car, and drive home. All the panic, fear, and doubt are gone. Why am I scared of going back to my own home? Witches don't have anything to be afraid of.

23

Money has changed my life.

A few weeks ago, I was living off Will's lunch, work food, and spoonfuls of peanut butter. And now? I have money to burn. And since I have it, why not burn it?

I bought a lot of stuff. New clothes that don't itch like the jacket I got before. New shoes. A dog scarf for Conrad. I bought a hat—a hat! I don't even wear hats! I don't know what's come over me, but I kind of like it. I get in my new Mercedes and drive to the mall in the next town over and I feel like a movie star. I definitely don't feel like a loser who lives in a glorified shack and sleeps on a forty-year-old mattress without a bed frame. Well, not anymore. I haven't been home in three days—I've been going to a cheap hotel and crashing there. I was worried my age and Conrad would be a problem, but the staff looks the other way as long as I stuff cash in their pockets. I have the money, so why not? People with money don't have to be miserable. People with money don't have to deal with their mom's boyfriend who has a short temper and a gun. And now I'm a person with money, so I don't have to suffer anymore. And I intend to keep it that way.

I call Benny's, my phone balanced against my chin and shoulder as I drive. I'm coming back from Walmart, but I'm late for work.

"This is Benny's, how can I help you?"

My stomach sinks. Julio. If it had been anyone else, I wouldn't be in trouble. But he's been getting so pissed at me for coming in late. Like all I have to do is flip burgers. "Hey, Julio, it's Katrell. I'm gonna be late, but I am coming—"

"Again?" Julio groans. "Katrell, come on. This is the third day in a row."

"I said I'm coming, what's the big deal?" I pull into a parking place three blocks from my house.

"The big deal is that you made a commitment when you said you could work these hours and you're letting us down." There's a tense silence. Then, "Is everything all right? This really isn't like you."

I heave a sigh and pull the Walmart bags from the front seat. "I'm fine. I'm coming, okay? I'll just be late."

"Don't bother," Julio says. "I'm calling Kayla to cover your shift. Use your days off to get yourself together, okay? I don't wanna have to fire you."

"Fine," I say through gritted teeth, unexpectedly wounded by Julio's words. "See you next week."

I hang up and let Conrad out of the backseat. He's wearing a bow tie I bought him, and there's a green sweater for him in one of the bags. He looks up at me, his ears standing up. "What?" I say, irritation making my words sharp. "You gonna fire me from being your owner?"

Conrad stares at me for a moment, his eyes cold, and then trots in the direction of home. So much for moral support.

I follow him, running my thumb over my house key. I wish I could just stay at the hotel. Everything was great when I was there—TV, movies, room service. Now it's back to my shitty house. But I can't live in the hotel forever. Will thinks I should either stay there or at her house as long as possible, but I have to come home. I don't know if Mom's run out of food in the three days I've been on vacation. Since I'm the only one working, I have to bring home food sometimes. For Mom's sake.

I have to walk three blocks because if I parked the Mercedes in the driveway, it wouldn't be there when I got back. Marquis said something about us being like "family," but I don't want to risk it. Conrad trots beside me, his head low, his eyes on the house. Used to, he'd dart around in front of me, sniffing mailboxes and barking at squirrels. But now he's focused, serious.

I bought him a new stuffed lamb. He won't play with that one either.

I climb the crumbling steps and open the front door. My heart sinks—Mom and Gerald are sitting at the kitchen table.

Gerald follows me with his eyes as I sit three Walmart bags on the kitchen counter. Mom's watching me too. No one speaks for a full minute.

I'm almost done putting the groceries away when Conrad growls softly. I turn, and Gerald has taken a few steps toward me. "You gon' explain where you been all week?"

"Nope."

There's a strained silence. "Heard you got a new car."

I debate my response. Rumors spread fast around here, so it's no surprise he knows about it. Plus, he saw me with Marquis. I decide to say nothing. Whatever he's guessing can't be close to the truth. I turn back to the counter.

"I also heard you're a witch," Gerald says. "That dog ain't normal."

I don't answer again. He's guessing pretty good. Better than I thought.

"You just gon' ignore—" He's cut off by a snarl from Conrad.

"You should be careful," I say, putting away a new set of sharp black knives. "If you come any closer, Conrad will get you."

Gerald doesn't say anything. There's a long silence, and then the front door opens and slams shut. When I look over my shoulder, Gerald's gone.

My chest swells with triumph. I was right—I don't have anything to be afraid of now that Conrad is a biting dog. Gerald's never hitting me again. Conrad looks up at me and I pat his head.

"Katrell."

All the triumph whooshes out of me when I see Mom's face. It's dark and serious, an expression I almost never see.

She points at the table and I sit down, suddenly sheepish. I go missing for three days and immediately start torturing Gerald—I bet Mom's mad. I texted her that I was at Will's the days I stayed at the hotel and she never answered. Maybe she didn't get my texts. Maybe she was worried about me.

"Mom, sorry I didn't come home, I—"

"The dog has to go."

I stare at her, stunned. "What?"

She points at Conrad, who's watching her with interest. "I told you, I *told* you not to do that ghost shit anymore. Gerald's so freaked out. He won't stay over with that dog in the house. I told you not to do that weird stuff."

I struggle for words. She didn't mention the car or my new clothes. She didn't say anything about me not coming home. And she wants me to get rid of Conrad because Gerald doesn't like him? Anger leaps into me like lightning.

"No."

Mom's eyebrows shoot straight up. "You talking back to me?"

"I'm not getting rid of Conrad." I stare at her, anger giving me strength. "You can't make me get rid of him. You know, Gerald shot him, right in front of me. Maybe he *should* be scared."

Mom's lip curls and some of my bravado fades. She's mad. She's mad, but I'm not giving in. I can't. Conrad's too important. I didn't bring him back to life just to abandon him because Gerald's a wimp.

"You ain't gonna talk back to me, girl," Mom says. "The dog gotta go. End of story."

I'm shaking with fear and anger and illness and something else. Hurt. Deep hurt, deep in my chest, in my bones. Will's always said my mom didn't care. She said it, but I didn't believe it. I'm so confused I barely notice Conrad coming up behind my chair. He lifts his lips and bares his teeth at Mom.

Mom backs up, just one step, and the spell is broken. I take a deep breath and stand. "You wanna try and make him leave? Be my guest."

I grab my backpack and go to the door. I pat my leg and Conrad turns from Mom, slowly, and follows me. I hesitate, my hand on the doorknob.

"I have the money for the rent this month, but you should start looking for a new job." I pause, my heart pounding at the idea of talking back to her. "Please."

I leave my house, Conrad beside me, and don't look back.

24

text Will in seventh period. *Do you wanna go shopping today?*

Things are tense at home, so me and Will have been going shopping a lot after school and then I go to her house or a hotel to sleep. We've been all over Huntsville: Bridge Street, the mall, fancy restaurants I never dared set foot in before. Turns out I like sushi. Who knew? It's been five days since Mom told me to get rid of Conrad. She hasn't texted or called. She's probably still mad. I'll have to apologize. And bring her some more food.

Will answers after a few minutes. *Can't. Going to the paint store with Cheryl after school.*

I stare at my phone in disbelief. Will's going somewhere with Cheryl? Somewhere she actually likes?

I'm gonna start a new painting, she continues. *Which do you like better, mountain lions or tigers? Cheryl says mountain lion but idk*

She's taking painting suggestions from her mom too? I expect to feel the familiar warmth, but it doesn't come. Will's choosing her mom over me. And I want that, right? I want Will to be closer to her mom. I do, don't I? But then why does my chest feel so hollow?

I answer Will (agreed, mountain lions are cool and easier to paint, probably), and after school I drive to the next town over. I sit in my car for a while, frowning down at my phone. Why am I in a bad mood? Will doesn't have to come with me everywhere. She's allowed to hang out with her mom. But when I look up at the Old Navy sign, the hollowness in my chest grows deeper. Will's the only one who will go shopping with me. I haven't been shopping with anyone else, not even Mom, in years.

I get out of the car, unease prickling the back of my neck. I'll buy some shoes and a dog hat for Conrad and forget about it. Maybe I'm just tired—I think my cold is getting worse. I've been sneezing and the back of my throat is hot and raw.

I stroll into Old Navy. No one pays any attention to me. I look like everyone else now. I've traded my ratty shoes and stained jeans for new pants and short boots. I'm still wearing Will's hoodie, but it's clean and smells like lavender—the hotel has a functioning washer and dryer that are free to use. Perks of having money.

I look at the jewelry first. I love jewelry. Big hoop earrings, silver necklaces, gold rings. Jewelry is the first thing to go when you need money. I work so hard and so long that I don't have time to dress up. I'm gonna buy dresses for summer and heels and as much jewelry as I want.

I touch a necklace with a red gemstone in the middle. It's cold against my fingertips. I should wear this to resurrections. I could tell people it was magic. I bet they'd believe me.

I pick it up, and someone moves closer to me. I move away, irritated—there's a whole empty aisle and they're crowding me. But as I move away, the person moves with me, uncomfortably close. I turn to tell them to back off, and frown. It's a woman, tall, gaunt, high cheekbones. She looks familiar. . . . When she faces me, smiling, my stomach fills with ice.

It's Five.

I gape at her, my brain stunned into static. What—what is she doing here? I told her family to keep her at home. I told them not to show her face. But here she is, a resurrected corpse, in broad daylight, in fucking Old Navy. My brain catches up to me and I grab her arm. She's alone—her family is nowhere to be seen.

"What are you doing here?" I hiss.

Five looks down at me. Her eyes are deep brown, but they have a sharp edge to them. Sort of like Mike's, but Mike's eyes are curious, wanting to get to the bottom of your lies. Hers are hungry.

"Hello, Katrell," she says. Her voice is soft and smooth, like a coo. "I need a new jacket. Mine is a little itchy."

"Listen, you're not supposed to be here." I'm talking low so no one will overhear us. What if someone recognizes her? I'll have a real shitshow on my hands then. "Where's your family?"

Five continues to smile. "How are you? Without Will today, I see. Oh, you look ill. Have you tried honey and a hot shower? Works wonders for a stuffy nose. I was a nurse, so you can trust me."

"Five, I swear to God—" I cut myself off when I see her husband, an overweight man who always looks surprised. I make a beeline to him. "Hey. Hey, look at me."

He visibly starts. "Oh, hi. I didn't—"

"What's she doing here?" I point at Five, who's still smiling serenely. "I told you not to bring her out in public. What if some-one sees her?"

The man looks everywhere except at me. A small child peeks at me from behind his legs, but slow rage is climbing up my neck. He better have a damn good reason for this.

"I feel so bad that she's in the house all the time," he says.

Not good enough. "Listen, if you do this again, I will take her back. Do you hear me? I'll put her ass back in the ground to rot. You take her home and hide her like the others. You understand?"

"She said . . ." The man's looking at his shoes, wringing his hands. "She said she wanted to come to Old Navy."

"I don't give a shit what she said, I said do you understand me? Because if you don't, I'll send her back to the graveyard right now."

The man nods, a bead of sweat dripping down the side of his face. "I—I understand."

"Good. Go home." I glare at him as he passes me, his hand tight around the toddler's hand.

"Come on . . ." The man trails off, looking down at the little girl.

Five smiles at him. "Katrell calls me Five, if that helps." She nods at me and joins her husband. "Goodbye, Katrell. I hope to see you again soon."

I watch them leave, my stomach in my toes. I text my other clients a harsh warning, but I don't feel any better after it's over. This is another issue, a big one. What happens if someone traces resurrected corpses back to me?

25

Mike peeks into my hiding place under the bleachers, smiling.

"I thought I'd find you here."

"What do you want?" I'm skipping third period and PE today. I need some time to think. Was Five a coincidence or should I worry everyone is disregarding my warnings? If they get caught carting around someone who should be dead, what does that mean for me? And that damn gun is bothering me. I can't leave it at home or at the hotel, so it's in the car, and I'm pretty sure it's loaded. I Googled how to unload a gun, but I'm scared to touch it. I should just throw it away, but I can't. I don't know why. I rub the bridge of my nose. I have a headache.

Mike keeps smiling. He's wearing a tan suit today; it's too big as always. "I see we've expanded to skipping history and PE."

I glare up at him. Maybe he'll go away if I don't talk.

"Why don't we go to my office?" he suggests. "It's warmer in there, at least. And I'll write you a note for both classes."

I hesitate, then nod. He's right; it'll be warmer inside than thinking out here.

I follow him to his office. He sits at his desk and I sit across from him. He should really get a more comfortable chair. The hard wood digs into my butt, sending ribbons of pain up my spine.

"Okay, so, good news first." Mike smiles at me again, his rows of perfect teeth practically gleaming. That'll be my next purchase. Braces. "You've only missed one day since we talked. Good job! We made a goal and you stuck to it. I'm proud of you."

I'm momentarily stunned by his sincerity. Mike sounds like he really means it, not like he's saying it because he has to. I don't know if I've ever heard the words "I'm proud of you." I clear my throat, fidgeting with discomfort. "Uh, thank you."

"You're welcome. I think you're doing great, Katrell. It's not easy to come to school, but you are, and that's something to be proud of."

I clasp my hands in my lap, a strange mix of happiness and mistrust boiling in my gut. "What's the bad news?"

"No bad news. Not really," Mike says. "I think since you're coming to school on time, we should make a new goal."

I shrug, but I'm a little interested. Mike may be annoying, but he's never boring. He'll probably tell me to do some meditation or something.

Mike pulls out a file from his messy desk and thumbs through it. "So, I heard some interesting news from your history teacher. She says you turned in your test blank."

What, do teachers just sit around and gossip about students all the time? "Well, you can't believe everything you hear, Mike."

Mike laughs, a sudden, loud outburst. "That's certainly true. For instance, I heard a rumor that you could talk to ghosts."

I tense, my heart rate kicking up a few notches. But Mike doesn't notice; he's looking at the file.

"In your case, though, she showed me the test." He's still laughing a little, his eyes scanning the file. "I was looking at your transcripts from last year, and they're quite interesting as well. You did great in English and creative writing—an A in both. Four Bs, a C in history. Not bad at all."

"So?" I'm warm now and ready to go. Last year was a lot different.

"So, when I look at your grades this semester, I'm a little surprised. You're barely passing any of your classes. Even English, which is something you excelled at last year, isn't faring well." Mike looks up at me, the humor gone from his sharp brown eyes. "Did something happen between last May and now?"

I struggle for a good lie. My head's pounding; I don't feel like battling with Mike today. He searches my face, then hands me a bowl full of peppermints.

"They're good for your throat," he says. "You sound stuffy."

I take one and unwrap it slowly. Mike waits, ever patient. I'm not getting away. I'll tell him a half-truth so I can go back to my spot under the bleachers. "Well, I . . . I told you I work a lot."

"Yes, I remember. You used to work thirty-hour weeks."

"Exactly. Not a lot of time to study."

"True. But see, you told me your hours were cut a few weeks

ago." Mike stares me down. "You turned in your test blank two days ago. So, logically, we can rule out work."

Goddamn, I thought he was a counselor, not a detective. I bite my bottom lip, trying to cover myself.

"If I may, I have a theory." Mike's staring through me, no longer smiling. "Something changed in your life this past summer, something big. It's something that's hard to talk about and something you think you can handle. But you're not handling it. Your grades tell me you're struggling, Katrell."

I look away. "Maybe I just don't care about school. Everything's not a huge deal."

"You're right. I could be wrong." Mike spins a pen between his fingers, his eyes on my file again. "But I don't think I am. I think you've dealt with this before. You failed seventh grade. On your second attempt, you passed with flying colors, and you've had great grades until now."

I chew on my lip. I failed seventh grade because Mom's boyfriend at the time was beating me senseless and I missed too much school. He was arrested for robbing a store a few months later, so I passed the second time. And I met Will around then too. That helped. "You sure are nosy, aren't you?"

He taps my file with the pen, smiling. "I'd say it's curiosity. And concern." When I don't answer, he nods and closes the file. "I'm here to help you, Katrell. You tell me what you need and I'll do my best to assist you. You don't have to tell me today, and the invitation doesn't expire. You don't have to do it all alone."

"Okay," I say after a few seconds. I wish I could tell Mike everything. He almost seems to care.

"Good!" he says, seemingly satisfied. "For our new goal, let's say you work on one class. How about English? I'll check in with you in a few weeks. Sound good?"

I nod and Mike smiles. He writes two excuses—one for history, one for PE—and we stand and walk to the door.

"Have a good rest of the day, Katrell. Oh, wait." He goes back to his desk and grabs another peppermint. He drops it into my hand. "Take care of your cold, okay? Lots of water, lots of sleep."

I put the peppermint in my pocket. In spite of the interrogation, there's warmth in my chest. Mike's good at making the day bearable. "Thanks."

I leave his office and head back to the bleachers. It was a nice break, but I still have Revenants and a gun to think about.

26

After school, I sit in my car and read a text from Will.

Want to come to my house?

Um yeah, I respond, even though I don't really feel like it.

Gotta drive with Allen. Will adds a throwing-up emoji. I raise my eyebrows in surprise. She's attempting to drive? With Allen no less? I'm impressed.

I start to tell her congratulations, but she texts again.

Just come over when you're ready. I was thinking, we should probably visit your first Revenant. What's her name again?

I stare at my phone, stunned. Shit, Two. I haven't visited her in a week and a half.

I don't answer Will. Instead, I crank up my car and speed to the apartment, cursing under my breath. I'm such an idiot—that poor woman's been alone for so long. I've been neglecting her so I could spend money and sleep at hotels. Guilt eats at me, but I push it away. She's fine. I'll just keep better track of her next time, that's all.

I climb the stairs to the apartment, winded when I reach the sixth floor. I bend over and cough into the crook of my elbow. Jesus, what's wrong with me? I get tired climbing six flights normally, but not so much that I'm wheezing. Maybe I need some cough syrup. This cold won't leave me alone.

I open the door to 6C. "Hey, Two. Sorry I've been AWOL—"

I cut myself off. Two is pacing and wringing her hands, muttering to herself. The room's a mess—she's shredded the blanket into thin blue strings and the mattress looks like it's been clawed by a rabid raccoon.

"Uh . . ." I trail off, at a loss. "Two? Are you all right?"

She looks at me sharply. "Katrell, have you seen Charlie?"

"No . . ."

Two grits her teeth and paces in a tight circle. "I can't find him. People just take and take. I can't find him. I don't know where he is."

I step into the apartment, my heart pounding against my ribs. She was so calm before—what's going on? Why is she so agitated? "Two, it's okay, I'm here. We'll find Charlie."

Two stops pacing. She looks at me, her normally dull eyes sharp and focused.

"Liar," she says.

A chill creeps up my spine. Something's wrong. Two's always been so relaxed and quiet. Is it because I left her for so long? I'll have to come back more often . . . with Will. She's freaking me out right now. "I—I'm gonna go, okay? Stay here. Try to stay calm. I'll come back tomorrow."

Two snorts and sits on the mattress. Her blue dress is covered in dirt and there are holes in it. There's a long rip up one seam that wasn't there before, and her bare feet are black, like she's been wandering around outside again. "Leave me, Katrell. You have work to do."

Work. I forgot to ask off so I could go to Will's house. I look at my phone—past three-thirty already. I'm going to be late for my shift.

I leave the apartment, ignoring Two's eyes on my back, and dial Benny's number. It goes straight to voice mail.

I frown at my phone. Benny's is always open at this time. What's going on? I text Julio and he replies right away.

Sorry I forgot to tell you. Benny's is closed

What? *Why? How long?*

Idk. There's a long pause, then: *someone broke in last night, completely trashed the place. We won't be open for a while. Sorry Katrell*

I look at Two, who meets my eyes. Cold realization fills my body and I can't stop myself from trembling.

How'd her dress get ripped?

🔥

I knock on Will's door, my head pounding. I have to talk to Will. I'm gonna tell her everything—seeing Five at Old Navy, the gun, Two, Benny's. I need a brainstorming partner, one who will actually talk back and give me an idea about what to do.

Will's mom opens the door. She brightens when she sees me. "Oh, Katrell! I didn't know you were coming over."

"Is that okay?" I try hard to keep my nervous trembling under control. "I need to talk to Will."

"Oh, sure! Will had to go driving with Allen for a bit, but they'll be back soon. Come in."

I step inside, nodding. Will's mom never calls Allen "Dad" or even "my husband." This family has issues, I swear. But at least Allen just has a dad complex and not a hit-your-kid-and-kill-their-dog complex. I'd take the former any day.

"Do you want some juice? Water? A sandwich?" Will's mom says, entering the kitchen. Normally I'd be thrilled at the offer of food, but I'm not hungry today. Not after seeing Two and her ripped dress.

"No, thank you. I'll wait for Will in her room."

Will's mom hesitates for a second. She nods to the table, where a set of polished decorative dishes sit in front of four chairs. "Let's chat for a second, okay?"

I don't move. Why? Normally she'd let me go straight to Will's room. What does she want to talk about?

Will's mom sits first and I slowly sink into the chair opposite her. She smiles at me. "How's school? Will told me you had a pretty tough test today."

"It's fine. Same as always."

"I feel like we should catch up a bit." She's still smiling, but she's reminding me of Mike now—sharp eyes ready to catch me in a lie.

"Um, okay." I fidget in the chair. "I've been okay. Just sort of tired."

"You do look tired," she says. "Probably catching a cold. Allen's been sniffling all week, poor thing. I can give you some medicine before you go, okay?"

"Sure, thanks."

There's a short, tense silence. Will's mom takes a deep breath. "So, I see you got a new car."

Suddenly this awkward conversation makes sense. Will's mom knows me, knows my mom and where I live—she knows I can't afford a Mercedes. It has to look suspicious as hell. I relax immediately. I thought she was mad at me for some reason. "Oh, it's not mine. I'm borrowing it from a friend."

She raises her eyebrows. "Oh? It's such a nice car, I was just surprised."

Me too, I want to say, but I smile instead. "Don't worry. I didn't steal it."

I expect her to laugh, but she doesn't. Her smile has slipped into a slight frown, like she's thinking hard about my words. "You know, I grounded Will recently. Did she tell you?"

"Oh, yeah. Is she still grounded?"

"No, not anymore. But she was sneaking out of the house at near midnight." Will's mom stares into my eyes. "I worry about that. She could get hurt."

Realization sinks my heart into my toes. Will's mom thinks I'm the reason Will got in trouble. And what's worse is that it's true. I didn't even think about Will's mom catching her or punishing her. I just begged her to come, begged her to leave the safety of her home and help me resurrect dead people. I didn't think about Will at all.

"Katrell, look at me, honey." I do, hoping I can keep the guilt off my face. "If there's something going on, you can come and talk to me. Anytime. No questions asked. Okay? But you have to meet me halfway. I don't want you or Will to get hurt."

"Okay," I say softly. "Can I wait for Will in her room?"

She nods, her expression sad. "Of course. Let me know if you want something to eat later on."

I go to Will's room in a daze, my head spinning. Have I been asking for too much this whole time? I didn't even realize it. Will has a nice life and I'm wrecking it. I sit cross-legged in the middle of her floor and wonder how she could not love a mother like that.

I'm dozing when the door opens. Will throws down her backpack and kicks the door closed with one foot. She sighs and collapses on the floor beside me.

"Hard day?" I ask tentatively.

Tears bloom in the corners of her eyes. "I hate driving. I hate it, and I hate it when he tries to teach me stuff. He's just doing it because he feels like he has to."

I take in her frustrated expression, her unshed tears, her aggravation at a symbol of love, and decide to keep all my resurrection problems to myself.

"Will, that's not true." I ease closer, and our arms accidentally touch. Will jerks away like she's been bitten. "Sorry, sorry. But listen, he's just trying to be a dad, you know? That's what dads do. They teach you stuff or whatever."

Will looks like she wants to bite my head off, but she stays quiet.

"Okay, how about this. I'll teach you how to drive. It'll be easier with me, yeah? Then Allen will be impressed and you won't have to drive with him."

Will wipes her eyes and laughs. "In your Mercedes? Yeah, right."

"I mean it! If you want to learn, I'll teach you." I pause to sneeze and blow my nose. A dull ache pounds behind my eyes. Add this cold to my list of issues. "I taught myself. It's not hard, I swear."

Will's eyebrows scrunch with uncertainty. "You're not scared I'll scratch your car?"

"Who cares? I have thousands of—" I'm cut off by another sneeze. I shudder and wipe snot off my face with my sleeve.

"Are you sure you're okay?" Will asks. "I've been thinking, ever since you started this resurrection stuff, you haven't looked too good. Didn't you feel bad when you started the letters too?"

"Yeah . . ."

"Maybe you should ease up on them? I know it does no good to tell you to stop altogether."

"What's that supposed to mean?" I tease.

Will rolls her eyes. "I've tried. You always have to do everything on your own."

I don't answer. In this case, I really do have to do it by myself. I can't ask for her help anymore. As far as my resurrection business goes, I'm alone.

27

I cough into my arm, shivering, as I move up in line to buy some more cold medicine. Conrad watches me from outside the gas station, his face pressed against the glass. I'm sure the employees don't appreciate him smearing his wet nose all over the window, but no one says anything. With the cold gleam in his eye and the flecks of blood in his fur, who would?

I feel like shit. My head and neck are killing me, and now I've developed a thick, wet cough. Will says I should take a break or stop altogether, but how can I? I have more money than I've ever seen in my whole life. Yesterday I bought a giant TV and put it in my room. The day before that, I bought a new laptop and a stereo system. I don't even have Wi-Fi. I don't like listening to music without headphones. And I still have thirty-one thousand, four hundred and thirty-six dollars. I had to get to fourteen thousand—that was the plan. But now I'm over, way over, and I can't stop. I need a new money goal. I need to decide what I'm going to do with all this cash. My head throbs constantly now; it's hard to think. I wish I could talk to Will about this.

I reach the front of the line and put the medicine on the counter. The cashier seems bored, completely uninterested in me or my purchase. "Is that all?"

"Yeah." My voice sounds like a sixty-five-year-old smoker's. Speaking of smokers . . . my gaze wanders to the cigarettes behind the cashier. "Actually, wait. I want some of those."

The cashier follows my line of sight, his eyebrows raised. "Are you serious? How old are you?"

I pull out three hundreds and stare into his eyes. "Does it matter?"

His eyes widen and, after a moment, he says, "What kind do you want?"

I cough into my arm and take a deep breath. "You pick."

He gives me a red pack and I slide him the three Benjamins. I slip the cigarettes into my pocket, grab the cold medicine, and leave the gas station, smiling.

Conrad and I get into the car and I pull out the pack of cigarettes. Marlboros. I open it and take one out, and put it in my mouth. Spongy paper sticks to my lips. I've never smoked before. I don't even have a lighter. But I'm filled with giddy excitement at the thought that money can do anything, get you anything you want. How can I stop resurrections when I have the whole world in my hands? I could have it, if I wanted. I just have to keep going.

"What do you think, boy? Do I look cool?" Conrad looks at me, his eyes dull and calm. "Ah, what do you know."

I take out my phone and raise it to take a selfie, but pause when I see my face. Dark bags are etched under my eyes and a delicate glob of snot leaks from one nostril. My cheeks are slightly flushed and I'm pale, paler than I've ever been in my life.

A car pulls up next to me as I lower my phone. I look to my left and the cigarette drops from my lips.

Marquis.

He's in a new car, a Lexus, and three other men are with him. He grins at me from the passenger seat. "Hello, sweetheart. Let's chat."

I sit, frozen, as Marquis and the men climb out of the Lexus. He leans on the driver's-side door, his cold eyes looking me up and down. "How you like the car?"

"Um, it's great." Shit, I really didn't want to run into him again. I glance at Conrad, whose body blocks the glove box. He looks at me, his ears raised.

Marquis's grin widens. "Don't be so nervous, I just got some business for you." He pulls a piece of paper from his pocket. I take it and scan it—it's a name and phone number. "You text that number, bring back who they say, and you'll get a pretty penny. Promise."

My mouth full of cotton, I nod. "Thank you."

Marquis laughs, so suddenly that I flinch. "Relax, I ain't gonna hurt you. We family now, remember?"

I nod, unable to speak. I don't think I want to be part of Marquis's family, business perks or not. The men surrounding him are huge, their arms crisscrossed with tattoos and scars. They stare blankly over my head, except for one. He's looking dead at me.

Marquis continues. "Since we family, I'll drop talking about business. You use my gift yet?"

I debate on lying, but I shake my head.

"I like you, sweetheart, but you gotta get tough. You keep making money, you'll keep making trouble. Right, Rock?"

The man who's staring at me nods. He has a huge scar on his right bicep. "You're absolutely right."

"Men beatin' on you is one thing, but you gotta think long term. Folks gonna want what you got. That's what my gift is for." Marquis laughs a little. "People think twice before taking from someone strong. You get me?" I nod, determined to stay mute through this, and Marquis pats my shoulder. "Good. Remember, this world ain't gonna give you nothing. You gotta take it. Don't be scared to take what you want."

Marquis jerks his head, and Rock and the two other men climb back into the Lexus. Slowly, Marquis reaches into my car and takes the pack of Marlboros from my hand. He smirks at me. "Bit young for these, yeah?" He takes a cigarette out of the box and places it between his lips, then puts the pack in his jacket pocket. Then he gets into the car and Rock drives away.

I sit in my car for ten minutes, stunned. Marquis's words turn over and over in my head. He's terrifying, but he's sort of right, isn't he? I've been so unsure, but the answer is right here. If I want something, I should take it. Why should I stop? But doubt eats at me. I hope Taylor doesn't shred her bed like Two does her mattress. I hope Taylor doesn't wander around at night without permission. Because if she does, I won't have to figure anything out—I'll be dead.

I come home from school and park where I always do, three blocks from my house. I haven't texted Marquis's contact yet—I'm too scared. If it's a man like Rock and his friends and something goes wrong, I'm dead. Everything is so damn complicated, and my cold keeps getting worse. I can't catch a moment to breathe.

I get out of the car with Conrad and walk home, coughing every few minutes. Maybe I need to get more natural light and that'll help my cold. I read that online somewhere.

Conrad walks close at my side, his head swiveling back and forth. A woman herds her kids into the house when I pass. Men sitting on their porches stand, shuffling their feet nervously. Guess they've heard about what happened to Demarcus. Or seen me hanging out with Marquis.

I freeze when I see someone sitting on my porch. Conrad doesn't bark or growl, so I cautiously approach. Mom, maybe? No, too tall. I get closer, and relax when I recognize the red letterman jacket—Three.

"Hey, what's up?" I look for his parents, the Joneses, but no one else is around.

Three stares at me dully. "I need a place to stay."

I stare at him, stunned. "What?"

"I need a place to stay," he repeats.

What's going on? I pull out my phone and call the Joneses, frowning at Three.

"Hello?" Mrs. Jones's familiar voice answers. "Who is this?"

"Mrs. Jones, it's me. I have Th—I mean, um, Danny here. What's going on?"

There's a long silence. Then, "Who's Danny?"

My blood runs cold.

"Y-your son? Daniel? He was killed and I—I mean, you know. Is everything okay?"

"I'm sorry. . . ." Mrs. Jones sounds distant, like she's in a fog. "I'm sorry, who are you? I think there's been a mistake. I don't have a son."

"Mrs. Jones—"

"Goodbye. I hope you find who you're looking for."

She hangs up.

I look at Three, shocked into silence. He slouches, his hands in the pockets of his letterman jacket. It's clean, like it's just been washed, but his hair is wild, sticking up in patches, and his tennis shoes are dirty with mud. How can Mrs. Jones not remember him? How can she not remember her son, who she loved enough to ask me to bring him back to life?

And what does this mean for me?

28

Three sits by Two, both pairs of dull eyes staring at me. I pace feverishly, trying to come up with a plan. Three's parents forgot him, but why? No, wait, I have to back up. I don't know if they forgot him for sure—maybe something else is going on. Maybe it's not my fault at all. I nod to myself, my head aching. I need more proof. I need to confirm it with the other Revenants.

I pull out my phone and take Three's picture. I'll ask Mrs. Jones if she recognizes him, and then I'll go from there. Don't panic, Katrell.

"It'll be okay," I tell Three. He stares at me blankly. Will's words crawl into my brain—*you don't know what you can and can't do.* God, I hope she's wrong. "Just sit tight, okay? I'll fix this."

Three doesn't respond. I pat his arm, squeeze Two's hand, and stand. I whistle for Conrad, and when he trots out of the apartment, I close the door on them. They stare at me the whole time.

I walk home, my stomach twisting in knots. Conrad pads beside me, his paws silent on the pavement. I have a headache. I need some Advil and a nap, ASAP.

I open the door and my lip curls when I see Gerald on my couch. Luckily, he's asleep. I ease the front door closed and open a kitchen cabinet to look for the pain reliever.

"Baby?"

I freeze. Mom hasn't talked to me since our fight, even though I've texted her three times. I turn and she's right behind me. She doesn't look mad; in fact, she's smiling.

"Where've you been?" she asks. "I missed you."

I hesitate, my head pounding. She's not mad? "Mom, I'm sorry about earlier—"

"It's okay," she says. "I was hard on you. Conrad's been part of this family for a long time, so I understand why you don't want to give him up."

I stare at her, confused. She was adamant earlier. What changed? "Th-thanks. I'll keep him in my room as much as I can."

"Good!" Mom smiles. "I knew we could agree. As long as you can keep him in your room, there won't be a problem."

I smile back tentatively. I can't believe I got away with talking to her like that. I'm seized with an urge to sit down and talk with her, like we used to when I was little. She knows about my power, so I can tell her everything, if I want. And I do want—I really need to talk to someone about Two and Three and Five, and maybe even Marquis. I really want her to brush my hair. "Mom, what are you doing tomorrow? Can we get dinner?"

"Very tempting! But tomorrow I have somewhere to go. I have a job interview."

Shock and happiness jump into me all at once. She actually listened to me. Will was wrong—she's trying. I just had to put my foot down. Everything is going to be okay. I can't stop grinning. Even Conrad wags his tail as he looks up at Mom. "Well, jeez, lead with that! Where? What time?"

"Tomorrow is Kroger." Mom sighs, crossing her arms and looking at the ceiling. "I wish the bank had worked out. Not as hard of a job!"

"You already interviewed for that one?"

"Yes. Shame I didn't get it. Or the office job, or Burger King."

Wait, she's interviewed for so many already? I haven't been gone that long. "Sorry they didn't work out. . . . But I'm sure if—"

"Oh, me too. Interviewing is *so* expensive. Ubers to get to places, new interview clothes, hair money . . ."

Some of my happiness is fading, slipping through my fingers. "Yeah, that does sound like a lot. Where did you . . . ?" I leave the question hanging, desperate for a response that won't ruin this good thing I've been waiting for for so long.

Mom returns her gaze to me. She's smiling, but her eyes are cold, like they were during our fight. "Well, it's like you said, I have to get a job and everything that comes with it. Maybe rent will be late, or maybe the lights will be cut off, but you told me I have to get a job, didn't you?"

I'm frozen, paralyzed by confusion. I'm still smiling, but it's because I don't know how to feel. I asked her to get a job, but I didn't think . . . I didn't know it took all this. I just walked to Benny's and asked for an application.

Mom reaches for my face. She touches my cheek with light

fingers, staring coolly into my eyes. "Why are you so surprised, Katrell?" Her voice is a smooth purr. "This is what you wanted."

Mom turns and retreats to her room, leaving me in the kitchen, stunned.

I wander to my room, trying to sort through my feelings. Mom is looking for a job, and that's a good thing, right? But she went on four interviews in a week? And failed all of them, even Burger King? Something isn't right. It isn't, but I shove the bitter disappointment and suspicion away. I have to look at the facts first. Mom spent the rent money I gave her, even if it was for a good cause, and she knows I have enough to cover it. Nothing has changed. At least not right now.

I lie on my side on my new mattress, still without a bed frame, and look at my phone. I have a new wave of pictures from Eight and Nine, but nothing from earlier clients. For a long time, I stare at the screen, my mind blank. Then I type my "have to" money for the month into the phone's calculator and multiply it by twelve. I stare at that number for a long time, then multiply it by five.

I told Will that a year of security would be enough, but it's not. It's never going to be enough if I have to pay rent and fund dates and job interviews. So I can't stop at just fourteen thousand—not if I'm going to take care of Mom. So, five years it is. I stare at the number, burning it into my memory.

$67,800.

I breathe out, ignoring the uneasiness in my chest, and text Marquis's contact. Three coming back or not, someone in this family has to go to work. It has to be me. It always is.

29

Will grips the steering wheel of my Mercedes like she's holding on to a life preserver.

"I can't do this."

"We haven't even started yet." Will and I are in an empty parking lot, practicing driving. Well, we would be practicing. Will has been sitting in the driver's seat, shaking, for five minutes.

"I'm gonna scratch your car."

"I don't care. I literally have thousands. I'll fix it."

Will looks at me, her eyes wide like a terrified horse's. "I'm gonna kill us."

Jesus. She's a nervous wreck. "Will, it's just driving. It's the easiest thing to learn, I did it when I was eleven. The dumbasses in our grade can do it. You can too." Will doesn't look like she believes me, so I continue. "Take a deep breath. One more. Better?"

Will nods. She takes another shaky breath. "Okay. Tell me what to do."

"All right, check your mirrors. Can you see? Good. Now pull forward, go around the parking lot for a while, then park."

Will nods, her eyes straight forward. She inches ahead, not over ten miles per hour, and stays perfectly between the lines in the parking lot. She does two laps, then a flawless parking job in a space in the middle.

"Will, that was great!"

She doesn't look at me, smiling sheepishly. "No, I messed up a little—"

"Stop, it was perfect." I want to wrap my arms around her and tell her to stop doubting herself so much, but I refrain. "Listen, you're doing great. You just need some confidence."

Will grimaces, but doesn't answer.

"We'll practice every day after school."

"Trell—"

"I don't wanna hear it. You're gonna get your license and then you'll get a car and you can drive me places."

Will smiles at the road in front of her. "Okay. But can we be done for today?"

"For today, sure. But tomorrow, we're working on parking in slanted lines. And U-turns."

We get out and swap places. I adjust the seat—Will's legs are almost twice as long as mine. I have to sit with the steering wheel practically in my lap. When Will has her seat belt on, I reverse and pull out of the parking lot.

"Where to?" I ask.

"Wherever," Will says.

We could go shopping. Or to that art supply store Will likes. She was saying she's out of spray paint. Which reminds me— "Have you heard back from the contest?"

Will shakes her head. "Not yet. They said they'll post the results soon."

"God, I hope you win. I wanna go to Kennings. Maybe they'll serve caviar."

"They're not that fancy," Will says, laughing. Suddenly, her face falls. "I hope Chelsea doesn't come."

I glance at Will out of the corner of my eye. "Has she been bothering you?"

Will doesn't answer.

"Will?"

Will picks at her nails. "She . . . she's been emailing me. And I've been ignoring it, but yesterday I went to the art room and the canvas I was working on was ripped up."

Hot rage builds in my gut. I grip the steering wheel with tight fists. "I'm gonna make her wish she was dead."

"Don't," Will pleads. "It's okay, really. I was gonna start over on that one anyway. She doesn't ever touch me. I can deal with everything as long as she doesn't touch me."

"If she touches you, I'll kill her." Will looks miserable, so I sigh and stuff the rage to my toes. "Fine, we can change the subject. Just know that bitch has it coming if I catch her being mean to you again."

"It's okay, I swear," Will says. "How's your cold? You sound awful, Trell."

Not the subject I wanted. I'm starting to get a little worried. I haven't had a cold last this long before . . . but it's fine. Probably. I don't want to think about it. "Fine, fine. Next thing."

Will rolls her eyes. "Okay, but we're going to talk about it later. How are the Revenants?"

My insides jump with unpleasant shock when I think of Three. I smile at Will, hoping she can't see through it. "They're fine. Looking great."

Will nods. "Good. We should visit the one in the apartment today. I bet she's lonely, all by herself."

Oh, she has company. "Let's do that later. How about that art store? Then your house?"

Will frowns and for a second I think I'm caught. Then she shrugs and leans back in her seat. "Sure. I need to get a new canvas anyway. And Cheryl'll love you coming over."

I don't say anything. Instead, I head to the paint store, trying to get Three out of my mind.

I toss and turn, hot, cold, shaking, and battling the worst headache I've ever had. It feels like something's in my skull, crawling around. I pant, my eyes tightly closed. Is this a migraine? Do I have brain cancer? I roll to my side, whimpering, and hold my head in both hands.

The bug in my brain stabilizes after ten minutes and I can think a little better. What is wrong with me? Wait, didn't I feel like this when Two was at the window? I sit up, one hand still on my head, and look to the window—nothing's there. I start to lie back down, but then notice something is missing from my room. . . .

Conrad.

I scramble to my feet, my heart hammering. Conrad doesn't leave my side when I sleep; what's going on? My door is slightly ajar—how'd he get it open? I'm shaking so hard I can barely push the door open wider. I creep into the living room, cautious, and the front door is open too. Oh shit. I grab the metal bat by the door, my only defense against a robber. I hold it aloft, then peek outside.

Conrad's sitting in the middle of the yard, alone, his back to me. I lower the bat, letting it dangle in one hand, flooded with relief.

"What're you doing?" I whisper, hurrying to him. The wet grass chills my bare feet. Conrad looks at me, quiet. There's something pink poking between his jaws.

"Here, give me that." I take the pink cloth from him and shine my phone's flashlight on it. My stomach drops. It's a piece of clothing, soft, faded from use.

It's soaked with blood.

30

As weak morning sunlight steals into my room, I hold the bloody cloth in one hand and thumb it over and over, fear eating at my stomach. It's pink, faded—like Mom's bathrobe. But I checked, sick with worry, and her robe was hanging in the bathroom like always. Intact, no blood. If it's not from her clothing, then whose? I don't own anything this color; I know, because I spent all night tearing up my closet to check. I don't get how this could have happened. I didn't hear anything last night, not even Conrad leaving my room. I look at him and he stares back, his brown eyes unreadable.

"Where did you get this?" I ask him. "Did you bite someone?"

He stares at me, unmoved. Conrad doesn't bite. He's never bitten anyone, except for the guys in the graveyard. But he was protecting me then. He's never growled at anyone either, until Gerald. And Mom. But that was one time—

I jump in surprise when there's a tap at my window. A shadowy shape waits for me to answer. Two again? I open the curtains and my heart sinks to my toes.

It's Four.

"Hey," he grunts. He's looking up at me with bored, lifeless eyes. "I need a place to stay."

I take him to the apartment and settle him in next to Three. I can't ignore this anymore—I'm fucked. Four came back too, so that means they're all coming back. I've resurrected nine people, including Conrad. Am I just gonna store them in here?

"Hey, Two," I bark. Two looks at me groggily. "Do you like staying here? In the apartment?"

Two shrugs but says nothing.

"What about you?" I ask Three. He shrugs too. Well, it's not a no. I can keep them here temporarily. It's a big apartment; I can fit eight people in here, no problem. Conrad will be with me. The bigger question is if I should stop the resurrections altogether.

My head pounds and I sneeze into my hands. I wipe my palms on my jeans. My chest aches with indecision. This is bad. Really bad. If they're all coming back, that means Taylor will too. Marquis will probably forget, but what about Rock and the other men? What about the clients he sends me?

I need to talk to Will.

I shake my head, rejecting the idea. I can't. I have to figure this out by myself. I've done it for this long—this is just a bump in the road.

I call Conrad and close the apartment door. I'll go to school so I don't get another unexcused absence and then I'll decide what to do about my Revenant problem.

I wait for Will at our lunch table, chewing on my bottom lip nervously. I've been over several scenarios in my head, but I can't focus. Should I try writing a letter to the affected families to restore their memories? But my letters have only ever worked on the dead. I tried to hex Chelsea in seventh grade and it didn't work. I could contact everyone and warn them, but what good would that do? Marquis will literally kill me if I tell him he's going to forget Taylor. I'm trapped. I'm trapped and if I could just get rid of this damn headache, I could think clearly. . . .

Will comes from her English class, a rare smile on her face. She sits down in front of me, out of breath.

"Hey." I hesitate. I want to say, *Will, I'm in trouble. Here's what's going on.* But it would be cruel, wouldn't it? This isn't Will's problem.

"I have something to tell you," Will says. She's grinning wildly.

I stuff down my whining. I'll tell her later. Maybe. "Yeah, what's up?"

Will pulls out her phone. "Trell, I can't believe it, but look! They sent me an email just now and I won the art competition!"

Shock, then happiness fills my whole body. "No way! Let me see!" I scan the email—Wilhelmina Tapscott, winner of the 2018 Kennings Art Competition. "Oh my God."

"I know!" Happy tears gather in Will's eyes. "I can't believe I won. I still can't believe it."

"We get our caviar after all!" Will and I laugh, and for a split second I forget my Revenants are coming back homeless.

"What should I wear?" Will asks as she pulls out our lunches.

She pushes mine to me, but I don't open it. My stomach is in knots, part excitement for Will, part dread. "It has to be something fancy. Kennings is super nice."

"What about that blue dress? You look great in that one."

"The dark blue one?"

"Yeah. We can go shopping today for shoes if you want."

Will nods, smiling to herself. "Not today. I have to tell Cheryl. She's the one who helped me sign up."

A strange mix of sadness and pride fills my chest. "Tomorrow, then?"

"Deal." Will's smile fades into a normal, comfortable one. Her eyes still sparkle with excitement. "Anyway, don't let me hog the conversation. What's up with the letter writing? I feel like we haven't talked to Nana in forever."

I stare at Will, confusion stunning me for a second. "What? I can't write a letter to her. You know I'd probably bring her back if I did that, right?"

Will stares back at me, her expression blank. She scrunches her eyebrows, like she does when she's trying to figure out a math problem. "Yeah, I . . . I'm sorry, I forgot for a second." Her voice sounds confused, likes she's in a fog.

Just like Mrs. Jones.

I start to speak, but I'm cut off by Justin sliding into the seat beside me.

"What the—"

"Yo, Katrell." Justin grins at me. "Got something to ask you, couldn't wait."

I look at Will with confusion and Will frowns. Justin never

approaches me at lunch. He's a year under me, so we have nothing in common, except he's a letter client.

"What?"

Justin leans closer. "So, I heard they call you 'the Witch' now."

Demarcus and his crew called me that first, but now all my clients do. "Yeah, I guess. Why?"

"If you mess with the Witch, you get hurt, huh?"

What? Admittedly, I like the way that sounds, but I have no clue what he's talking about.

Justin must see my confusion because he clarifies. "Did you do that to Chelsea?"

"Do what?" Chelsea and I don't have any classes together. I'm too lazy for advanced classes and she prides herself on flunking every single one Mire High has to offer.

"Her arm's broken," Justin says. "And she's got scratches all up her neck."

"Oh. Well, I didn't do it. Wish I did."

"Come on, I know you did," Justin says. "According to Chelsea's friend, a dog broke into her room last night through her window and tore her up. You got a big dog, don't you?"

My stomach fills with ice. The pink material in Conrad's teeth.

"Conrad doesn't bite," Will says. She looks at me for reassurance, but I can't speak.

"That's not what Demarcus told me," Justin says. "Says a huge dog fucked him up for screwing with Katrell."

Will searches my face. "Is that true?"

I stand and yank Justin by his arm. "Come here, I gotta talk to you."

I drag him out of Will's earshot and away from the cafeteria. When we're by my English classroom, I let him go. "How many people know about this?"

Justin shrugs. "I don't know, a lot of people? I hear all sorts of shit about you, Katrell. Heard you're running with Marquis these days."

Yeah, and not for long if I don't fix things. But I have to stay calm and approach this like I did Two. Scientific method. "Okay, first, do you know who I am?"

Justin makes an ugly face at me. "Umm, yeah? Are you okay?"

I almost crumple with relief. Mrs. Jones didn't know who I was, but Justin does. Will does. Okay, I can work with this. "Do you know why we know each other?"

"Yeah, I pay you to see my uncle Kenny." He opens his mouth to say something else, but his eyebrows scrunch and he closes his mouth again. "Wait, why did we stop doing that again? You told me you couldn't do it anymore, but I can't . . ."

All the relief from before turns to ash.

I dig out my phone and find the picture I took of Three. I meant to send it to Mrs. Jones, but I've been so tired and everything is falling apart around me. "Justin, this is important. Do you know Daniel Jones?"

Justin's brow furrows again. "Who?"

Shit. Shit, they know each other, they were on the football team together, Justin gave me the Joneses' number— Calm down. I've got to stay calm. I turn my phone around and show him the photo. "Do you know this guy?"

Justin shakes his head and I want to throw up.

"Anyway," Justin says, "I just wanted to know if you fucked up

Chelsea. You're a badass, Katrell. Remember me when you come up, yeah?"

He pats my back, laughing, and heads back to the cafeteria. I watch him go, my head throbbing. It's not just the Joneses—everyone's forgotten about the Revenants.

Even Will.

31

After school, I hand Will the keys to my car. "Your turn to drive," I say, grinning.

Will groans, but with some coaxing, she gets into the driver's seat. I hurry to the passenger seat, pushing Conrad into the back. He grunts, but sits quietly behind me.

"I don't know how to back out."

"Yes, you do."

"Okay, fine, there's too many people to back out now."

"Okay. We'll wait."

Will makes an ugly face at me and I laugh, the last part turning into a thick cough. She reaches for me, like she's going to pat my back, but lets her hand fall to her side. "Are you all right? You sound horrible."

"Fine," I wheeze. I drink some lukewarm water from my water

bottle and it soothes my sore throat. "Now, look, you're clear, right? Put it in reverse and look in your mirrors."

Will shakes her head slowly, her hands gripping the wheel like a vise. "I can't believe you did this when you were eleven."

"What can I say? I'm a badass." I cough again and a searing pain shoots between my eyes. I rub my temples. "Anyway, go ahead. Back out, try to do it straight."

Will nods nervously and does the slowest reverse I've ever seen. Slow, but flawless. She successfully pulls out of the parking space and beams at me.

"See! You know how to drive, you just get nervous." I place my water bottle between us and grin at her. "We'll practice every day until you get it."

Will smiles tentatively at me. "Okay. Thanks, Trell."

Will puts the car in park and we switch places. I blow my nose and blink tears out of my eyes before pulling out of the school parking lot.

"So . . ." Will trails off. I glance at her. She's no longer smiling. "Are we gonna talk about Conrad?"

My chest tightens. I swung by my house before driving practice. I didn't want to leave him alone too long since I know he can get out of my room now. I can practically feel his eyes boring into the back of my head. "What's there to talk about? Dogs bite sometimes."

"Not Conrad," Will insists. "Conrad never bites, not since I've known him."

I don't want to talk about this. I grip the wheel with both hands. "Um, first, where do you wanna go? To your house?"

"Trell—"

"We can watch a movie, maybe? That'll be fun."

"No." Will's glaring at me. "Something's wrong and you're not telling me." She grips her knees. "What happened? Start from the beginning."

I stay quiet for a minute, my resolve crumbling like sand through my fingers. I can't hide it anymore. Not from her. "Okay, first, I have to ask you something. Don't freak out."

Will's hand shoots to her mouth, but she pauses and puts it back in her lap. "Okay. Go ahead."

"What's Two's real name?"

Will's quiet, so I glance at her out of the corner of my eye. She has that foggy, confused expression again. "Wait, who is Two?"

Fuck. I close my eyes and take a deep breath. "Do you remember why your mom grounded you?"

"I was sneaking out." I can practically see the gears turning in Will's head. "I was sneaking out to meet you. . . . What were we doing? Wait—" Her eyes widen and she grips her knees tighter. "The resurrections. You were resurrecting someone. Two, I mean Rose, was first. No, Conrad—" Will cuts herself off, horror crossing her face. "Why did I forget?"

I breathe a sigh of relief. Will hasn't forgotten completely. Probably because she saw so many resurrections. But will I have to keep reminding her? How long will she remember?

"Trell." Will's voice is shaky, but she's looking right at me. "Why did I forget? What's going on?"

I pull into Will's driveway and put the car in park. I drove here automatically; I don't remember the drive at all. Will's mom waves at us from inside the house. Will's dad sits on their porch, a book on his beer belly, fast asleep. I turn to Will, dread making me want to vomit.

"The Revenants' families forgot them, and they don't remember even when I remind them. And now Three and Four are living in the apartment with Two."

Will's eyes get so big, I'm scared they'll pop out of her head. "Oh, Trell. Oh no. I knew something would go wrong."

I quickly fill her in about the phone call with Mrs. Jones and Justin's reaction, and she groans.

"What're you gonna do?" she asks. "You have to find a way to get their memories back."

I shrug, wincing as the action aggravates my sore chest. "I don't know how. I've been thinking about it, but I can't. . . . Anyway, I'll figure it out. No problem."

"No problem?" Will's voice creeps up in pitch. "It's a *big* problem. What are you gonna do with them?"

I think of Marquis and his contacts. "That's not really what I'm worried about."

Will stares at me for a moment. "Wait, there's more, isn't there? There's something else?" I look away, biting my lip, and Will shakes her head. "No, you tell me everything right now. I knew you've been acting weird."

Slowly, painfully, I tell her about Marquis, the gun, Two's dress, and the incident with Five.

Will stares at me, speechless. She opens the glove box and there it is, the metal glinting in the afternoon light. "Holy shit," she breathes.

I hurry to continue. "But it's not so bad, if you think about it. See, the Revenants can live in the apartment. They don't hate it. They don't eat or breathe or feel pain, so I can just sort of put them there until I figure it out. And I can look for a solution as I go."

"What do you mean, 'as I go'?" Will blinks at me, seemingly in disbelief. "You're not saying you're going to do more resurrections, are you?"

I shrug helplessly. What else can I do? "I mean, I was thinking about it. Benny's got trashed, so I don't have a job, and I have to pay rent and stuff. And I was thinking, one year of 'have to' money isn't enough. So, I mean, I can figure it out. I'm sure there's a solution."

Will opens her door and gets out of the car. I follow her, unsure, and watch as she paces in her front yard, her teeth tearing her nails to the quick.

"No," she says. "No, no, no. No, I can't let you. This has gone too far."

"It hasn't," I say, already defensive. I barely believe myself, but if I give in now, everything really will fall apart. I have to believe there's a solution and I just haven't found it yet.

"You're in over your head." Will keeps pacing in a tight circle, looking at the ground. "You have to get rid of that gun, you have to find out how to return their memories, and you absolutely have to stop doing resurrections."

"I can't stop," I say. My mind goes painfully to Mom spending the rent money on interview clothes. "I have to have money. You don't know what's going on."

"I don't know what's going on because you won't tell me." Will stops pacing and stares at me, really looks at me. "Do you not trust me? Why didn't you tell me?"

"I do, I do trust you." My eyes sting, like I'm about to cry. "But I just didn't want to involve you in this. It's . . . it's dangerous. You'll get hurt."

"So it's okay for you to do it?" Will's exasperated. "You know you sound crazy, right?"

A surge of bitterness hits me. "Well, sorry I don't have a perfect life I can shit all over like you do. I have to do what I have to do."

Will's eyes grow round and there's a tense silence. "This is about your mom, isn't it? You're doing this for her."

"No, I'm not." I'm spitting my words, like I'm actually mad at Will. I'm not, though, I can't be. Will and I don't fight. We just don't. "Maybe I want some money for myself, did you think about that? Maybe I deserve some payment for putting up with so much bullshit for so long."

"No, this is about her." Will nods like she's so perfect and can pinpoint all my issues. "I'm sorry, Trell, but you shouldn't do this for her. She doesn't care about you. She never has. She'll bleed you dry if you let her."

A vicious amount of grief and hurt hits me all at once. It's not true. It's not true, and Will doesn't have a right to talk about Mom like that. "If you wanna talk about moms, let's talk about how you treat yours. You always treat Cheryl like shit, you know that? That poor woman bends over backward for you and all you do is ignore her."

Will looks like she's struggling for words. "That's none of your business."

"Well, seems like you're all in mine, telling me to stop resurrections."

"At least I'm not selling faulty shells," Will growls.

"Excuse me?" My voice is deadly calm. I'm giving her one chance to stop what she's doing. I'll forgive her if she apologizes now.

Will, who would normally back down, looks me in my eye and says, "I should have stopped you from doing resurrections after Conrad. Because they don't work."

"What?" I point to Conrad, who's watching our exchange with perked ears and tense body. "I brought him back from the dead. He's perfect."

"You're crazy, Trell. That's not the same dog. Not even close."

A surprising amount of pain hits me in my chest. "Take it back."

"Look at him. He doesn't eat, sleep, or breathe. He doesn't play with toys. He doesn't do anything except stare at you and me. And now he's biting people. Trell, you know Conrad doesn't bite. He would never bite anyone. You didn't bring him back. You haven't been bringing anyone back. They all just sit around and stare at you and can barely function. This has to stop."

A mix of fury, rage, and grief wells up inside me. "You don't know what the fuck you're talking about, Will. Conrad is fine and so are the other Revenants. Back the fuck off."

"Or what?"

Will isn't a bear in a cage anymore. Will is a bear who's pissed off, who's stretching her frame to its full height for the first time in years.

I'm not afraid of her. All I feel is fury, raw pain and anger, and I want to hurt her, make her feel this too. "It's not my fault you're weak, Will. I always have to save you, you know that? Who spent weeks talking to a brick wall because you went mute? Who coaxed you into talking to your parents so you could have a halfway normal life? Who taught you how to fucking drive? And this is how you treat me?"

Will steps back like I've hit her. Tears build in her eyes. My chest throbs with pain knowing that I hurt her, but I can barely feel it through the fury.

Will's shoulders tense and she stands up straight. The tears are gone. "I'm not your pet, Trell." Her voice is a quiet growl. "You always act like you're doing me some big favor. And I'm happy we're friends, but you can't just expect me to go along with everything you say because it comes out of your mouth. You're in deep and I'm trying to help you, but you're too stubborn to accept any ideas other than your own."

"I know what I'm doing!" I'm screaming. I'm screaming at Will, even though I know she's scared of loud voices. "I always know, damn it! I have two deadbeats at home and you and Conrad and I've always known what to do. Why is it suddenly not good enough, huh? You're supposed to support me. You're supposed to be on my side."

"I can't be when you're being so selfish."

"I'm selfish? Me? Wow, okay. Thanks for having my back, you've done a great job. After all I've done for you—"

"I'm trying to help you!" Will's frustration bubbles over and suddenly she's screaming too. "Look at yourself! This is killing you! You look like shit, Trell. You're selling your body and soul for money and it's not right."

I'm momentarily stunned by her raised voice, but I'm quickly consumed by bitterness again. "Well, excuse me, Wilhelmina, not everyone has a loving home and parents they can be dicks to. Sorry I don't have the money to say, 'Hey, maybe this is a bad idea.' Sorry I don't have the luxury of being a good person."

Will starts to say something, but Conrad raises his lips in a snarl.

We're both stunned into silence. Conrad has never growled at Will, not once.

Will's mouth closes into a tight line. "Fine. Fine, if that's what you want. Go resurrect a thousand people, but I don't want anything to do with it. I'm done."

"Fine," I snap. I tug at Conrad's collar and pull him into the front seat. I slam the passenger-side door. "Don't talk to me ever again. If you're not my friend, you're my enemy. Got it?"

Will doesn't say anything. Instead, she turns and marches into her house.

I get in my car and drive around for twenty minutes, mad as hell. Then I stop in front of my house and burst into tears.

Will was my best friend. She was my only constant in this world. And now she's gone? First Conrad, now Will? I hug Conrad's neck, wailing, but he doesn't react. He's like a heated statue. Will's words enter my brain—he's a shell. It's not true. It's not true. Will's wrong. She's wrong about Conrad, about the resurrections, about Mom. She's wrong about me.

Bitterly, I wipe my eyes and look at my texts. One from Marquis—*you talked to the customer I got you yet sweetheart?* My hand tightens around my phone. Marquis is right. If you want something, you have to take it. I can't be afraid anymore. If Will wants to abandon me, fine. I'm not going to stop, no matter what she says. I'm sitting on a gold mine and if she doesn't like it, too bad. I don't need anyone anymore.

32

I cough, hard, and pick at my wilted salad. The librarian glares at me, for eating or coughing, who knows. I glare back and chew my salad extra loud.

It's been two days since Will decided her moral high ground was more important than me. She was absent from school yesterday and didn't talk to me at all today. Not even a hello. Not even an acknowledgment. Four years of friendship ended just like that.

My salad tastes like acid and glue.

I throw it in the trash. Fuck Will. If she can drop me just like that, fine. She can't tell me what to do or how to live my life. I let out another wet cough and check my messages. Marquis's client finally texted me back last night. They called me "the Witch" in the text. They want to meet tonight.

Revenant Ten coming up.

"Hi, Katrell."

I nearly drop my phone. Mike grins down at me, hands on his hips. I take a deep breath and close the text.

"What do you want, Mike? You gave me a heart attack."

"I came to get a book, but saw you sitting here." Mike's grin gets even wider. "Good timing, because I need to talk to you."

"Again?" I shake my head, weary. "Leave me alone. I'm busy."

"Sulking over your fight with Miss Tapscott?"

I narrow my eyes at Mike. How does he know everything?

"I'll write you a note for algebra," he says.

I stand up and shoulder my backpack. "Deal. Lead the way."

Mike laughs and we go to his hole-in-the-wall office. He sits at his desk and pulls out a file while I ease into the wooden chair. My whole body aches, so I have to be careful.

"First, let's talk about your grades," Mike says. "Our goal was to improve in English. I talked to your teacher and she says you haven't turned in your essay for this week."

I look at my new shoes, exhaustion and shame coursing through me. "What, you brought me here to talk shit about me?"

"No." Mike's voice is gentle. "Sometimes we don't meet our goals. That's okay, because we can always readjust. Let's make a new one, okay?"

I look up at Mike and he's smiling kindly at me. I blink a few times to clear my eyes. "Okay," I say softly.

"Great! We can do something smaller, more focused. Maybe the English goal is too vague. Do you have something you'd like to do?"

I stare at him, lost. My brain is a mess of heated static. "I don't know."

"That's okay. Maybe a hobby you want to pursue? It doesn't have to be about school."

I stare down at my lap, thinking of the time before the past seven miserable months started. I used to have roller skates, and I'd go to the Walmart parking lot to practice on the weekends. I used to watch makeup tutorials on YouTube and practice in the mirror at home. I used to write poetry. I'd fill pages and pages of notebooks with poems and lyrics to made-up songs, and every once in a while, the words would make me feel a tiny bit better. They were even good enough to hang on Cheryl's fridge. I used to do a lot of stuff before Mom lost her job and I had to pick up the slack. I meet Mike's sharp eyes. "I . . . I want to write a poem."

Mike smiles, a quick upturn of one side of his mouth. "Sounds like a plan. You don't have to show it to me, but what about writing one before next week?"

I nod. I can do that. I'm rusty, and I haven't read any poetry in months, but I bet I could try something. "Okay."

Mike leans back in his chair, looking like a cat who's successfully caught a bird. "This is great, Katrell. I'm confident in you. And if you can't write a poem, we can switch to something else." He glances at a stack of papers on his desk. "Also! Have you had a chance to think about trade school?"

Is he serious? I don't have time for that. I've got too many balls in the air. "No. I've had a lot going on."

Mike's hawk eyes search my face for more, but I stay stubbornly quiet. He sits up straighter, shuffling his papers. "I understand. It's a busy time of year, with holidays and such." Thank God

Mike's throwing me a bone. "But if you get a second, take a look at the pamphlet. You might like something there! It's okay if you don't want to go to college, but it's good to have a plan in place for the future, right?"

"Yeah," I say, wiping my nose on the sleeve of the hoodie Will gave me. "A plan sounds good. Can I go now?"

"One more thing." Mike doesn't say anything else until I look up at him. He's no longer smiling. "Again, Katrell, I want to ask: Are you okay?"

Oh boy, here we go. "I'm fine. I just have a cold."

"You've had a cold for a while now, since our last meeting. Has anyone taken you to the doctor?"

"Thought I couldn't miss any more school." I try to laugh, but Mike doesn't join me.

"A visit to the doctor is an excused absence."

Yikes. Mike's not messing around. I straighten, more alert. I need to be careful so he doesn't trap me in a situation I can't talk myself out of. "I'm okay. It sounds worse than it is. And I don't have a fever or anything, so I'm good."

Mike's eyes have me frozen. I see why they call him Slenderman; he's terrifying when he wants to be. "We trust each other, don't we, Katrell? I wouldn't lie to you and you wouldn't lie to me. Right?"

"Right," I croak.

"So, I'm not going to lie to you—I'm starting to get concerned. You've lost a lot of weight alarmingly fast. You've had a cold for a long time. You look like you haven't slept in weeks." Mike stares into my eyes, into my soul. "I know something is going on at home, and I will have to make some calls if this continues. If something's happening, you can talk to me and avoid some unpleasantries. Okay?"

"Okay," I say, my voice shaky. I can't tell if he's trying to be kind to me or if this is a thinly veiled threat. Either way, I gotta get outta here.

"Good!" Mike's grin returns and I cautiously relax. He writes a quick excuse for algebra and gives it to me. He opens the door and I shuffle out of his office. "Let's make this a weekly thing, shall we? Until I know you're all right."

"Aw man, Mike—"

"I'll write you a note for PE."

"Done." I'd rather dodge his questions than go to PE. It hurts to run and I'm so tired. "See you next Friday?"

Mike smiles. "See you on Monday, Katrell. Have a good weekend."

I rest my head on the steering wheel, panting. I just completed the resurrection for Marquis's contact, but boy was that a bad idea. I'm about to throw up.

I've been busy. I got serious about Googling the gun and I figured out how to unload it and load it again. It has five bullets in it, and I have a holster I bought at a pawnshop. If I'm gonna have it, I might as well know how to use it. I also went to the apartment to check on Two, Three, and Four. There's something I didn't notice before—they talk to each other. Two is usually quiet, but Three and Four chat. Three talks about school a lot. He even mentions Mike.

I wrote a poem. It was about betrayal. I ripped it up.

My phone dings and I pick it up, my heart racing. It quickly returns to normal when I see the text isn't from Will. She hasn't texted me since our fight.

I heard you're a witch and you can help me.

Guess it's time for my second resurrection tonight.

I set the meeting for an hour from now; the place is the usual graveyard. Then I close my eyes for a short nap. "Conrad, watch the car," I grunt. He doesn't make a sound, but I'm sure he heard me. I'm sure he understands. It's not like what Will said. He's still Conrad. He has to be.

My alarm goes off and I sit up wearily. Two a.m. One more resurrection, and I can go to bed. I open the car door, but suddenly I'm on the ground, on my side. I blink in confusion, my head pounding sluggishly. I get to my hands and knees, panting, the world swimming before my eyes. Get it together, Katrell. You can do this. Just one more.

I take an icy breath and get to my feet. I lean heavily on the car until the world stops swimming, then let Conrad out of the passenger side. We walk to the center of the graveyard, where a hooded figure is waiting.

He's a huge man, with a big gut and small, beady eyes. He's holding . . . a flowerpot?

"You the witch?" he asks. His voice trembles slightly.

"Depends. Who's asking?"

"I—I am." He tugs at his collar and shifts the pot to his hip. "I got your number from a buddy of mine. Said you can bring people back. He said you'd look like death and have a big-ass dog."

My reputation precedes me, I guess. "You got money? It ain't free."

I expect him to lean his flowerpot down, but instead he pulls off his backpack and opens it. I can see the pointed edges of stacked bills from here.

I nod. "What's the name?"

"Caroline. She's my great-aunt. I—I need to talk to her. She hid something of mine."

Not the usual request, but okay. "Where's her grave?"

"Here." He holds up the flowerpot.

"What?"

"In here. She was cremated."

Oh, it's an urn. I cough into my arm, frowning. I've never resurrected anyone who was cremated. It's worth a try. I reach for the urn, then grab paper and a pen. I write the message, short as always.

Caroline,

> *Wake up.*

—Katrell

The words glow bright red, as usual, but then they fade back to black. Uh-oh. I try again—same result. One more time and nothing happens. I wait thirty seconds, sixty, ninety. Nothing.

Turns out I can't resurrect everyone.

"What's wrong?" The man leans over my shoulder, frowning at the three notes. "He said it happened pretty quick."

I shake my head, standing. "Sorry, looks like I can't do it without a body. Who knew, right?"

The man gapes at me. "B-but Caroline—I need what she hid from me. I need to know where it is!"

"Sorry." I shrug. "I feel bad I wasted your time, so no charge. Good luck finding your thing or whatever."

The man snatches my shirt collar so fast I barely have time to process it. One second I'm on the ground, ready to go home, the next I'm dangling in the air. He brings my face to his, so close I can see the sweat beading on his forehead and the blackheads on his nose.

"You better do your job, bitch." His breath smells like vomit. "If you don't bring her back, right now, I—I'll kill you."

I stare at him, rage eating away at my stomach. Another man thinking it's his right to lay his hands on me. Men always think they can put their hands on women with no consequences. I'm so tired of this. I'm so tired of being used as a commodity.

I reach for the gun at my hip, but Conrad charges and chomps down on the man's arm. I fall to the ground as the man screams, flailing and kicking at Conrad. But my dog holds on, his teeth bared, his eyes almost glowing in the dark. I let Conrad terrorize the man for a few seconds, but when he starts crying, I give in. Pathetic. They all think they're bad until Conrad comes along.

"All right, Con, enough."

Conrad doesn't let go.

I watch in disbelief as he bites into the man's shoulder, ripping and tearing. Blood spurts from the wound, soaking them both. The man kicks over the urn and ashes fly into the air.

He didn't stop. He didn't listen to me.

"Conrad!"

Conrad freezes, his jaws still clamped around the man's shoulder. The man is sobbing, pushing against Conrad's chest with his good arm.

"Conrad, enough. Let go."

Slowly, he rises away from the man, and turns. His whole chest is stained red and flecks of Aunt Caroline stick to his mouth and paws. He walks to me, his eyes never leaving mine.

I look at the man, then at his backpack. I hesitate, but scoop it into my arms. I didn't do the resurrection, but he attacked me. I deserve his money. This is payment for not letting Conrad kill him.

I open the passenger door for Conrad, then get into the car. I look at my dog. He returns my stare, his eyes dull and lifeless. It's okay. Nothing's wrong—he probably just didn't hear me. The man struggles to his feet and limps away, crying. I toss the backpack in the backseat, crank up my car, and get ready to go home.

33

When I get home, I hose the man's blood from Conrad's fur.

He stands still under the cold water, even though it has to be freezing. It's like Two said: Revenants don't feel anything.

The water runs over him, long after he's clean. I can't find the strength to turn off the tap. I'm washing a man's blood off my dog. I'm wearing a gun I can't shoot on my hip. I have six thousand dollars plus whatever's in the backpack in my Mercedes. What is happening to me? Everything used to be simple. I would go to Will's house and her mom would make us food and we'd talk to Clara sometimes. Mom was working too, once upon a time, and sometimes she had good boyfriends who were kind to me. I was happy, wasn't I? Or was I? There's always been a Gerald, hasn't there? I've always had to use every cent I made for her and not for me. The only thing I've ever been able to control was my power, and now even that's betraying me. Maybe I've never been happy. Maybe I never will be.

I look up at the sky, feeling the tears at the edge of my vision. I wish I'd never fought with Will. She was the only person who always stuck by me, even through all my bullshit. I wish she'd tell me what to do. I'd listen this time, I swear. But I blew it. Yawning sadness threatens to consume me, but I shove it down until I'm numb and cold. One thing at a time. Wash Conrad, take some Advil, go to bed.

Finally, I cut off the water and Conrad shakes the excess from his fur. I need to get him inside quickly so he won't catch a cold. If he can even get sick now. I don't know. There's a lot I don't know.

When I unlock the front door, Mom's waiting for me.

She smiles and gets up from the table, but I don't smile back. I'm tired as hell and freezing. Conrad's wet. I just want to be left alone.

"Hey, baby," Mom says. "Where've you been? Out with Will?"

"Don't worry about it." It comes out sharper than I intended, so I continue. "I'm sorry, I'm tired. I'm going to my room."

"Wait, wait." She pats my arm. "I was thinking we could get that dinner you wanted."

Hope flutters in my chest. It's pitifully weak, but it's there. "Really?"

Mom nods, smiling. "Yep! We can go to that place you like, the one with the shrimp. You used to even eat the tails when you were little. You said you didn't want to waste even a little bit. Do you remember?" Mom laughs and it drags a smile out of me too.

"Yeah, I do." I still eat the tails, actually. We just haven't had shrimp in a long time. "How's the job hunt going?"

Mom shrugs. "Not great. But I'm looking to get away for a bit. I was thinking we could go on a trip. Wouldn't that be fun? I've always wanted to go to Gatlinburg."

The smile is frozen on my lips. Gatlinburg. A trip to an amusement park. She doesn't have a job. Gerald works part-time at Wendy's. She wants me to pay for it.

Like someone lit a match, all the sadness turns to rage in an instant.

"I'm not giving you any more money." I'm snarling at her, because all I can think of is Will saying, "She'll bleed you dry if you let her." I have to put my foot down, right now. I have to stop enabling her, and then it'll be okay. "You can go to Gatlinburg if you want, but you better pay for it."

Mom looks stunned, like I just slapped her. "Excuse me? I am your mother, and you will not talk to me like that."

"I always take care of you," I growl. "I always have, but I'm not doing it anymore."

"Oh, I see." Mom laughs again, but it's bitter, hollow. "You get a little bit of money and now you can't look out for your own?"

"I have—"

"I hear things, Katrell. How Marquis is sweet on you, and you suddenly got that car and all this money. And I don't say a word, no I don't, because I want you to be happy. I let you keep your dog and I let you stay out all night doing God knows what, and I never say a thing. And all I ask is for you to do one thing for me and you won't?"

My brain is foggy with confusion. Mom knows about Marquis and she didn't say anything? She knew I was hanging out with a drug dealer and didn't say a word? Will's mom caught her sneaking out and grounded her. My mom just sat by and collected money at my expense. My emotions are out of control. I want to hit her, really hit her and make her bleed. I want to cry and say I'm sorry, I'll give you the money because I do have a lot and I really am in over my head because I can't spend it and hiding it in the house is useless. I don't know what to do.

"If you're gonna act like that," Mom says, her eyes narrowed, all traces of her good mood gone, "there's gonna be some changes around here. The first thing is that dog gotta go. I let you keep it for a while, but if you can't mind me, you can't keep it. Second, you're gonna stop taking drugs."

I gape at her. "I—what? I'm not taking anything."

Mom grabs my arm, so suddenly it makes me flinch. "I'm not an idiot, Katrell. You got them bags under your eyes, you're losing weight." Mom squeezes my arm, tight so it hurts. "That's gotta stop. You ain't gonna use drugs in my house if you can't share the drug money you make."

"Let me go." My voice doesn't even sound like mine; it's fierce and even, almost a growl. The confusion is replaced by fury. Fire bubbles up in my chest and my hands curl into fists. In "her" house? Where she doesn't pay rent half the time? Where she dicks around all day while I go to school and work? I'll do fucking meth in front of her if I want. This is *my* house. Everything in it belongs to me.

Mom squeezes my arm even tighter. "This is your fault, Katrell. This wouldn't be happening if you weren't so selfish. You know that, right?"

I'm so mad I can barely see. I'm selfish? *I'm* selfish? I've given her everything I've had for sixteen years. All of me, for so long.

"Let me go," I say again. Conrad steps beside me, lifts his top lip, and snarls at her. There's fabric between his teeth from his attack on the man earlier. "If you don't let me go right now, I don't know what's going to happen."

Slowly, Mom releases me. She backs away and I grab Conrad's collar and tug him into my room. He doesn't stop snarling until she's out of his sight.

"Gerald was right," Mom says softly. She's watching me with contempt, like I'm not even her daughter. Like I'm a bug she can't seem to squash. "I've spoiled you."

I close my bedroom door on her. I sink to the floor, my back against the wall. My throat burns and my eyes sting, but I don't have any tears left to cry.

The pain in my head is excruciating.

It's like there are bugs crawling, pinching. I toss and turn in agony. I claw at my head, trying to scratch the bugs out of my brain. Make it stop—someone, help me. Conrad watches from a corner of the room, his eyes burning in the dark.

When the attack is over, I slump on my mattress, spent. I pant, overheated and freezing at the same time. My sheets are soaking wet. Fuck, what am I going to do? I press one hand to my forehead, but I can't tell whether I have a fever or not. *Will was right*, a voice whispers in my ear. *This is killing you.*

What does Will know? She accused Conrad of being a shell. He's not, he's a good dog. He protected me. He bit someone I didn't know. He didn't come to my aid when I was thrashing with my headache. He wouldn't listen to me. He's a good dog.

I think I fall asleep, because the next thing I know, it's morning and light is seeping through my curtains. I blink against the sun, my stomach in knots and my head foggy. I have to go to school. I can't be late again. How many absences do I have? Four and two-thirds? I try to lift my head, but a sharp jab of pain grounds me again. It's gonna have to be five absences now.

I fall asleep again and wake up shaking but more alert. I grab my phone—9:33, Monday morning. Late for school. Fuck, Mike's gonna be pissed. We're supposed to meet today too. I groan, roll out of bed, and head to the bathroom for a shower and to brush my teeth. When I'm done, I look in the mirror. I look like hell. Dark bags are under my eyes and I'm pale. Scratches from my finger-nails snake up and down my temples and forehead. My edges are curly from sweat. Mike's right; I have lost weight. A lot of weight. I pick at my shirt, noticing for the first time that it dwarfs me. It's at least two sizes too big. No wonder Mom thought I was on drugs.

Things are falling apart.

"Get your shit together, Katrell," I tell the skeleton me in the mirror. My reflection's eyebrows scrunch in determination. Okay, I can do this. I fought with Mom—so what? She didn't mean it. She was upset, I was upset—it's okay. Families fight sometimes. Things are fine, or they will be after some time. My reflection bobs her head, agreeing with me. I'll focus on school, which is the immediate issue. I'm already late, so I can take some time to get myself together and fool Mike. I'll put on some clothes that fit, put on makeup, eat something. I can do this.

I put my plan into action, and by 10:45, I'm ready to go to school. I'll be honest: I look like a bad bitch with my makeup, new leggings, and size-too-big dress. I even shaved my legs. I'm ready for anything. I kiss Conrad's cheek and tell him to be good, then head to my car. I tiptoe past Gerald, who's fast asleep on the couch. Mom is nowhere to be seen.

When I get outside, the apartment building catches my eye. I should check on Two, Three, and Four. I have time—I just have to be at school before noon. I pocket my keys and slip through the chain-link fence, climb the stairs, and open the door to apartment 6C.

"Hey, it's me. How're—" I let out a cross between a yelp and a scream. It's not just Two, Three, and Four in the room—

Five and Six are here too.

I stare at them, openmouthed. I had no idea. They didn't come to me, they just set up camp here. Five gets to her feet, smiling, but Six ignores me completely.

"Hi, Katrell," Five says. She has a coy smile on her lips, like she's keeping a secret from me. "I didn't have a home anymore, so I came here."

"How . . ." I scan the room in disbelief. They're all watching me, waiting. "How did you know where to go?"

Five doesn't say anything. She just smiles.

Things just keep getting worse. So it's true, it's not a fluke—all the families really will lose their memories. I resurrected someone else this weekend. Will was right. Oh goddamn it, Will was right.

"Katrell, where's Will?" Four asks. "She never visits anymore."

"Katrell hurt her feelings," Six grunts. "Katrell's mean."

How do they even know about my fight with Will? Only Conrad was there. They were here.

"I wanna go to school," Three complains. "Katrell makes us stay here. I hate it."

"Me too," Four says. "I'd like to go back to school. Though I think college isn't for me."

"Y'all sure are chatty today," I growl. They fall quiet, like I just scolded them. I rub my temples. This can't be happening. I cover my eyes, my head pounding, and try to think. All I can hear is Will's voice: "You're in deep."

"I brought you something," Three says, pulling my attention back to him. He holds out his hand and I cross the room to take the gift. He drops something cold into my palm. I bring it closer and my body freezes.

It's a necklace studded with diamonds.

"Where did you get this?" I demand.

Three smiles, but it's more of a sneer. "It's for you," he says.

"Where did you get it?" I repeat. My knuckles are white around the necklace. "Tell me."

"Here's another gift," Five says. She brings me a pair of pearl earrings. She's beaming. "I know you'll love them. I know you like jewelry."

This can't be happening. I pull out my phone and check the Mire news, but there's nothing new from last night.

"You should be grateful," Four says. "It's hard to get into houses. People don't leave their windows open anymore."

I drop the necklace and earrings like I've been burned.

"What are you doing?" I clutch my hair, my chest tight with panic. They robbed someone. They took things without asking. They moved from where I put them.

They all stare at me, dead-eyed, none of them smiling any-more. I shake my head, panting.

"I have to go to school." My voice sounds ragged, foreign. "Please, stay here. Don't move. Stay in the apartment."

No one answers at first. Then Two inclines her head and blinks slowly.

"Have a good day, dear," she says. "If you see Charlie, would you tell him where I am?"

I nod, frantic, and close the door behind me. After school, I have to find something to remove fingerprints from stolen jewelry.

34

That night, I decide to open Mike's pamphlet.

He wasn't mad at me for being late. I lied and said I overslept, and he said it was okay. But he seemed disappointed, which sucks. I wish I could tell him what I'm dealing with here. Rogue Revenants and Will being an asshole and headaches sent straight from hell to fuck me up. But I just have to smile and say I overslept, because who would believe the truth?

I lie on my side, touching the glossy finish of the pamphlet. I doused the necklace and earrings in rubbing alcohol and threw them in a trash can in the park. I wore gloves. I also bought more cough syrup. I locked the Revenants in the apartment with a chair under the doorknob and they complained, actually told me no. This is the most vocal I've ever heard them. They're not docile and lifeless like Two. They don't want to just sit there. They stole jewelry from someone.

Will was right. I have to stop.

An ache spreads through my chest and tears build in my eyes. Everything's falling apart. Nothing makes sense anymore. It's all going bad, one thing after another. The Revenants are doing whatever they want, wandering around, stealing. If they'd just stay put, this wouldn't be happening. If the families hadn't lost their memories, I'd be in the clear. The Revenants are one more problem on my long list. If they'd disappear, I could have some space to think about everything else.

I wonder how you kill a Revenant.

I wipe my eyes and open the pamphlet. I can at least be productive if I'm gonna sit here and be miserable. The pamphlet is all about trade school, and what you have to do to get certifications. Plumber. Welder. Construction. Boring. Does Mike think I want to push dirt around for the rest of my life? Please. I start to close the pamphlet, but one job description catches my eye—electrician. I read it half-heartedly, then with increasing interest. Average annual salary is fifty thousand. Twenty-five dollars an hour. Some electricians work inside, out of the heat and cold. I could do that. I pull up some information on my phone and Google tells me math and English are the best traits for an electrician. The best part is that trade school only costs eleven thousand dollars, max. I have that stuffed in my gutted copy of *War and Peace*. Fifty K is a lot better than minimum wage. I browse electrician attire, getting more and more excited. Sometimes they wear little hard hats. I would look cute as fuck in a hard hat.

A text pops up in front of my research. *Are you the Witch?*

I hesitate, my thumb hovering over the notification. I didn't meet my goal of sixty-seven thousand—I'm only at forty-seven now. But I have the car and a new mattress, and the toilet doesn't leak anymore. I have enough. And I really don't need to add to my Revenant problem. I need to figure out how to subdue the ones I've got before I take on anymore.

Not looking for more clients

Five thousand

Ha, like that's a lot.

No

Twenty thousand

I stare at my phone for a long time, then sit up. My head swims for a moment, but after the spell passes, I stand.

"Come on, Conrad." I place the pamphlet on my desk, beside my old red headphones. "We gotta do one more job."

I stand in the alley behind Fernando's Laundromat, frowning. The client asked me to meet him here, which is odd. Usually we meet in the graveyard. I touch Conrad's head for comfort. He doesn't move; instead, he stares straight ahead.

At a man approaching us.

I stand still, one hand on Conrad, the other on the gun. Conrad lifts his ears and lets out a small growl. The man gets closer and closer, until he walks under a streetlight and I recognize him.

Gerald.

"What do you want?" I can't hide the disgust in my voice. "Go away. I'm meeting someone here."

Gerald puts his hands in his pockets and leans against the brick wall of the coin laundry. He's unsmiling. "So it's true. You're the Witch."

"Oh come on, *you're* the client?" I shake my head. "You don't have twenty thousand dollars, you can barely buy Taco Bell. Bye."

"You leave when I tell you to leave," Gerald snaps. Conrad lifts his top lip and exposes his teeth. Gerald steps closer to me, his expression grave. "I knew something wasn't right 'bout you. I knew it. So this how you getting all that money? Bringing folks back from the dead?"

I glare at Gerald, wishing with all my might I could hit him. I cough into my arm before answering. "Yeah, genius. So smart. Now leave me alone. I've got the worst cold of all time and you're not helping."

Gerald steps even closer, uncomfortably close. Close enough to grab me. "I think you playing with fire, Katrell. And it just got worse for you." He finally smiles and a shiver snakes up my spine. "I want some a that money."

I can't help but laugh. "What? You think I'm just gonna give you my money? Go home, Gerald. You're high."

"I talked to your mom." Gerald smirks as my laugh dies in my chest. "She said you were ungrateful and wouldn't share your money. And you are. So you gon' share, because she's your mother and I'm sick of you disrespecting her. I ain't no kin to you, I get that, but when you disrespect her, we got a big problem."

I study his face, a combination of revulsion and fascination swirling in my stomach. He really is sprung, isn't he? He really likes her. I can't believe it. He was so freaked out by Conrad, and yet here he is, threatening me because Mom cried to him that we fought. For the first time, I feel something other than disgust for Gerald—pity. He's absolutely pathetic. In a few months, she'll have someone else and he'll have nothing left but his damaged pride.

"Fuck off, Gerald. Go get a job, and then you'll make your own money."

Gerald grabs my shirt collar and jerks me once, hard. "You listen to me, Katrell. I'm the adult here. You making money running game on folks, and we want some. An' you gon' give it to me 'cause I'm the adult and you the child. You understand?"

I glare into his eyes, the pity gone. Hatred boils in my chest. I clench my hand around the butt of the gun.

"You'll have to pry it from my dead hands, you lazy fuck." I cough again, hard, and spit a glob of mucus in his face. It rolls down his cheek, slow, and I have to suppress the intense desire to laugh.

I see his fist coming, I'm expecting it by now, but I don't expect the pain that comes from it slamming into my nose. I scream and he pushes me to the ground, punching and kicking me. I want to get up and fight back but there's a pressure in my chest and I can't breathe. I start coughing, hacking, and the remaining air rushes out of my lungs when he kicks me in the ribs.

"You feel like listening now?" Gerald kicks me again and I can't hold back a whimper. Conrad is barking and snarling, the sound reverberating through my head. "Spare the rod, spoil the child, remember?"

I pull myself into a sitting position, my whole body aching from the cold and Gerald's assault. I'm tired of this. I'm so tired of this. I pull out the gun Marquis gave me and point it at Gerald.

"Gerald," I say, my voice muffled with my blood, "think carefully about what you say next."

I can't even savor the terror on his face. Even if I win today, there's tomorrow. He loves Mom, so he won't leave. I'm trapped, like I've always been. I'm tired. Conrad paces beside me, snarling viciously. We must look like quite a pair—a short, pudgy girl with a gun she's never fired and a snarling dog who used to be gentle. What happened to us? We're unrecognizable. Gerald must be shitting himself, the poor bastard.

"Listen carefully." My voice is flat, tired. Marquis's words run through my head: If someone won't respect you, you make them respect you. "You're never going to hit me again. You're never going to speak to me again. Okay? Because if you do, I'll blow your kneecaps out."

"O-okay, Katrell. You got it." Gerald's voice trembles. His hand moves toward his hip and Conrad barks savagely, lunging at him. He steps back in fear.

"Throw your gun away, you idiot. I'll fucking shoot you."

Grudgingly, Gerald tosses his gun to the side.

I cough into my elbow, mucus and blood climbing my throat. I spit the mixture out wearily. "Get out of here, Gerald. Get out of my life."

Gerald backs away, uncertain. I lower the gun and put it back in its holster. I never even took the safety off. I touch Conrad, but he jerks away from me. His eyes are on Gerald and he's snarling so loud and hard, foam flecks his lips.

"Conrad?"

Conrad's body is vibrating with fury. His eyes are focused and cold, staring straight at Gerald. Gerald backs up another step and Conrad lets out a guttural snarl.

"Conrad, it's okay," I say slowly, reaching for his collar. "He's leaving. It's okay."

Conrad looks at me for one breathless second. Then he lowers his head, tenses his muscles, and charges.

I watch in stunned disbelief as Conrad knocks Gerald on his back and closes his jaws around Gerald's leg.

The screaming is horrible. Gerald struggles to get away, but Conrad is relentless. Gerald grabs a pocketknife from his jeans and stabs at Conrad, but Conrad doesn't react. He bites farther into Gerald's leg and tears his pants leg away. Blood is everywhere, on Conrad, on Gerald, pooling beneath the grisly fight.

"Call him off!" Gerald yells, trying to hold Conrad at arm's length while Conrad snaps at his face.

"Conrad, stop, boy! Let him go!" I step closer, fear making it hard to breathe. He's not stopping. He's ripping skin and muscle off Gerald's right arm.

"Call him off!!" Gerald's screaming, crying, trying to get away, but Conrad is too heavy. Gerald manages to reach his gun and empties three shots into Conrad. My stomach clenches, but nothing happens. Conrad's still snarling and biting into Gerald.

He won't stop.

"Conrad, no!" My head buzzes, bugs running rampant. I double over, gasping. I call to Conrad again, but he ignores me and lunges at Gerald one more time.

"Call him—" Gerald's voice is cut off with a wet gag as Conrad's teeth close around his throat.

It's like everything is happening in slow motion. My dog jerks his head and blood jumps from Gerald's throat. Gerald writhes, his hands flying to his neck. Conrad pulls his head back, stringy muscle and sinew dangling from his jaws. Gerald's hands go limp and he's still. Conrad turns to me, blood dousing his entire front half.

His face is twisted and bloody from the bullets—one in his eye, one in the middle of his head, one in his neck. He shakes, like he's dispelling water after a bath, and three bullets clink to the ground. In seconds, his face morphs back to normal. No blood. No holes. No sign that he'd ever been shot.

His eyes burn orange in the dark.

35

I sit in my room under a heavy blanket, watching the five o'clock news. I've been watching the news all day—I didn't go to school. How could I? Gerald is dead.

There was nothing about him on the morning news, but at eleven, they said there had been a murder and the police were investigating further. At one, the Mire police came to the house and talked to Mom. I stayed in my room. She cried for hours after they left.

"Breaking news," the anchor says. "This is a public alert for the Mire metro area. There are reports of a rabid dog loose in Mire. Please keep pets indoors and make sure their rabies shots are up to date."

I look at Conrad, who's sitting in the corner of my room. He's quiet, staring at me with lifeless eyes.

I watch TV for another hour, waiting for the six o'clock news.

This time, the anchor has a police officer to interview. The news anchor has bright red hair and small, focused eyes. The officer is in full uniform and has a tall mop of curly black hair. He looks like a small buffalo.

"Can you tell me more about the rabid dog situation?" the anchor asks.

The cop stares into the camera gravely. "There have been reports of a large dog attacking people around Mire. We urge citizens to be cautious and mindful of their surroundings. The animal is large and dangerous, and can cause serious harm to anyone it attacks."

Well, they've got something right.

"How did this happen?" the anchor asks. They spend a few minutes talking about rabies and how it's spread. Irrelevant, since Conrad doesn't have rabies.

"We need to wrap up, but can you confirm that a dog is responsible for the death of Gerald Miller?"

The cop shifts uncomfortably. "I'm not at liberty to say."

"So his death was an accident, not foul play?"

"Again, I can't say. We're not ruling anything out." The cop shoots a warning glance at the anchor before returning his focus to the camera. "However, if anyone has any information, please call the police department at the nonemergency number."

I close my eyes. They're raw, burning with exhaustion. What am I going to do? Conrad killed Gerald. For ten minutes after he died, I couldn't do anything. I stood there in a pool of blood, too shocked to scream. When I came to my senses, I got in my car, wiped my fingerprints off Marquis's gun, and buried it in Two's old grave. I couldn't look at it anymore. If I'd thrown it away earlier, maybe things would have been different. If I'd thrown it away, maybe Gerald wouldn't be dead. I left Gerald's gun next to him—I didn't want to touch it. Then I rushed Conrad home and gave him three baths and brushed his teeth. He just let me, just stared straight ahead. Conrad hates baths. Hated. Before he died, he hated baths. Before he died, he wouldn't bite anyone. Before he died, he was a good dog.

Everything is falling apart.

My phone buzzes and I look at it, a dull pounding behind my eyes. I jerk a little—Will. Will's calling me.

I'm paralyzed with indecision. Will hasn't wanted anything to do with me since our fight, but she's calling . . . I should answer, but I can't. I can't talk to her and hear her say "I told you so." Because she was right all along and I didn't believe her and now someone is dead.

The call ends and I press my head to my knees. It feels just as raw as my eyes. I had several attacks through the night, the kind where it feels like bugs are rummaging around in my brain. Those coupled with the bruises from Gerald's fists and I'm so weak I feel like I'll pass out any moment.

Faintly, I hear Mom answer a knock at the front door. People have been in and out all day, offering Mom quiet condolences and food. She's been really hamming it up, bursting into sobs with every new visitor. But maybe she did love Gerald. He loved her. Maybe they were destined to be together and I ruined their happiness. I guess we'll never know.

As the news ends, I wobble to my feet. I have to get out of here.

Someone will talk about Conrad and it'll all be over. I have to take him with me. Gerald shot him point-blank, but he just shook it off like it was nothing.

Conrad can't die. The Revenants can't die. I can't fix this.

I have to run.

I start packing, but hesitate when I get to a dress two sizes too big for me. I'm well and truly fucked. But then again, everyone is forgetting about me and the work I've done. Maybe everyone will forget about Conrad too. I'm up to six out of ten. The only loose end is the guy who asked me to resurrect ashes and I couldn't do it. I glance at Conrad. He's staring into my eyes.

I need to calm down and think. A sharp pain stabs my chest when I try to take a deep breath, so I settle for pacing my room until I get winded. I don't have to leave, not yet. I'll wait until the rest of my clients forget, then figure out what to do with the guy who won't forget me. And I'll have to figure out what to do with the orphaned Revenants, especially now that I know bullets can't kill them. But one step at a time. I need this headache to go away so I can think and Advil isn't cutting it. I'll go to the doctor; fix my cold and get Mike off my back for missing today. Two birds with one stone.

I go to one of my hiding spots, a hollowed-out copy of the Bible, to pick out some money for a visit to urgent care. I don't have insurance, so just an office visit will cost me at least a hundred bucks. All for a damn note so I can stay home from school and not get locked up in a group home. I open the book and stare at its contents.

It's empty.

I had twelve hundred in here. Twelve hundred dollars. I close the Bible, a slow burn starting in my feet and climbing into my stomach. I check the piggy bank on my desk and it's empty too. The burn climbs to my chest. I check the rest of my hiding places and they're all fine, so at least Mom didn't clean me out. Fifteen hundred dollars, gone.

I leave my room, seething, and go to her room. The click of Conrad's nails follows me. I don't knock; instead, I snatch open her door and say, "Where is my money?"

Mom's sitting on her bed, but she jumps to her feet when I storm in. She glares at me, hatred burning in her eyes.

"Somebody gotta bury him," Mom says. "It ain't free."

"Use your money then. Don't use mine."

"You got plenty to spare, with you slinging an' all."

"You don't know what the fuck you're talking about."

"You swear at me one more time, Katrell Louise, and I'll—"

"You'll what?" The burning is up to my face, overwhelming me. I close my hands into fists. I want to break something over her head and knock some sense into her. "You'll hit me? News flash, your shithead boyfriend has been doing that all along."

"Don't speak ill of the dead." Mom looks like she's either going to cry or strike me but can't decide which to do first.

Pain stretches all over my body because here it is, my proof that Will was right. She really doesn't care. She can see the fresh bruises on my face, but she doesn't care. My knees get weak, but fury burns me up from the inside out and dulls the pain.

"You're such an idiot!" I'm screeching, wrapping up the sorrow in anger and pouring it all on her. "I've put up with your bullshit for so long and I'm tired of it. You never pick me, you know that? It's always Gerald, or Kaleb, or whoever you're fucking at the time—"

Mom slaps me, hard.

The burn is at the top of my head. I ball my hand into a fist and hit her back.

Mom falls to the ground, one hand on her cheek, her eyes wide with shock. I'm panting, wheezing, the burn still full force and not abating. "Listen to me. You fucking listen, okay? You don't own me. You don't get to say a fucking word to me. You're too late to act like a parent. Since I'm the adult here, you listen to what I got to say.

"You don't do shit around here, you know that? You stay at home all day and do nothing. I go to work every day of my god-damn sophomore year, I'm failing all my classes because I'm so tired, and you just take my money and blow it on stupid shit. I'm not gonna fucking take it anymore. You know Will's mom cares about her? Do you know how shitty I feel when I come home to you, who can't be bothered to protect me from your asshole of the week? Look at my face, Mom. Fucking look. What happened to 'you and me'? You've been watching them beat the shit out of me this whole time and you didn't do anything. I've been in hell for years and you don't even care.

"I want my money. All of it. It doesn't belong to you—you don't get to just take what you want from me anymore. Do you hear me? I work hard and you're just a freeloader." I'm in a frenzy. I'm sweating, hot, burning. I grab shot glasses and the wolf figurine and the silver-backed brush from Mom's vanity. "This is mine, all of it." I throw them to the floor in front of her. She flinches as the glass shatters and the delicate brush splits in two. "This house is mine and everything in it. I bought it, me, not you. You bring a man in my house again, you'll wish you were dead. Do you hear me? I said, do you hear me?"

I'm interrupted by a harsh cough that makes me lean over in pain. When I'm done, I straighten and point at Mom. "I want my money. All of it. Now."

"It's gone," Mom says, her voice barely audible. "I spent it to bury him."

I curl my lip in disgust. "Then get it back. I'll give you three days, but you better have it back."

"Or what?" Mom's voice trembles. "Or you'll kill me like you killed him?"

I glare at her, rage and sadness and a pathetic amount of love turned hatred making me want to vomit.

"What do you think?"

I'm done. The burn is ebbing, back down from my head to my stomach to my knees. My whole body hurts. My head's killing me. There's a dull buzzing, bugs about to move. I step backward and almost stumble over Conrad. In my tirade, I forgot about him. He's growling softly, showing all his teeth. His eyes are locked on Mom.

I turn away from her to leave.

"I hate you," Mom says. Her voice is broken—she's crying. "I hate you so much."

I leave her room.

"I wish I'd never had you!" Mom screams. "I should have left you at a fire station when you first started seeing stuff that wasn't there."

I walk through the kitchen, Conrad behind me.

"You're a monster."

I slam the front door behind me, cutting her off.

I sit on the porch and watch everyone mill around, coming home from work or leaving for work or walking to church, and burst into tears.

I don't know how long I cry, for finally realizing that Will was right, for hitting my mother, for turning into a monster, but eventually I'm spent. I blow my nose into the hem of my sweater—my snot is tinted red. I wipe my face free of tears and stare at my bare feet for ten minutes, my mind painfully blank. Then I stand, brush off my clothes, and go inside to get ready for school tomorrow.

36

I stand in front of Mike's office, swaying slightly. I'm dizzy and cold, and I feel so guilty. I can't believe I had a meltdown on Mom. Maybe I was too harsh on her. It's my fault, some of it. I didn't apologize for letting Conrad kill Gerald. I should have apologized. But I don't know how to take back what I said. I don't know if I can fix this.

I look up at the COUNSELOR plate on Mike's office door. Maybe he knows about how to apologize to your mom. And your best friend. Mike looks like he knows a lot.

I knock on his door, breathless for several fearful seconds. The door swings open and Mike looks down at me, his eyebrows raised. His surprise melts into concern.

"Katrell, I didn't expect you."

"I know it's not Monday," I say, my voice a hoarse croak. Pain shoots down my throat every time I talk. "But I was hoping I could ask you for some advice? If that's okay?"

"Sure," Mike says, and my chest soars with hope. Maybe Mike can help me fix this. My head hurts too bad to think anymore.

Mike lets me in and we sit in our usual places. The wooden chair digs into my butt, worse than usual. My bones ache with every movement, even breathing. I've got some sort of superflu, I bet. Mike searches my face with his razor eyes. He's more on edge today; his shoulders are tense. I hope this isn't a bad time.

"Okay, Katrell, what would you like to talk about?"

"I got into a big fight with my mom." I pause to cough wetly into my arm. "A big one, Mike, huge. I said some awful things. And I want to fix it, but I don't know how."

Mike nods slowly, still staring at me. "Well, sometimes people argue. That's normal, healthy even. No one can get along a hundred percent of the time."

Me and Will used to. We did, but maybe it was because I was treating her like a pet, like she said. Maybe I'm wrong about everything. My head throbs dully.

"What was the fight about?" Mike asks.

I hesitate, trying to sort out what I have to lie about. But it's hard, harder than normal. "Mom, she tries, but she hardly ever thinks about me, you know? See, she has all these boyfriends and she always picks them over me. Sometimes they're nice, but sometimes—" I cut myself off. That's too far.

"Anyway, she just makes me so mad. It's supposed to be me and her, you know? That's the way it's always been. But Will told me that Mom doesn't care about me, and that hurt my feelings because it might be true." I hesitate. Mike's face is blurring. I blink to clear my eyes. "Sorry, does that make sense?"

"It does." Mike's voice is gentle. "You care about her a lot."

"Yes!" I knew it. I knew Mike would understand. This was a good idea. "I do. I love her. I have to, she's my mom. We're family."

Mike nods again. "It's true that she's your family, but that doesn't mean you're obligated to love her."

I blink in confusion. "What? Of course I do."

"You know the saying 'blood is thicker than water'? Well, there's another version. This one is 'The blood of the covenant is thicker than the water of the womb.'" Mike meets my eyes. "It means that just because you share DNA with someone doesn't mean you're bound to them for life. If they hurt you, it's okay to be angry with them. If they're toxic, it's okay to get away from them. The bonds you form with others, like through friendship, can be and often are stronger than family ties."

I try to process what he just told me. Is Mom toxic? Wait, am I toxic? How would I know?

I must look troubled, because Mike continues. "But that's not what you asked, I know. You want to know how to make up with your mom."

I nod. "Yeah, I . . . I said something terrible."

"People do terrible things out of anger," Mike says. "It's normal. As far as making up, be sincere. Say you're sorry and mean it."

"That's all?" I could have thought of that.

Mike smiles. "It's harder in practice. You have to talk to her in person, so it'll take some courage. I'd say try after you've both cooled off."

I nod, tired but relieved. Mike didn't help me much, but talking to him has made me feel better. Since me and Will fought, I don't have anyone to talk to.

Mike is quiet for a few seconds. "Was that all you wanted to talk about today?"

"Yeah," I say. "I've been really stressed, you know. I just snapped on Mom and I am sorry, I really am. I hope she forgives me."

Mike doesn't say anything for a while. Then, "I'd like to talk about something else."

"Sure." The longer I stay here, the less I have to go to class. I'm so far behind I can't catch up. It's pointless.

He pauses, just for a second. "Katrell, I don't want you to get upset, but you do not look well."

"Oh." I look down at my clothes. I'm wearing Will's hoodie, and it's got bloodstains from my split lip on it. I haven't washed it. It's also huge on me and hangs like a curtain.

"Can we go to the nurse's office?" Mike asks. He's already standing. "We can finish our conversation there."

"Oh, sure." I stand and the room lurches to one side. I hang on to Mike's desk for support. When I can see straight, Mike's expression is anxious. "I'm fine, just a little dizzy," I assure him.

We walk to the nurse's office, which is pretty close to his. Still, I'm out of breath by the time we get there. Mike opens the door for me and I shuffle into the room.

"Hey, Stacy," Mike says to the nurse. She turns from her desk, perched on a rolling stool. "Katrell isn't feeling well."

"It's just a cold," I tell her.

"Hmm, have a seat." I sit on the one creaky cot in the cramped office and Stacy sticks a thermometer in my mouth. Mike watches from the doorway like a worried, skinny giant. The thermometer beeps and Stacy checks it. "Whew, not feeling well indeed. You've got a fever, young lady: 101.6."

Oh. Guess it's the flu after all.

"I'll call your parents," Stacy says, rolling to her desk on the stool. "Can't stay here with a fever."

"I'd like to call her mother, if that's okay," Mike says. He and Stacy share a long glance, like they're communicating telepathically.

"Okay," Stacy says slowly. She gets up from the stool. "I'll be in the cafeteria for a bit. Come get me if a student comes in."

Mike nods and Stacy leaves. He comes to my side and gets to his knees, so he's shorter than me.

"Katrell." His voice is painfully gentle, like he's talking to a kid. "I want to be transparent with you, okay? I'm going to tell you what I'm about to do."

My shoulders stiffen. "I just have a cold. Or the flu, maybe. It's not a big deal."

"You've been sick for weeks," Mike reminds me. "Katrell, I'm going to be honest, I am worried about you. I'm concerned by what you told me."

"I didn't say anything." Beads of sweat pop out along my hairline. I'm so cold, it's unbearable. Did I say too much? I thought I did well. My head hurts, making it hard to think, but I'm sure I didn't say anything bad.

"You said your mom always chooses her boyfriends over you. That means you've been in a situation where you needed her to choose you and she didn't." Mike hesitates. "You're unwell, even though I mentioned the doctor weeks ago. You're wearing a lot of makeup and your lip is split."

"I fell," I whisper, begging him with my eyes. Mom didn't do this. She just slapped me, she didn't beat me like Gerald did.

Mike's sharp eyes soften. They're almost sad. "I'm sure you did," he says. "But I need to talk to your mom and make sure, okay?"

I shake my head, tears rising in my eyes. This can't be happening. I shouldn't have come to him. I forgot he's a damn bloodhound. I forgot we weren't friends and his job is to ruin my life.

"Hey, it's okay." Mike holds out his hands to me. I want to take them, but keep mine folded in my lap. "Listen, we trust each other, right? I'm being transparent. You're not in trouble, not even a little. This isn't your fault. You've done well, okay? You've done really well, Katrell. You love your mom and you work hard for her. I'm proud of you."

I sniffle, a tear spilling over the rim of my lower lid. I blink and more fall. I'm filled with confusion and gratitude, misplaced loyalty and exhaustion. I don't want Mom to get in trouble because of me. She's all I have left. It's me and her, always, like she said. We have to protect each other. Mom called me selfish, and she's right. It would be selfish to tell Mike the truth.

Mike moves to Stacy's desk and grabs a box of tissues. He hands it to me and I grip the box tight. I can't believe I'm crying in front of Mike. What an embarrassment.

"It's okay," Mike says softly. "It's okay to cry, Katrell. You've been through a lot. It's time to rest, don't you think? It's time to let me help you."

I wipe my eyes with the sleeve of Will's hoodie. "N-no, I'm okay. What are you going to do after you call Mom?"

"I'm going to talk to her about getting you to a doctor. Then I'm going to come to your house with my friend Kathy. She's just another counselor, don't worry. I'm just going to talk to your mom, no one is getting in trouble. And then we'll go from there."

I look away, wanting to believe him. That's not so bad. Them coming to my house is risky because it's a dump since I've been too sick to clean, but I'll text Mom and give her a heads up. She can out-talk anyone—she'll be okay. I look back at Mike and nod. His face softens.

"It's going to be fine," he tells me. He gets to his feet. "Lie down, I'll get Stacy. Just rest, okay? I'll take it from here."

I lie down on my side, easing my aching head onto the thin pillow, and Mike brings me a blanket. I watch him leave the room through half-closed eyes and then text Mom. She doesn't answer, as usual. She's still mad, probably, but I hope I gave her enough notice. I close my eyes fully and fall into an uneasy sleep, full of nightmares of screaming and Gerald's blood and Conrad's eyes glowing in the dark.

"How is she?" someone says.

"She's been out for a while. Did you get the mom?"

"No. I called three times, but she didn't answer. I'm worried. I have to report abuse and this seals the deal on that."

My eyes pop open. Mike and Stacy are talking a few feet away, their backs to me. Someone placed a heavy quilt over me and a cool washcloth on my forehead. I take the washcloth away—it's stained with my makeup.

"Poor girl," Stacy says. "You think the mom did it?"

"No," Mike says. "But I think she stood by and let it happen, and that's just as bad."

I glare at Mike's back. Help me, my ass. I knew it was too good to be true. They're trying to pin everything on Mom. I curse under my breath. I always have to fix everything.

I pretend to be asleep until Mike and Stacy leave. Then I jump up, grab my backpack, and go to the parking lot. I unlock my car and slide behind the wheel. Conrad looks up at me from the backseat. His brown eyes are lifeless, dull. I take a wet, shallow breath, thinking. Mom'll take care of cleaning—I just have to go to the doctor. That's what Mike wants, right? I'll take myself and everything will be fixed. I have cash in my car, over six grand, so I'll go straight to urgent care. I nod to myself, determined, and crank up the car. Urgent care it is.

37

end up at the apartment building.

I was going to urgent care, but I had to stop driving because my head was hurting so bad I couldn't see. I guess I passed out, because the next thing I knew, it was after five and the sun was gone and almost all the doctors' offices nearby were closed. I was close to the apartment, and I haven't checked on the Revenants in a while, so here I am. My head throbs as I climb the stairs. I'll check on them and then go to urgent care. Those close at eight, I think. I have to hurry—I want to avoid the ER. And I want to be better for Will's art show. It's tomorrow. I want to go. I want to apologize.

When I open the door to the apartment, the Revenants look up at me. Some of them have dirt on their clothes and one of Six's shoes is missing. They've been leaving again.

"Hi, Katrell!" Five says, bouncing over to me. "Did you rest well at school?"

I blink at her tiredly, my head throbbing. "Yeah. It was fine."

"Oh, good," Three grunts from the floor. His shoulders droop and he stares sullenly at his feet. "You get to go to school and we don't. How nice."

"Did you apologize to Will yet?" Four asks. "You should. You were really mean to her."

"Downright cruel," Five agrees.

Six stands and holds his hand out to me. "A gift," he says. He drops a diamond-studded bracelet into my hand.

I have a terrible headache.

"Mom isn't giving your money back, you know," Three says. He's sneering at me. "Serves you right. Should have put the money in the bank."

"Your fault," Four agrees.

"This will help you since Mom won't give it back," Five says. She gives me a worn leather wallet. I open it and see a photo of an elderly neighbor, Mr. Jenkins. The wallet has three credit cards, two twenties, and a picture of a little girl with braids.

I'm going to throw up.

"Katrell's mad," Three says, laughing. "She's always mad these days, huh?"

"Hey," I bark. The Revenants immediately go quiet and the life leaves their eyes. They're like overgrown, frustrating dolls. Dolls who go out at night and rob houses and old men. "Listen, didn't I tell you not to leave here? So why are you still giving me this junk? Stop it. Stop leaving."

"You know, this is actually good for you," Five says after a moment. Her mischievous expression is back. "No one can remember us."

"Yep," Four agrees. "We're ghosts."

"No one can see ghosts except Katrell," Six says.

I shake my aching head. They're maddening. I'd tear my hair out if it was long enough. "What the hell are you talking about? Can you just stop leaving? Please?"

"I'm saying, if we're ghosts, we can take as much jewelry as we want. We can take whatever we want." Five grins at me, a nasty, cold smile. "You can be rich, richer than you already are, Katrell. We can do that for you."

I stare at them, cold shivers racing down my spine. I'm struck by the horror of what they're saying . . . and the horror that, just for a second, it doesn't sound like a bad idea. "Why . . . why would you say that? Who even said I wanted you to steal shit for me? Just stop, okay? Stop leaving."

They stare at me in silence. Then, softly, Three says, "We only do what you want us to do, Katrell."

🔥

I drive to Will's house because I don't know what else to do.

There are bugs in my brain again. Moving around, biting, buzzing. When Conrad was attacking Gerald and he wouldn't stop, I got this same pain. When Two showed up at my window. The night before they gave me the jewelry. It's the Revenants, it has to be. They're running amok and I'm paying for it.

I can't go to urgent care like this. They'll send me to the ER, and I'll really be in trouble then. But where can I go? What should I do? So, I'm at Will's because it's all I can think of. Maybe I can apologize, and everything will be a little easier. Will's house is lit up, and I can see her dad pacing back and forth in the living room window. Will's room is dark, though. Is she not home?

I pick up my phone, hands trembling, and try to get to her name. I'm shaking so bad the phone bounces out of my hands and onto the floor, by my feet. I swear and close my eyes. Deep breaths, Katrell. Just like I tell Will when she's having a panic attack. Just like I used to, anyway.

When I open my eyes, no calmer, I look at Conrad. He sits next to me, silent, staring out the passenger-side window as if he doesn't have a care in the world. As if he hasn't turned into an immortal, vicious dog I can't control. As if everything is fine and not falling apart.

"What should I do, Conrad?" I whisper.

Conrad continues to stare out the window at Will's house. I look past him, into the living room window. Her dad paces, his eyes glued to the TV, and her mom washes dishes in the kitchen.

And there's Will, in her pajamas, sitting just a few feet from her dad. A sketch pad in her lap. Calm. Happy.

Something sharp and painful sneaks into my chest and I squeeze my eyes closed so I can't see her. I can't ask her for help, even though I want to, I really do. I can't screw up her happiness. I don't have the right, not after our fight.

After a few minutes, I can breathe again. When I open my eyes, Conrad's looking at me. His eyes are quiet, cold. I wonder if he sees the same in mine.

"Come on," I say, my voice quiet. I crank up the car and kick my phone under the driver's seat with my heel. "Let's go."

I'm at the apartment again.

I almost went home, almost went in, but our house was cold, dark, lifeless. The opposite of Will's. So, I'm here, at the apartment. Conrad and I can sleep here tonight. Maybe if we just stay away from other people, Conrad won't attack anyone. Maybe I can still fix this.

"Okay, boy," I say, opening the passenger-side door after I grab my backpack, "we gotta lay low for a while. Give me a second to figure things out."

Conrad looks up at me, ears pricked, then jumps out of the car. He trots up to the chain-link fence and stares intently at the apartment building. I lock the car and start to climb the fence, but Conrad nudges the gate.

It's unlocked.

I look up at the building, dread swirling in my chest. The Revenants aren't sitting quietly like I told them to. They're always leaving.

And one is waiting for me on the front steps.

I walk through the gate, my arms heavy, defeated. It's like I'm going to face a firing squad. Conrad trots ahead of me and meets the Revenant. It pats his head and looks up at me. Torn blue dress, distant, uninterested eyes—Two.

I sit next to Two on the stoop, my chest and head and nose aching. I cradle my head in my hands, looking down at the concrete steps. At least it's Two and not one of the others. Three would probably sneer at me and make fun of my weakness. Who knows what Five would do.

"Two," I say, weariness dragging at my tone, "why are you outside the apartment?"

Two doesn't answer for a while. When I finally turn to look at her, she's watching me closely, studying my face. Finally, she says, "I wanted out."

I lean back on my hands, a bubble of sudden laughter ripping from my chest. "Oh yeah, of course you do. We all do, don't we? We just want out." The laugh dies as quickly as it came. I look up at the moon, the stars, and tears build in my eyes. "Everything is out of control, Two."

"Yes," Two says, petting Conrad's head. "I know."

"If you and the other Revenants would just stay in the damn apartment." My fingers curl, trying to grip the cold concrete. "No, if your families hadn't forgotten you, it would all have worked out. Everything would have worked out if that hadn't gone wrong."

Two is silent. Conrad is silent. Two dead bodies listening to my pathetic rant.

"Everything would be okay if . . ." I trail off, the words dying on my lips. I'm so stupid—there's something I haven't tried yet. I fumble with my backpack and pull out a pen and my battered notebook. I flip to a clean page, shivering with cold and anticipation. It's time. It's over. My moneymaking idea didn't pan out, so it's time to cut my losses. If I can drop some dead weight, I can think about what to do with Conrad. The homeless Revenants have to go. It sucks, but not everything works out the way you want the first try.

Maybe next time.

I touch my pen to the page.

Rose,

It's time to return to the land of the dead.

—Katrell

As soon as I sign my name, the ink glows hot. I drop the page, expecting it to ignite, but nothing happens. I turn the page over, my heart hammering. The ink is black and dry, just like what happened at the graveyard with the cremated woman.

No.

I try everything. Letter after letter. Some long, some short, some just Rose's name over and over. It's not working. The letters don't work. I don't have a way to kill them.

I'm screwed.

"Katrell," Two says. I look up at her, dread swirling in my stomach. Her eyes glow orange in the dark. "Are you trying to get rid of me?"

Panic surges into me all at once. I want to scream, or run, but I'm paralyzed. She's so close. She's sitting so close; she could snap my neck if she wanted.

Instead, Two's eyes lose their glow and she looks away.

"It's okay," she says. Her voice is so quiet, I can barely hear her. "I want to run away too." She shrugs her bony shoulders, still patting Conrad's broad head. "But people who are trapped have nowhere to run."

Two stands and walks into the building. She pauses and looks back at me. She's smiling at me gently, sadly.

"Good night, dear. I think you know what you have to do."

38

I try to hide my coughing as Will gives her acceptance speech.
She's wearing a dark blue dress, the one I suggested, and a string
of pearls rests around her neck. Her hair's pressed into pretty,
loose curls. Her parents are at the front of the audience, beaming.
Will shuffles her notes nervously, and I send her mental positivity.
Not that she can feel it, I'm sure. I'm hiding so far in the back she
can't even see me.

I've been sleeping in my car, slumped against the steering
wheel, in a staring contest with my former pet. I don't know what
I'm going to do. Conrad killed Gerald, and what if the killing
doesn't stop? I can't do anything about it. Conrad was shot three
times and kept going. I wrote seventeen letters to Two and she's
still alive. They can't die. They can't die and they won't listen
to me.

I'm overwhelmed.

Two's right. I know what I need to do. I need Will's help.

Will finishes her speech and everyone claps. She nods at the audience, clearly embarrassed, and joins her parents in the front row. Will's mom and dad talk to her, excitement on their faces. Will looks at her feet every so often, but mostly she looks them in the eye, smiling. Good for her.

A short white man in a suit takes the podium. "Thank you, Miss Tapscott, for your beautiful words, and especially your beautiful art." He smiles at the crowd. "We'll be open for another two hours, so feel free to browse our talented winner's paintings. There are details on our website if you're interested in purchasing. We have refreshments in the back. Congratulations again, Wilhelmina!"

The crowd claps again and everyone breaks into small groups, chatting. A woman tries to talk to Will, but Will tenses up and backs away after only a few seconds. Her parents rescue her, and Will turns toward me, relief on her face. I don't have time to hide—she sees me immediately. She jerks to a stop and stares at me, her mouth slightly open.

Okay. Now or never. I swallow, my throat burning, and take a few tentative steps toward her. She doesn't run away, so I close the gap until we're inches apart.

I clear my throat. "Hi, Will."

"What're you doing here?" She sounds curious, but her words are tinged with caution.

"I wanted to come. I mean, I promised." I cough into my arm, breathless with nerves. "Your art is really good and I wanted to support you. And I'm sorry I didn't get you a gift, but I will soon. Promise."

A number of emotions cross Will's face, but she settles on anger. Uh-oh.

"You didn't have to come." She sounds strong and harsh, so unlike herself. "You shouldn't have, after everything you said to me."

"Will, I'm sorry—"

"I don't forgive you."

I stare at her, stunned. I blink back tears.

"You are selfish, and cruel, and you only care about yourself." Will's mad, actually mad. I don't think she was this mad during our fight. "You said some really shitty things to me, you know? You made me feel horrible. And I'm just trying to help you. That's all I've ever done."

"Will . . . ," I say weakly. "I just—"

"No, I'm not done. Stop trying to talk over me like you always do."

I shut my mouth and listen.

Will angrily tucks a strand of hair behind one ear. "I bet you're here just because you miss having someone to take all your bullshit. I can't believe you'd seriously hurt people, all for money. And then get mad when I call you out! And you show up to my art show, all sad and sick and looking for sympathy." She suddenly goes quiet. "Okay, I'm done. You can talk."

"I didn't come here because I wanted you to feel sorry for me," I mumble. I can barely look her in the eye. She's right. She was always right. "I just came to say I'm sorry and I want us to be friends again. That's all."

"After all you said?" Will snorts. "You'll have to try harder than that."

"What can I do?" My voice is a pitiful whine. "I'm sorry, Will. So sorry. And you were right, about everything. That's why I came to apologize. Because I was wrong and really shitty to you for no reason."

Will studies my face for a while, like she's struggling for words. Then she heaves a sigh. "What went wrong?"

Relief floods into me, so strong my knees start shaking. "Everything."

"Looks like we need to talk." Will motions for me to follow her and leads me to an empty bench and we sit down. The bench is in a private part of the museum; no one's hanging around. They're all gathered up front, where the snacks are. I'm already exhausted. I want to just lie down and die, but I have a lot to tell Will. And a lot to figure out in terms of my future and the Revenants.

We're sitting in front of one of Will's paintings she did with spray paint last year. It's four animals in a forest: a fox, a bear, a deer, and a rat. They're running, their shadows blurred against the forest floor, their mouths open in joy. I read the caption underneath: *"Flight." Wilhelmina Tapscott, $2,500.* I remember when she painted it, in her garage. I held sheets of paper where she told me to and ruined one of my best shirts with green spray paint. Will says I'm the fox, but I've always felt more like the rat at the bottom of the painting. Small, tired, and unexpectedly vicious.

Will nods to me. "Well, go ahead."

I try to swallow, but my mouth is as dry as sandpaper. "First . . . do you remember . . . ?"

Will nods and I'm filled with relief again. "I started forgetting after we fought, so I wrote down everything I could. Now I remember it all." She hesitates. "But let's not avoid it. Gerald is dead."

I look at my feet. "Yeah. Sorry I didn't answer your call. It was . . . a hard day."

Will's quiet. Then, softly, "Did you kill him?"

Tears spring into my eyes. "I might as well have. He was hitting me and I had him at gunpoint. I wanted to kill him, but I let him go. He was leaving, but Conrad . . . Conrad wouldn't let him go." I can't lie to Will. Or myself. "Conrad's out of control, Will. He won't listen to me anymore. I don't know what to do. I'm in over my head, like you said. And Mike is on my case and I got into a fight with Mom—" My voice hitches and I can't stop the tears from coming.

Will doesn't move. She's as distant as Conrad—a warm statue. Somehow, that breaks me more than anything else. I'm sobbing, really crying. I can't take this anymore. I came to Will's show for help and I hoped we'd make up, but she's still mad. She doesn't want anything to do with me. I don't have anything left.

When I'm spent, sniffling and exhausted, I wobble to my feet. "I'll go," I croak. "Sorry for ruining your sh-show. I'll just go."

"Wait," Will says. My heart soars with hope. "Wait, that can't be everything. Start from the beginning. I don't want anyone else getting killed if I can help it."

Not exactly an olive branch, but better than nothing. I sink back onto the bench and wipe my eyes. Over the next hour, I tell her everything—Conrad's disobedience, the Revenants robbing people, the excruciating headaches, throwing the gun away, the failure of the letters to destroy Two. I even tell her about my fight with Mom and what she said. Will listens with increasing alarm, and by the time I'm finished, her eyebrows are almost to her hairline.

"Okay, first problem is Conrad. We need to deal with him," she says.

"Don't kill him," I beg. Tears well up in my eyes again.

"We can't kill him, according to your story. But he can't be out attacking people either. Where is he now?"

"Locked in my car."

"Good. We'll put him in the apartment so he can't get out. We'll make a barricade."

I nod slowly, liking the idea. "Okay, yeah. And we can buy time to think?"

Will nods. "And for you to rest. I'm sorry, but you look horrible."

"Oh." That's all I can say. Why is she helping me if she doesn't want to be my friend anymore?

Will stands, her face determined. "Let's go. I'll do some brain-storming. Even if letters or bullets won't work, they have to have a weakness—we just need to think about what it is."

"Thank you, Will." My voice is hushed with awe. She's always been a calming force in my life and everything fell apart after we fought. Maybe the person with the superpower is Will.

"Come on. Let's tell Cheryl and Allen."

Will and I walk over to her parents. They're visibly shocked to see me.

"Oh, Katrell," Will's mom says. She exchanges an unsure glance with Will's dad. "Nice to see you again. Will, did you . . . ?"

"We have some business to take care of," Will says, her voice even. "Can Katrell spend the night with us tonight?"

Spend the night? Why? Is she still mad at me or not?

"Um, yes, of course." Will's mom seems confused, but she smiles at me. "You're welcome anytime, Katrell."

"Thanks," I say, my voice hoarse and brittle. Will's dad frowns deeply.

"We're gonna pick up some clothes and then we'll be back," Will says to her parents. She tugs at my hoodie sleeve. "Come on, Trell."

I wave at Will's parents as Will drags me out of her own art show. When we get to the car, Conrad is where I left him, lying down in the backseat. When he sees Will, his tail wags furiously. His tail hasn't wagged in two weeks.

I fish the keys out of my pocket and smile weakly at Will. "Wanna drive?"

Will shakes her head. "No, you go ahead."

I climb into the driver's seat, pressure behind my eyes. Will doesn't trust me to be her driving instructor anymore. And I guess that makes sense, but I just want things to go back to normal. For once, I want there to be something I haven't wrecked.

Will buckles her seat belt and looks at me, her expression grave. "Let's go."

When we get to the apartment, the Revenants crowd by the door to greet Will.

"Will! You're here!"

"Hey, Will! How are you?"

"How was your show?"

"Is Katrell being nice to you again?"

Will looks at me, stunned, and I shrug. "They annoy me about you all the time."

"Trell, how many of them are there?" Will's voice is a horrified whisper.

I gesture weakly to the Revenants packed in the doorway. "Um, seven here, but ten in all."

Will doesn't say anything, but presses her lips into a tight line.

I push through the Revenants, trying to get into the apartment. "Get out of the way, make room."

The Revenants back up and let us in. Conrad trots inside too, settling beside Two. The apartment has a new member—Marquis's daughter, Taylor. My stomach churns uncomfortably.

"Will, did Katrell apologize to you?" Five asks. "She was very mean. She's sorry, even if she didn't say it."

"Um, yeah, she apologized." Will looks at me, her eyebrows raised. I shrug again.

"Will, your art is beautiful," Six says, his expression serious. "You're so talented. I hope you'll allow Katrell to buy some of your work."

"Yes," Four agrees. "We would like some for our apartment. We admire it greatly."

"By the way, that dress looks lovely on you," Five says. "Really complements your eyes."

"Stop badgering her," I bark. The Revenants fall silent, some with surly expressions. I rub my temples, a massive headache blurring my vision. "Look, since y'all are always acting up, I'm locking you in. No more leaving the apartment."

They immediately start whining and I get a sharp pain behind my eyes. I double over, groaning, and Will takes a small step toward me. When I can straighten up, I glare at them. "You better be good. All of you. I mean it, I'm sick of your shit."

"Katrell is so mean," Three says sullenly. "Mom was right. She's a—"

"If you say it, I'll cut your head off," I say through gritted teeth. Everyone is silent. I go to Conrad and get to my knees before him. "It's just for a little while, Con, don't worry. Just until I get things figured out," I assure him. He stares at me blankly. There's a speck of red on his collar.

I hug him once, tight, then stand. I stagger out of the apartment and Will follows me. We close the door on the Revenants, Conrad included. The last thing I see is Conrad staring at me.

Will locks the door and we drag an abandoned armchair and other debris in front of it. When the pile is secure, we admire our handiwork. I'm wheezing from the exertion and spots swim in front of my eyes.

"Are you gonna make it to the car?" Will asks.

I nod, panting, and Will steps away from the door and heads toward the stairs. She nods at me, the ghost of a smile on her lips.

"Let's go home," she says.

39

Will and I sit in her room, in awkward silence.

Will's room is the same as it was a week ago—pale walls, stuffed animals everywhere. But things are different. We're different. She can't even look at me.

"If you want, you can sleep in the guest room," Will says.

She knows I hate the guest room. She knows I feel better when I'm closer to her.

"Will, if you don't want me here, I'll leave." I sound pathetic with my congested sinuses. "I'll go back to my car and sleep."

Will doesn't say anything, so I get to my hands and knees, panting.

"Wait," she says. Her voice is soft, sad. The Will I'm used to. "Wait, don't go. I don't want you to go, Trell."

"It sure seems like it," I say miserably.

"I just—you really hurt me, you know? You said I was your enemy. You said I was a burden on you."

"That's not what I said." I wipe my nose on the hem of my shirt. "I mean, I did say you were my enemy. And I'm really sorry about that, I didn't mean it. But you're not a burden on me."

"That's how it sounded. You lumped me in with Gerald and your mom and a dog." Will pauses and I'm horrified to see tears well up in her eyes. "I'm doing the best I can, Trell. I know it's not easy being friends with me. I know it must suck that I can't be normal, and Chelsea picks on me, and I can't stand for people to touch me. I just thought you were cool with it. But maybe I've been taking advantage of your kindness."

"No, it's okay," I say quickly. "I don't mind, honest. I just get so mad sometimes, and I took it out on you. Which was wrong, and I know that."

"It's not okay. You were right. I'm weak."

"I didn't mean to call you weak. I just—"

"Yes you did." Will's looking at me calmly, not upset. "You meant it and it's true. I am weak. But I've been thinking about what you said, about Cheryl and Allen and everything. And I want to try to be better."

"Yeah?"

"Yeah. I've been leaning on you this whole time, and I haven't been there when you needed me. So, I want to try to be better. But I want you to be better too. You get what I'm saying?"

I nod, my throat like sandpaper. I can do that. I can be better, if that's what will keep her close to me.

"I'm so sorry, Will." I sniff, trying to avoid crying again. "It really hurt, what you said about Conrad. I didn't want it to be true. But it was. And now Gerald's dead because I didn't listen to you."

"I'm not too upset about that, if I'm being honest," Will says, a dark expression crossing her face. "But I am worried about Conrad snapping at people other than Gerald. When he growled at me, I was scared of him. Really scared. I thought he was going to rip my throat out."

"I'm sorry, Will. I'm sorry for everything." Sure enough, the tears come and won't stop. "I'm s-sorry I didn't listen, and hurt your feelings. And I'm sorry I talk over you, I didn't even realize I was doing it, and that's so shitty of me. And I-I'm sorry all this happened because n-now you have to clean up my mess—"

"Hey, it's okay." Will goes to her bathroom and brings back a roll of toilet paper. She gives me some until I calm down enough not to weep with every word.

"Mom was right," I whimper. "I'm a monster."

Will sighs. "Your mom is a manipulative asshole. Sorry, it's true. She doesn't get to tell you who you are. She barely knows herself."

Will's right, as always, but "monster" cycles in my head over and over.

"Listen, Trell," Will says. Her dark brown eyes are soft. "I forgive you, okay? I want to be friends again. I want to help you, because you're right—you've always been there for me. I'll do whatever I can."

I nod, too overwhelmed to speak. I don't know what I'd do without her. She's all I have left.

"Okay. Now stop crying. You're freaking me out."

I laugh, misery mixing with happiness. Will's back and I'm not letting her go again. She's my lifeline. If I have her on my side, I can do anything. Even solve this Revenant problem.

"Can I ask you something weird?" Will says.

"Yeah, sure. What's up?"

Will fidgets nervously. "I was wondering . . . if you want a hug."

I'm shocked into silence. Will has never touched me on purpose. She's never held my hand or even picked a hair off my shoulder. Will hates being touched in any way, because when she was little, any time someone touched her it was with a fist. She used to have meltdowns when people bumped into her by accident in the hallway at school. But now that I think about it, she hasn't had a meltdown like that in years. She's going to movies with her mom. She's looking her parents in the eye. She's trying to be better. She's been trying for a while, and I didn't notice.

"Yeah," I say, opening my arms. "Of course I do."

It's sort of awkward at first—I haven't hugged anyone in a long time either, so we both stare at each other for a few uncertain seconds. Then Will takes a deep breath and gently, carefully wraps her arms around me. I stay still, my arms pinned to my sides. Her grip is warm and strong, and just for a second, I don't feel so awful. Just for a second, I'm filled with overwhelming peace. I have to blink several times so I don't start crying again.

After a while, too soon, Will pats my back. "Let's go to bed," she says softly. "Sorry, Trell, but you look like garbage. And your forehead is burning a hole in my shoulder. You need to rest."

"Okay," I mumble. I pull away from her and we lock eyes for one moment. I'm overwhelmed with the feeling that I need to tell her how much I appreciate her, how much I missed her when we were fighting, how proud I am of her finally, after four years, being able to touch me, but all I can do is manage a wobbly smile. She smiles back, gives me a pillow from her bed, and ushers me to my usual spot in the middle of the floor. As soon as I put my head to the pillow, I descend into a dark, merciful sleep.

40

I don't dream, but noises float in my ears. The sound of rhythmic water, soft voices cooing for me to sleep. Faint scratching of a pen against paper. There are smells too, Will's body wash and food cooking and the familiar scent of the hoodie I borrowed from Will the night Conrad died and everything changed. Still, I sleep. Sometimes I come close to consciousness, close enough to see red light behind my eyelids, but the darkness consumes me every time.

The final sensation is touch. Someone's touching my shoulder, gently. A voice says, "Katrell? Are you okay, honey?"

I blink slowly, my eyelids heavy with exhaustion. Light floods my vision and I squeeze my eyes closed again, groaning.

"Katrell, it's past five-thirty," the voice says. I recognize it . . . Will's mom. I open my eyes again and her blurry shape focuses.

She's on her knees, one hand on my shoulder. She smiles kindly at me. "Hey, sweetie. You okay? You've been asleep for a long time."

I blink groggily, trying to force my brain to catch up to what she's saying. It's after five-thirty . . . in the morning? No, Will's room is lit with warm orange sunlight. It must be Sunday afternoon. I fell asleep around nine p.m. on Saturday, so I've been asleep for twenty hours.

I sit up, yawning. Exhaustion still drags at my bones, but I'm feeling a lot better than I was at Will's show. My chest doesn't hurt as much and my head only throbs dully. No bugs for now.

"How are you feeling?" Will's mom asks. "Will told me not to bother you, but you've been sleeping for so long. Sorry, I just wanted to make sure you were all right."

"I'm okay," I say, rubbing granules of sleep from my eyes.

"Are you hungry? You didn't eat dinner last night."

I shake my head. "No, I'm fine."

I'm surprised when Will's mom puts the back of her hand to my cheek. It's soft and cool. "Baby, your fever is bad. Have you gone to a doctor?"

Tears well up in my eyes. I didn't think anyone cared, not really. Mike has to tell me to go to the doctor because it's his job, but Will's mom doesn't have to do anything. She doesn't have to be so nice to me. I bet she doesn't think I'm a monster.

I shake my head and wipe my eyes. "N-no, it's just a cold. I'll get over it soon."

"Let's go together tomorrow, okay?"

"I don't have insurance—"

"Not a problem." Will's mom smiles at me and I'm shocked

when she pulls me into a hug. "We gotta get you feeling better. We're all worried about you."

"Th-thanks." I lean into her, wishing she'd never let me go.

She must sense my hesitation, because she holds me for a long time. When she does let go, she's all business. Her smile is replaced with fussy determination. "Okay, let's get something going here. Brush your teeth, take a shower, then meet me in the kitchen. I know you don't feel like eating, but you need some food in your system. Can't get better on no energy."

I nod, a little dazed. I'm not used to anyone bossing me around. Usually I'm telling Mom to do this stuff.

"Will is out with Allen, driving, but she'll be home soon. Then we can do something fun, if you're up for it. I have popcorn and a movie with your name on it." She pats my leg and gets to her feet. "Come on, into the shower. Let's go."

Will's mom helps me up and I stumble into Will's bathroom. I stand under the hot water until I'm dizzy and scrub the sweat and dirt from my body until my skin is soft and clean. I get out of the shower, ready for bed again, and pull on a pair of Will's pajamas. I sit in the middle of my nest of sleeping bag and blankets, exhausted. Will said she would help, but I'm scared something's going to happen to her. I need to find a way to make sure she doesn't get hurt.

Footsteps approach. As they get closer, I recognize the voices of Will's mom and Will. Home from driving.

Will opens her bedroom door and grins when she sees me. "I thought you'd sleep forever."

"I would have if Mrs. T. hadn't woken me up." I cough into my arm; it's wet and thick.

Will sits next to me on the floor and her mom comes in with a tray of food. She puts the tray before me: a bowl of soup, a grilled cheese sandwich, and a glass of water. Two blue pills and a thermometer rest next to the soup.

"You don't have to eat it all," Will's mom says, "but try to eat some, okay? First, let me check your temp."

I put the thermometer under my tongue and Will's mom presses her hand to my cheek again. I lean into her hand, exhausted. I just want to go back to sleep. The thermometer beeps and Will's mom frowns at it.

"102.4. I'm taking you to the doctor today, Katrell. I think the urgent care on Wilson is open on Sundays."

"No, thank you. I feel okay. Better than yesterday."

She pats my arm. "You don't have any choice, honey. I'll call and tell them we're coming. Come find me if you start feeling worse. And try to eat, okay? We'll leave in an hour." She stands and leaves the room, closing the door behind her.

I stare after her, stunned into silence. I guess I'm going to the doctor today.

Will nods at the tray of food, a small smile on her lips. "Better do what she says. She's been worrying me all day because you wouldn't wake up."

I get an unfamiliar warmth in my chest. I pick up the tray and stir the soup with the spoon. It's the most unappetizing thing I've ever seen, but I choke down a mouthful. It's warm, but tasteless. I take another mouthful of bland broth, but I already feel like I'm going to throw it up later.

"How was driving?" I ask Will, tearing off a piece of crust from the sandwich.

"Good." Will's watching me tear the sandwich into small pieces. "Allen says I can get my license soon. If I want."

"Yes, you definitely want!" I cough, hard. Too enthusiastic. I take a deep breath, as deep as my clogged lungs will allow. "I mean, it's such a good thing. You should."

"You don't have one and you get around fine," Will teases.

"Yeah, but I'm not exactly a role model." I grin and dip a piece of the grilled cheese into the soup. When I put it in my mouth, it tastes like cardboard. I put the sandwich down, finished.

"You're not eating much," Will says after a minute.

I shrug. "Not hungry."

"You're always hungry. At least, you were."

"I've got the worst cold of all time. I'm just not feeling it. Everything tastes like dirt."

Will narrows her eyes at the tray with a picked-apart sandwich and uneaten lukewarm soup. "I don't think that's it."

"What do you mean?"

She crosses her arms. "I've been thinking about everything you told me yesterday. I don't think you've been resurrecting people this whole time."

"Uh . . ." I know I have a fever, but Will's not making any sense. "Explain."

"Conrad attacks people you see as a threat. Gerald, the guys in the graveyard. He growled at me when we were fighting, and something bad happened with Chelsea. Also, the other Revenants say what you're thinking sometimes, right? They know things they shouldn't. So, I'm thinking they have a piece of their original personality, but really, they're just extensions of you."

I stare at Will, in disbelief. They're . . . me? "But that doesn't make sense. Why is Conrad so mean now? And why did the Revenants rob people? I would never do that."

"Maybe they do the things you can't. Like you wanted to kill Gerald, but couldn't. So Conrad did it for you."

"But Conrad won't listen to me anymore. None of them do. If they're me, shouldn't they listen to what I say?"

Will points to the picked-over food. "I think as you get weaker, your control over them gets weaker. You were okay at first, right? But the more you took on, the worse you got. So now that you're sick as hell, they're stronger. They're taking advantage. They're out of control."

I stare at the food uneasily. "If that's true, I just have to get better?"

"Yeah, and don't resurrect anyone else until we figure out how to send them back. It's too much strain on you."

I nod, my head aching dully. She's right. She has to be right. It makes sense now—they talk about things I'm thinking about. They hate the people I do. They love Will and even scolded me after our fight. I've been talking to myself this whole time.

But if they are me . . . that means I robbed Mr. Jenkins. I stole the jewelry. I killed Gerald. I'm definitely not hungry now.

"You okay?" Will asks tentatively.

I nod, even though I feel the opposite of okay. "Everyone forgetting about the Revenants . . . do you think that's my fault too?"

Will nods and my stomach sinks further. "Probably. I think this whole thing ties back to your emotions. Like maybe you wanted people to forget, in case it got out somehow?"

"No." I can't find the strength to look at her. "When they stole the jewelry, Five told me I could be rich. She said only I can see ghosts. Because if no one can remember them . . ."

I trail off, ashamed. This is all my fault. I did this, all of it, and now I don't even know what to do to fix it.

"Hey, it's all right." Will hesitates but touches the back of my hand with hers. She pulls away almost immediately but looks a little pleased with herself anyway. "That's just what Five said. And so what? Everyone wants to be rich. They're just taking basic emotions and running with it. Okay?"

I look at Will, gratitude almost overwhelming me. "Okay."

Will smiles at me. "Okay, good! So, game plan—you get better, we find a way to return the Revenants to being dead bodies. And we never do this again."

"Agreed." I rest my head on the edge of Will's bed, feeling a little bit better. At least she's on my side. "Thanks, Will. I really was overwhelmed."

"Well, you are my best friend," Will says. She smiles at me. "And you did say my dress complements my eyes."

"Shut up." I close my eyes, grinning, on the edge of sleep again. All I have to do is feel better and things will get better. I can do that. The tension eases from my shoulders, and I take a shaky, shallow breath. I'm the most relaxed I've been in weeks. Maybe the Revenants are relaxed too.

"Katrell, Will," Will's mom calls. Probably time to go to the doctor.

"Yes ma'am?"

"Did you mean to leave him outside?"

Will and I look at each other, confused.

"Who?" Will answers.

"Conrad," Will's mom says. "He's in the front yard."

My stomach drops to my toes and a wave of nausea hits me. Will's eyes grow wide with horror. We run to her window and look out—Conrad is there, staring up at us. He lingers for a few seconds, then turns and trots down the road until he's out of sight.

41

I grab my phone, my keys, and Will's hoodie, and run from her room.

"Wait!" Will calls, but I'm already in the kitchen, wheezing, panic threatening to choke me. How did Conrad get out? The door was barricaded. The apartment is six floors up.

"What's going on?" Will's mom's eyes are huge. "Katrell—"

"Stay here!" I bark. "Don't leave the house, okay? Tell Will I'll text her later."

I run outside and jump into my car. In seconds, I'm peeling out of the driveway, my heart in my throat.

I check the apartment first—a window is busted out of the sixth floor. Conrad fell six floors and still got up. He's invincible. I drive around looking for him. For hours. No Conrad. No puddles of blood or carnage either, thankfully. I stop at the gas station where I bought the cigarettes around nine o'clock, wheezing, and get out to buy some cough syrup. Where the hell is that dog?

I pocket the keys and head toward the gas station, but someone calls my name. I turn around—

Something hits me in the face.

I stare up at the stars, stunned. Liquid trails from my nose to my chin. Someone jerks me upright by my shirt collar—a man I've never seen before. I blink in disbelief, my nose throbbing. What's going on?

"Think you're hot shit, huh?" The man shakes me, hard. "Think you're bad enough to steal boss's stuff?"

"What're you talking about?" My voice is muffled by blood. "I didn't—"

He raises his fist to hit me again, so I shut my mouth.

"Sit there," another man commands. I know this one—Marquis's friend Rock. Four men approach me, no, five. One smiles coldly down at me.

"Hello," Marquis says.

I don't say anything, silenced by the sudden realization that if Marquis doesn't remember the resurrection of his daughter, he sure doesn't remember giving me his brand-new Mercedes. Marquis paces slowly in front of me, his goons keeping a sharp lookout.

"Now, here I was thinking someone has to have massive balls to steal from Marquis, but what do I find? A little girl." He laughs, a cold outburst. His friends don't join in. Rock looks down at me, dread on his face.

I try to swallow, but my mouth is dry. "Marquis, I can explain—"

"Oh, can you?" Marquis laughs harder. "There's not enough time in the world for you to explain how you got my car."

Shit. I glance behind me—the cashier who sold me the cigarettes earlier is stubbornly staring at the back wall. I look at Marquis's crew, pleading with my eyes. They look away, stone-faced.

"I should kill you an' take my car. But that wouldn't solve nothin', now would it?" Marquis continues to smile. His grill reflects the gas station lights. "I don't believe a little girl's clever enough to steal something that belongs to me. So, if you tell me who gave it to you, I'll let you off easy. What do you say?"

I let out a pitiful cough in response. Fuck, what should I do? Has he really forgotten everything? All the times we talked to Taylor as a ghost?

"Don't you remember Taylor?" I ask, hoping the name will trigger any ounce of humanity he has left. "Our letters?"

Marquis stares blankly at me, but Rock visibly starts. He stares at me, frowning, and his eyes widen. Hope springs into my chest. Maybe he'll convince Marquis to let me go.

"Who?" Marquis says. My hope dies a little, but I keep staring Rock down. Recognition, pity, fear—I'll take any of them. Anything to get me out of this. "Is that who gave you the car?"

"Marquis," Rock murmurs. My heart hammers against my ribs. "I think—"

"Quiet," Marquis barks, and my hope dies for good. "Can't you see we're talkin'?" He brings his attention back to me. "Is this Taylor the one who gave you the car?"

I throw the "appeal to his better nature" idea out the window. Time to lie through my teeth. "No. Do you know a lowlife named Gerald?"

Marquis raises his eyebrows. "Depends. If you mean the ugly-as-fuck meth head who owes me money, then, yeah."

"He had your car." The lie comes easily, especially because they can't ask Gerald if it's true. "When he got killed, I thought I could take it. I didn't know it was yours, honest."

Marquis doesn't say anything—probably considering my story. He turns to Rock. "You think she's telling the truth?"

I glare at Rock, hoping for intimidation. He nods and I have to hold in a smile.

"Hmm. That's interesting, 'cause Rock's got the best judgment outta anyone I ever seen." Marquis nods to himself and my stomach flips when he opens his arms. "All right, I'll bite. I'll believe you."

"Th-thank you—"

"Wait now, don't get excited." Marquis's grin widens. "I think Gerald was a dumbass and stupid enough to steal from me, especially 'cause he didn't have anything to lose. I was comin' to collect; shame someone axed him before I could. But you? Come now, sweetheart, you have to know better than to drive a stolen car."

My heart pounds in my chest, in my head, in my ears. I'm starting to get that pain, when the bugs are gearing up for flight.

"Usually people who cross me get dead. But it's your lucky day—I'm in a good mood. A good beating will knock the stupid outta you, I bet."

Marquis bends down to my level. Fear takes root in my bones. His eyes are soulless, just like my Revenants. "I'm doing you a favor. Free education."

He snaps his fingers and two of his men hook their arms under mine and jerk me to my feet. The pain in my head gets worse and I groan with fear and agony.

"Empty her pockets," Marquis orders. They yank my keys, phone, and wallet from my borrowed pajama pants and hand them to Marquis. He takes the money from my wallet—eight hundred dollars—and smiles at the pink jewels on my phone case. "Cute. I'll keep this for . . ." He trails off, his grin giving way to confusion. "Huh. Anyway, I'm gone. Rock, you with me. You three, teach her what happens when you play with Marquis's belongings. Easy on the face, though. She might need that in the future."

I watch, half-blind with pain, as Marquis pockets my phone and strolls to the Mercedes. Rock whispers something in the nearest goon's ear and his eyes widen slightly. He shoots an uneasy glance at me while Rock joins Marquis in the Mercedes. They drive away with the only car I've ever owned and the six thousand, seven hundred dollars I hid in its interior.

As the car disappears from sight, a figure at the edge of the parking lot catches my eye. A tall man. Is he coming to help me? Or to just watch a beating?

The guys Marquis left behind don't see him approaching. They're all looking down at me, glaring, ready to follow Marquis's order. The one Rock talked to holds one hand up. "Wait. Listen, y'all know this is the Witch, right?"

The guy on my left drops me like he's been burned. I sag to one side, hanging from the other one's grip.

"Shit," the guy who dropped me hisses, backing up. "The one who talks to dead people?"

"The one who iced Gerald," the first one says.

"Shit, man, what should we do?"

"What we're told," the man who's still holding me barks. He

tightens his grip on my arm and I whimper with pain. "I ain't believin' in no legend. I *do* believe Marquis'll kill me if I don't do what he says."

The two other men hesitate, looking at each other. I say nothing. I'm watching the tall man approach, along with a woman and a kid my age. More shadows approach behind them. My stomach sinks with fear and resignation.

The Revenants are coming.

"I don't know, man, she might hex us."

"What all can she do? Nobody knows nothin' about her. She's a ghost."

"I heard Gerald looked like hamburger meat, man. I ain't tryin' to die."

"Enough!" the man holding my arm roars. He swings and punches me in the gut. I double over, vomit surging from my stomach to the pavement. He throws me to the ground, where I curl up in a weak ball. From between the legs of the men surrounding me, I can see my Revenants surrounding us, their eyes burning in the dark.

"She's a fucking kid, for God's sake. Get some balls and start kicking."

I cringe from the men, but the kick never comes. Instead, Four steps into the light, smiling, his eyes bright orange.

"Men always think they can lay hands on women," Four says. His hands are in his pockets, his shoulders relaxed. My headache ramps up in intensity.

"Stay out of this, buddy," the man who's poised to kick me warns.

Five steps into the light next, also smiling. "It's always the same ones too. Inferior to their victims in every way."

The men see the rest of the Revenants now. They back away from me, but it's too late—they're surrounded.

"They always think because they're bigger, they can get away with it," Six says.

One of the goons pulls out a gun. "Get back. Get back!"

"Why is that, you think?" Five asks. "Fragile male ego? Power dynamics?"

"Does it matter?" Eight says. He steps closer, grinning.

All three of them pull their guns and fire at the Revenants.

Holes appear in the Revenants' chests, faces, mouths, but they keep coming. The men whimper and huddle together.

"They're scared," Three sneers. One of his eyes is a vacant hole, but the other remains bright orange. "How pathetic."

"Pathetic. Do you know how much we endure?" Six says. "Beatdowns in our own kitchens. Black eyes, loose teeth. And they're scared to get a little more in return."

The men are trembling. Their guns are empty. The pain in my head is excruciating.

"Your fault," a young voice says. Taylor emerges from the dark, her eyes orange and a huge grin on her face. "Katrell's mad. You're in trouble."

"Please," one of the men whimpers. He looks to me, his eyes wild and bulging in fear. "We'll let you go. We won't tell anyone, I swear. Please."

I stay silent. I know what the Revenants are going to say.

"If you mess with the Witch, you get hurt."

The Revenants swarm the three men.

I get to my feet, shaking, my heart pounding in my head. The bugs are tearing my brain apart, like the Revenants are tearing into the men. I stagger away, walking anywhere but here. I can hear the men's screams in my ears, even after the lights of the gas station are long out of sight. I don't know how far I go, but eventually I collapse and darkness fills my vision.

I wake up in a ditch. Wet grass and sludge stick to my face, my hair. My toes are numb. I blink up at the cloudy sky, my brain a mess of static and pain. I lie there for several minutes, freezing, my breathing harsh and loud in my ears. Eventually, one thought pushes to the forefront of my mind.

I still haven't found Conrad.

I sit up, wincing as the action aggravates my ever-present headache. I know where I am—Wilson Street, ten minutes from home. I shuffle in that direction because I don't know what else to do.

As I walk, fragments of last night enter my head. The Revenants attacking Marquis's friends. Marquis stealing his car back. The way the Revenants' eyes turned orange, like Conrad's did when he killed Gerald.

When I killed Gerald.

Will's right—the Revenants are me. Those are the thoughts I have, uttered by their mouths. They killed them. Was it self-defense or murder? Was I just mad they took my car and my money?

My head is killing me.

What day is it? I need to go home and then to school. Mike's gonna be on my ass about missing school. I can't get my last absence—that'll send me and Mom to court. Wait—Mom. Most of the fog lifts from my brain. The Revenants are killing everyone, and Mom and I just had a heated fight. She's in danger. They'll kill her.

I hurry home, panic giving me strength. I stumble up the crumbling steps, my heart pounding jaggedly against my ribs, and touch the door. It's open.

"Mom?" I step into my house, my nerves fried. No answer—all the lights are out. Please don't let there be any blood. Please.

I drag myself through the living room and into the kitchen. Mom's not there. A TV is playing—mine or Mom's? I go to her room, struggling to get air into my lungs. I open the door, but she's not here either. Her TV is off. I turn to go to my room, then pause. The trinkets on her vanity are gone.

I stand in the doorway to her bedroom, cold fear settling in my chest. Mom's clothes are missing from the closet. Her jewelry box is open and empty. Her bed is unmade. The only suitcase she owns, the one she's held on to while we hopped from city to city to avoid her boyfriends when they got too violent, is gone.

She skipped town.

I step into her empty room, trembling, my mind blank. There are no bloodstains, no ripped-up clothing, because she's gone.

She left. She left me here, alone. An ugly thought pushes past the shock—how did she skip town with no money?

No.

I sprint to my room. It's a wreck; someone's rifled through all my stuff. I open *War and Peace*—empty. The Bible—empty. The shoebox in my closet—empty. The crease in the mattress, the loose floorboard, the piggy bank on my desk—all empty. I methodically check every hiding place I've ever had. They're all cleaned out. Not a single dollar left.

Mom stole all forty-one thousand dollars from me.

I hold on to my desk so I don't fall into a dead faint. She really left. She really skipped town without me and took all my money with her. Will's words crush me and I'm on my knees, then flat on the floor. She doesn't care about me and she never has. When I was little, I was cute enough to inspire churches and nonprofits to give us food, money, housing. When I was in middle school, I served as a target so her boyfriends wouldn't hit her. Now that I'm in high school, I can work and support her. And I did support her. I sacrificed everything for her. I worked long hours and failed all my classes and smiled at her with blood in my teeth. I turned into a monster for her. And it wasn't enough.

I have nothing left. Everything has crumbled in my fingers. No, Will's grandma was right—I've burned everything to the ground.

Footsteps approach, thundering down my hall. I almost hope it's the police, so this nightmare can end. I can't take this anymore.

"Trell?" Someone kneels next to me. "Trell, look at me."

I do, and Will's face swims into focus. I give her a small smile. "Hey, Will. Guess what? I burned it all down. Just like Clara said."

Will touches her hand to my forehead. She swears under her breath and pulls out her phone. "Hang on, it's okay. I'm calling Cheryl and Allen and Mike. It's okay, it'll be okay."

"She left, Will," I say, even though Will's speaking urgently into her phone. "I'm all by myself now. That's what I get, right? Everyone is dead. Everyone."

"I'm here," Will says, her free hand finding mine. I hold it, tight. She has calluses on her fingers, probably from painting. I didn't know that. "Let's try to sit up, okay? Cheryl's coming. She's gonna take you to the doctor."

Will practically pulls me to my feet. We stagger outside; cool air hits my face. I want to go back inside. I'm freezing. I turn to Will to tell her this, but I'm interrupted by a hard, painful cough. I look at my hands; they're red with blood.

"Oh man." Will stares at my hands, her face pale. "Oh man, okay. Trell? Just hang on for a second. Cheryl's coming. It's gonna be okay."

Everything is blurry. Will's hands pull me to the cold ground. My head swims with pain and confusion. Someone touches my temples, speaking softly.

"Katrell, can you hear me?"

"Help her, please," Will's voice says from somewhere near me. She sounds close to tears. "Mike, she's coughing up blood, please—"

Mike? My eyes pop open. I'm leaning heavily against Will, and Mike is kneeling in front of us. I blink some of the confusion away and offer him a weak smile.

"Hey, Mike. So sorry about school. I'm on my way, promise."

"Don't worry about that, Katrell," Mike says. His voice is

gentle, but shaking. "Wilhelmina, I'm going to call an ambulance. Keep her calm for me."

No. No—I can't go to the doctor, not like this. I don't remember why, but I can't. I stagger to my feet and back away from Mike and Will. "No, no, you can't. How am I supposed to pay for an ambulance? Mom is gone, she took all my fucking money."

"Don't worry about that," Will urges. "I'll pay. We just have to get you to a hospital—"

"No!" I'm screaming at her, at both of them. "No, just leave me alone! I'm fine. I don't need a doctor, or you, or anyone. Just leave me alone."

"Katrell, listen to me." Mike is so serious, comically serious. He looks like a beanpole with a drawn-on suit and frown. I get an urge to laugh. "You're delirious. You're burning up and you're hurt. Stay calm, okay? Let's wait for the ambulance, okay?"

"Goddamn Revenants wrecking my life and now you. And you know what, this is your fault. You just had to go to my house to yell at her, and now she's gone. Everything was fine. Everything was going okay!"

Will tries to come to me, anxiety twisting her face, but Mike isn't listening to me. He's already on the phone. "Yes, please send an ambulance. A student is hurt."

Fury wells up inside me and I feel strong, stronger than I have in weeks. I snatch the phone from him and throw it on the ground. Mike looks at me, stunned.

"I said stop ruining everything!" I'm screaming at him. My breath comes out in white clouds. I'm a dragon, a fire-breathing dragon. Someone has to pay for all the pain this hell has caused me. "I'm not someone you can just swoop in and fix, okay? My mom said she hates me, Gerald knocked me around, and there's a bunch of dead people ruining everything, and there are bugs in my head—"

I cut off my rant, realizing that bugs mean Revenants. They're here, close to me, about to fuck my life up. I search my yard wildly and there he is, chest stained red, eyes burning, drool and coagulated blood leaking from his jaws.

Conrad.

Fear replaces the fury. I stand in front of Mike, shielding him.

"No," I groan. "No, not again. No more, okay? You're killing me. Please."

Conrad drops something from his mouth. He takes a step closer, then another.

"Not Mike, please." Tears well in my eyes. "I didn't mean it, I didn't mean what I said. He gave me peppermints. He's a nice guy."

Conrad lowers his head and pulls his lips up in a growl, his eyes on Mike.

"Stop, please." I'm crying, sobbing. "I wrote the poem. I'm gonna be an electrician. I read the pamphlet and I can do that. They wear cute hard hats. Please, Conrad, just leave him alone. My head hurts so bad."

Conrad charges, teeth bared.

I'm supposed to be protecting Mike, but he pushes me out of the way. Conrad leaps over me and bites into Mike's arm.

The noise is awful. Mike, who has been so kind to me, writhing in pain and screaming. I hold my head, in agony too, but my pain is from the weight of messing with something I didn't understand and hurting everyone in the process.

"Katrell, run!" Mike screams. He wrestles with Conrad as my dog snaps at his face.

I don't run. I can't. I scramble to my feet and dash to Conrad. I yank his collar, the collar he's had for years, with all my might. It snaps in my hand, twenties I taped to the inside flying everywhere. Unbalanced, Conrad lets go of Mike's arm, and I use the last bit of strength to grab the scruff of his neck and throw him to the side. I stand in front of Mike, sadness boiling in my gut.

"Go away!" I scream at Conrad. He takes a hesitant step back, his ears pinned to his head. It's the first time since he's been dead that he looks like his old self. "Leave us alone! Will told me to be better, do you hear me? She told me to be better!"

Conrad backs up until he's at the edge of the yard. Mike is groaning and Will is calling my name, but I keep my eyes on Conrad until he disappears behind the neighbor's house.

My knees almost give out when the bugs disappear. Mike's face is crumpled in pain. Will is on the phone, her voice shaking, both hands putting pressure on Mike's arm. Mrs. Tapscott's car is racing down the street. My head in a fog, I wander away to see what Conrad dropped when he first appeared.

It's my phone.

I pick it up, ignoring the blood on the pink rhinestones. My fist tightens around it and some clarity comes with the pain. Marquis had my phone, and if Conrad brought it back, Marquis probably isn't breathing anymore. Rock either. This is wrong. I didn't ask Conrad to bring it back. I could have gotten a new phone. My breath heaves from my chest, fury and despair making my mind sharper. I was wrong; this isn't Mike's fault. This is on the Revenants.

Slowly, like a pot of boiling water, rage rises in my chest and replaces the crushing agony of Mom leaving, the fear in Mike's voice, Will's soft crying. The Revenants wreck everything. They go around killing people who get in my way, but I never asked them to. Where do they get the right to ruin my life? Where do they get the right to disobey me? I created them, I raised their sorry asses from the ground where they were rotting. And this is the thanks I get? Constant bugs in my head, blood in my lungs, and the only people who care about me hurt and bleeding.

I leave the front yard and head to the apartment, seething. It takes me almost ten minutes to climb six flights of stairs, but when I do, I'm fighting mad.

The Revenants turn in surprise when I kick open the door.

Five brightens when she sees me. "Katrell, hello! Busy night, huh?" She picks at her nails, cleaning blood from beneath them.

"I hope we can get out again soon," Six says. The whole front of his shirt is stained red. "I need more natural light. I read that online somewhere."

"Stop." My voice is quiet.

"We should get Conrad a new collar," Taylor says. "His is wrecked now."

"A cute little dog suit!" Five squeals. She looks at me and smiles. "It'll match the one Mike always wears."

"Enough!" My voice silences the Revenants. The bugs are about to take flight, their claws pinching my brain. I grind my knuckles into my temples. "Enough! I have had enough!" I slam my fist into the wall. A few Revenants flinch. "I hate this, I hate all of you! You keep moving around, making the bugs in my head go wild, and for what? Killing people you think are a threat? Enough. Enough!"

"We only do what you want—"

"This isn't what I want!" I'm screaming, the rage boiling over and burning me and everyone around me. "I want this to stop! I want you to disappear!" I point at them, fury clouding my vision. "I want all of you to die. You should all just die. Your family is gone, no one cares about you, so you should just die and leave me in peace."

Silence permeates the room. Every Revenant eye focuses on me. Every eye turns orange.

"You're selfish, Katrell," Three says, stepping closer. They all move, quietly, their shoulders tense and eyes locked on me. I back up, the rage melting and slowly replaced by fear.

"You only think about yourself." Four's eyes are dead, burning.

"You're a monster," Six says.

Two watches me from the mattress, the only Revenant not moving. Her eyes are orange, but filled with sadness and resignation.

"Men always think they can put their hands on women without being punished." Five puts her hands in her bloodstained pockets and grins at me. "But maybe you deserve it."

I back out of the apartment, my knees shaking with fear. I've done it. I've finally made my last mistake. The Revenants lunge at me and I take off running down the hall.

Fingernails scratch my arm and I yank free. They're all screaming, laughing, their words filling my head with pain.

"Stupid."

"Greedy."

"Worthless."

"Monster."

I stumble to the stairwell, but Six catches me and sinks his teeth into my arm.

His teeth are scalding, made of fire. I scream, trying to get free, and Three slams his fists into my ribs. I push away and stumble down one flight of stairs. I ignore the pain, wheezing. Hands tear at my clothes, my back, my scalp. They chase me down three more flights, and I can't breathe, mucus chokes my lungs, so I slow down and then they have me. One of them kicks me so hard I tumble down the last flight of stairs and collapse in a heap at the bottom.

Legs surround me. I look up, blood swimming in one eye, and all I can see is my own fire burning me to the ground.

"You should just die," Five says, smiling. "And leave us in peace."

They descend upon me and my world goes dark.

43

There's a lot of light for being dead.

You'd be surprised. There's a lot of pain too. Apparently, the whole clouds and white gates and God coming to greet you scenario is wrong. So is the eternal darkness thing. It's just sunlight and pain, the kind of pain that's so bad you can't scream, the kind that almost feels like it's not happening to you.

"What are you doing? Stop! Leave her alone!"

The Revenants have killed me. It's ironic, isn't it? Death by my own creation. Is it murder or suicide? What will happen to them once I'm gone? Maybe their families' memories will come back. That would be nice. Maybe they'll disappear slowly, writhing in agony. That would also be nice.

"Trell, talk to me, answer me!"

I hope Mom gets far with my forty-one thousand dollars. At

least the police won't get it. But I would have liked to give it to Will. She deserves it.

"H-help, please, m-my friend is hurt, she's hurt bad—"

Will told me to be better. And I wanted to, I really did, but look at what I've done. I lost all my money. I chased my own mother out of our home. The Revenants killed people, people who had lives and dreams and loved their dead daughters. Maybe I deserve it. Maybe I deserve to burn to death.

"Trell, please, hang on. I'm right here, I'm not leaving you."

Some of the pain fades. Someone's touching my cheek, my forehead, my hand. Someone's wiping blood from my mouth. The light fades and everything is dark. Sirens scream in the background and footsteps echo around my ears, but they're muffled. Oh, I was wrong. Dying isn't so bad after all.

It's kind of nice.

44

I wake suddenly, violently, blinded by bright lights.

Where am I? Am I dead? It's so bright. Something's in my throat, in my nose. I reach up to take it out, but a hand stops me.

"Trell!"

I look to my left and Will's there, her face filled with joy and relief. She touches my cheek, then my forehead.

"Are you okay? Can you understand me?"

Will's touching me? She doesn't do that. Will doesn't like being touched.

"I'm gonna call the doctor," Will says.

The doctor? Where am I? It's so bright. There's something in my nose.

"Stop, don't pull it out," Will says. She moves my hand from my face. "It's to help you breathe."

Something to help me breathe. Slowly, my surroundings come

into focus—a thin curtain, sneakers on linoleum, beeping machines in the corner. I reach for words to describe where I am, but everything slides from my brain like Jell-O.

Will leaves and I'm struck with panic. I whimper and pain stabs at my throat. Shoes gather under a translucent curtain, and when it's pulled back, Will isn't there. It's just three old white men in white coats.

"Will?" My throat is in agony. I groan and claw at my neck. Some of the details are coming back—I'm in a hospital. These are doctors. Will's gone, they probably won't let her see me yet.

I was attacked by my own Revenants.

"Easy," a tall doctor says. He's got a massive beer belly. "You'll probably be confused for a bit. Can you tell me your name?"

I swallow painfully, needles stabbing my throat. "Katrell Davis."

"Good, good." The doctor nods and the ones behind him scribble on clipboards. "How're you feeling? Sore?"

I nod. The pain's coming back in jumps—my fingers, my toes, my ribs. My throat. My nose. As the pain gets sharper, so does my mind. I survived the Revenant attack and I'm in the hospital. But where are the Revenants now? How long have I been out?

The tall doctor turns to one scribbling on a clipboard. "Up her dose after I'm done." He turns back to me. "All right, let me listen to you for a second. Won't take long, promise."

I'm too weak to protest. The doctor listens to my heart, my ragged breathing. He shines a light into my eyes and swipes a high-tech thermometer across my forehead. He frowns at the number.

"Well, the good news is you're no longer critical. But you are very sick, young lady. You have one of the worst cases of pneumonia I've seen in someone your age. Your body is weak from your injuries too, so you're in bad shape. You need rest, and lots of it. Okay?"

Pneumonia. The coughing up blood makes sense, I guess.

"I'm going to up your pain medication to make you more comfortable. Someone will come and talk to you later, and you can have visitors later too. Rest now, worry about all that when you've recovered a bit."

I want to protest, to say I have to talk to Will and ask about what happened and where the Revenants are, but a wave of exhaustion hits. My eyelids sag and then ease shut as a nurse messes with the IV dangling from my right arm.

"Sleep," the doctor says gently. "And welcome back."

When I wake up the second time, I feel like myself.

Panic hits me immediately.

I sit straight up in the hospital bed, terror threatening to drown me. The Revenants. They're out there, loose. I have to find them. If I don't, the body count will keep rising. What if they attack Mike again? Or hunt down Mom?

"Katrell?"

I look to my right and find Will's mom. Before I can say or do anything, she wraps me in a gentle hug. Some of the fear melts away as she clings to me.

"Oh, sweetie, I was so worried." She breaks the hug and holds me at arm's length. "How do you feel?"

Weak. More than anything, more than the pain, weakness

drags in my bones. I feel like I could sleep for months and still be tired. I clear my throat and try to speak.

"Tired." My voice is brittle and scratchy, but usable. Not too much pain.

"I bet." She rubs my arm. "Rest, okay? Lie down and rest."

"Where's Will?" I croak. I let out a hoarse, painful cough.

Will's mom rubs my back gently. "Easy, easy. She's gone to get a snack. She'll be right back."

"I need to talk to her." I cough again, streaks of pain rocketing through my chest.

"You need some water first."

Will's mom grabs a pitcher from the bedside table and fills a paper cup. I let her bring it to my lips. The water is so cold and soothing, I empty the cup in seconds. She pours another and I down that too. I'm surprised when she touches my forehead and bends to kiss the top of my head.

"I was so worried, Katrell," Will's mom murmurs into my damp hair. She wraps one arm around me, so gentle, so careful, and hugs me to her chest. "Please rest. Sleep. Take all the time you need. I'm here and so is Will. We're not going anywhere."

I want to ask why, why would she give up her time and energy for me, but Will moves back the curtain. She's clutching a Walmart bag full of snacks. Will's mom squeezes me one more time and moves away.

"I'll give you two some time," she says. She turns to Will, who sits in the chair next to my bed. "Don't push her too much, Will. She's still tired."

"Okay, Mom," Will says.

My eyes widen and I look to Will's mom, expecting to see surprise on her face. But she just smiles and leaves the cubicle, closing the curtain behind her.

"Nothing can kill you, not even seven wild Revenants," Will tells me, opening a bag of dill pickle chips. "You're like a cockroach."

"You called her Mom." I can't keep the disbelief out of my voice.

Will's hand shoots to her mouth, her eyes wide with surprise and a little despair. "You're kidding. Tell me I didn't."

"You did, just now." I cough weakly, but manage to smile after a few breathless moments. "I'm proud of you."

"Don't be," Will says miserably. "I didn't mean to. When we were in the ambulance with you, I was so scared and I called her that. It just slipped out."

"Ambulance?" I cough again, my head pounding. "Back up, I have no clue what's going on. How did I live through that?"

"You're welcome," Will says. "I mean, I found them beating you to death and I stopped them."

"How?"

"I just told them to stop. They seemed really confused, but they didn't hurt me. They all ran away when they saw M—Cheryl coming. What happened?"

I think about what I said, how the Revenants turned on me so quickly, and a cold shiver races up my back. "Later. Please." I cough miserably into my elbow. "Sorry, it's so hard to breathe. Where are they now?"

Will chews on her lip. "Well, there's good news and bad news."

Shit. "Tell me the good news first."

"So, after the doctors said you were stable, I checked on the Revenants in the apartment. There were more than last time, so I guess all of them have left their families. I asked them to please not leave and they agreed. They really like me. I mean, I guess you do."

"So they're not . . . ?"

"They're not hurting anyone, no. The police came and checked out the apartment, but after that, the Revenants just went inside and sat down. They've been kind of sleepy, I think? Which makes sense because you were asleep. But now that you're awake . . ."

Worry eats at my stomach. "Is that the bad news?"

Will's face falls. "No. Bad news is, I've found all of the Revenants except for Rose, Daniel, the tall woman with the scary eyes, and Conrad."

Two, Three, Five, and Conrad. Conrad's still out there, on the loose. Shit.

"But I don't want you to worry," Will says. She squeezes my hands. "You need to relax. I'll take care of the Revenants."

"They're my problem—"

"I don't care." Will's eyes shine a little and she looks at her hands. "Trell, I don't know if anyone told you, but you're not doing so good. Broken arm, fractured ribs, broken nose. You weren't breathing for ten minutes in the ambulance. You were in a coma for three days."

I stare at Will, speechless. I've been out for three days?

"I was so scared. I was so scared you wouldn't wake up."

"I'm sorry." My voice is subdued. I really almost died.

"It's okay. Just don't do it again," Will says. She wipes her eyes and takes a deep breath. "Okay, your turn. Tell me everything that happened after you left my house. When I found you, you were a wreck."

I tell Will what happened, in excruciating detail. When I get to the end of the story, I remember the fiasco at my house. Bile creeps up my throat. "Will, is Mike okay?"

"He's fine, don't worry. He just has a broken arm. And he had to get a rabies shot."

Relief floods me and so does a surge of exhaustion. "Thank God. I thought . . ."

"I know. Conrad's dangerous, really dangerous."

"That's why I don't want you to—" I'm cut off by a coughing fit, one so bad I spit out red-tinted mucus into the trash can by the side of my bed. Breathless, head pounding, I finish weakly. "I don't want you to confront them. Let me do it."

"Yeah, right," Will says. "You're in horrible shape. Just stay here and rest, okay? I'm not doing it tonight, I promise. I'm going to try and find Rose, Daniel, and the tall lady and convince them to go to the apartment."

"But how are you going to stop them? They can't die. Conrad was shot, he fell out of a sixth-story window . . . he's invincible."

"No, they're not. While you were out, I did some investigating. When I went to the apartment, there was a burn mark on Four's arm. Conrad's wounds healed, right? So why didn't the burn heal?"

"So . . ." I'm trying to think, but the combination of exhaustion and hospital drugs makes it hard to think. "What are you saying? We have to burn them?"

"Exactly. Think about your letters. What happens when you write them? They catch on fire."

Hope flares in my chest. I thought there was no way to stop them—thank God. "I tried to resurrect someone who'd been cremated and it didn't work."

"Good!" Will's grinning, determination all over her face. "This is great news. I asked Allen to get some gasoline, so tomorrow I'll have a weapon. I told him it was for an art project, so I don't think he'll catch on."

"We. *We'll* have a weapon."

"Not a chance," Will snorts. "Now go to sleep, please. Watching you cough stresses me out."

I laugh, which turns into another coughing fit. After I've caught my breath, Will pulls a blanket up to my chin and I close my eyes. I want to tell her to please let me handle this, but exhaustion drags at my bones. With Will's hand next to mine, I fall asleep in seconds.

45

I'm half-asleep when someone knocks on my door.

"Come in," I mumble. It's the next day, and they've moved me from the curtain ICU to the room ICU. Which isn't really better, but at least I don't have to hear the squeal of sneakers on tile floors and my neighbor wheezing a death rattle. Will and her parents have been with me almost 24-7, but they left to get some sleep an hour ago. I tried to watch TV in their absence, but turned it off when the news anchor said there was a manhunt for a massive rabid dog.

The door opens and Slenderman himself walks in. Mike and I grin at the same time.

"Looks like someone's alive!" Mike's holding a gift basket under one arm, complete with balloons and a stuffed dog. He places it on a table at the foot of my bed and sits in a chair at my bedside. His left arm rests in a blue sling and there are a few cuts on his neck, but otherwise he looks fine. Thank God.

"Barely," I croak. I glance down at my left arm. It's wrapped in a hard black cast. I guess if Mike has a broken arm, it's fitting I do too. Poetic justice and all that.

Mike's grin fades a little. "Are you feeling better? I visited earlier but the doctor said you were really hurting."

I look at Mike's chin so I don't have to stare into his sharp eyes. "I'm better, I think. I get my own room, so that's cool. I don't have to share anymore."

"Silver linings, huh?"

I try to answer, but launch into a coughing fit instead.

"Are you okay?" Mike asks when I can breathe again.

"Look at me. What do you think?" I wipe my mouth with the hem of the blanket. It's stained pink with my blood. "What're you doing here?"

"Is it a crime to visit my injured student?"

"I *guess* it's okay." I yawn, exhausted again. The medicine in the IV is strong enough to keep the pain at bay, but it also makes me so tired. That or it's the pneumonia.

Mike looks like he wants to say something, but settles on something else. He smiles at me gently. "So, I heard someone wants to be an electrician."

"Who?"

"You!" Mike laughs at my shock. "You don't remember? You said you wanted to be an electrician. And there was something about wearing cute hats."

"Oh God." I can't believe I told him that. I barely remember the minutes that led up to the attack. It's all a haze. "What else did I say?"

Mike's face transforms in an instant. The easygoing joking vanishes. "You said dead people were ruining your life."

I close my eyes, my heart pounding. "You should forget you ever heard that, Mike."

Mike is quiet for a long time. "That dog—it was yours, wasn't it?"

I don't say anything.

"I didn't tell the police it was yours. But it's the same one that's been attacking everyone, right?"

I take a shallow, watery breath. "There are some things you aren't meant to know. This is one of them."

"No." Mike's voice is a quiet, frustrated whisper. "Katrell, I've tried to be patient with you, but this is it. You have to tell me. No more secrets."

I open my eyes and Mike's staring dead at me, refusing to let me go. For a moment, I consider telling him everything, about Marquis, about the resurrections, about the Revenants. But I can't. I can't burden him with my secrets. They're already too much for me to bear—it would be cruel to share them with him. "I can't. I'm sorry."

Mike shakes his head. "I'm not taking that for an answer. The time for letting things slide is over. It was over the moment you landed in the hospital. Let me help."

I shake my head, not trusting my voice.

Mike's eyes soften. "You really can't tell me about this, can you?" When I shake my head again, he nods. "Okay then, we'll change gears. How did you get these injuries? When I saw you at your house, you were hurt, but not this bad. Not nearly this bad."

"I . . ." I hesitate, then fall silent. I can't tell him my undead creations are in their rebellious phase and beat me senseless.

"Are you protecting someone?" Mike asks. "Your mother?"

"No," I say forcefully. "She didn't . . . she didn't do anything wrong."

"I doubt that, Katrell." Mike's being gentle with me again. "I saw the heavy makeup, the way you sometimes flinch from people."

"It wasn't her," I say quietly. I can tell him this at least. Gerald's dead, so it doesn't matter. "My mom had a boyfriend, Gerald. A real piece of shit."

"He hit you?"

"Yeah. A lot." I'm surprised when tears sting my eyes. I blink them away impatiently.

Mike's face fills with sadness. "Oh, Katrell. I'm so sorry."

Relief floods through my chest. I've never told anyone in straight terms before. Will knew without me telling her. Mom saw it. Mike's the first person I've actually told. Some tension eases from my shoulders and exhaustion fills my whole body. "It's okay," I say, coughing wearily. "It's not like it's the first time. Or the last, probably."

"I'm going to do everything in my power to make sure it's the last time." Mike's voice is grim. "Where is Gerald now?"

"Don't worry. He's dead." I look Mike in his sharp eyes. I can't tell him about the Revenants, but I can give him a hint. "You may have seen him on the news. Gerald Miller? He was killed by a rabid dog."

There's a long silence while Mike rapidly pieces together what I'm saying. A dark expression crosses his face, then confusion and sadness.

"I'm sorry, Katrell," Mike says. I steel myself. He's going to say he's gonna turn me in to the police or something. I'm surprised when his eyes fill with tears. "I'm so sorry I failed you."

"What? Mike, you didn't—"

"I suspected something a long time ago. I saw the transcripts and the makeup and I knew. But I felt like I had to be sure." Mike closes his eyes and a few tears spill out. He swipes at them. "You suffered so much because I had to be sure. You should have never been in that position. You shouldn't be in this hospital. I'm sorry."

Gratitude rises in my chest. Mike's always been on my side, even if his methods were annoying. I just didn't see it before. "Thanks, Mike. It's okay, it's not your fault. You gave me peppermints, and those were damn good."

Mike laughs and I smile at him. "Very true," he says. "But, I need to make sure you're safe from this point forward. No more bruises. No more visits to the hospital."

"It's fine. Gerald's gone. I'm grounded here for a while and then I'll go home."

Mike hesitates and my stomach sinks. "Katrell, I don't know if anyone has told you yet, but it's unlikely you'll go back home."

My heart stutters in my chest. The heart monitor starts beeping faster. "What? What did you just say?"

"You know you're not in a good situation. And no social worker is going to let you go back to a place where you're unsafe. I won't either."

"What social worker? Who called them?"

"The hospital did. You're a sixteen-year-old minor who was nearly beaten to death. That's not something the hospital can let go."

Goddamn snitches. "Okay, fine, whatever. But I have a home already. I don't need a social worker."

Mike meets my eyes. "Has your mother visited you since you've been in the hospital?"

I flinch. Mom is still gone, and it's been four days. Maybe five or six. Time is kind of muddy—it's all been one disaster after another.

"We, as in me and your new social worker, tried to contact your mom several times while you were unconscious," Mike says. "We couldn't reach her. When we returned to your house, she wasn't there. We still haven't been able to get in touch with her."

I don't say anything, just chew my lip. Do they think Mom did this to me? They can't—Mom is way too weak to break my arm and ribs. I'd blame it on Gerald, because he's come close, but sadly he's dead.

"This is a big problem." Mike's still looking at me. "Do you understand what I'm saying? Even if your mother isn't responsible for your injuries, she has abandoned you."

I suddenly can't get enough air. The word "abandon" runs through my head over and over. It's not true. It can't be true. Mom's coming back for me. "Don't say that, Mike." My voice cracks and now I'm the one crying, my already sore throat constricting further. "Don't say that. It's not true."

Mike holds my hand and I cling to it, my breath short, my head aching. "I'm so sorry, Katrell," he says. "Your mother is gone. And if she comes back, you deserve better than what she can give you."

I sob, holding Mike's warm hand. Despair washes over me. I was trying to avoid it, trying not to think about it, but here's the ugly truth—Mom is gone. She skipped town and didn't take me with her. How could she do this? How could she leave me after all we've been through? Sixteen years, through all the boyfriends and towns and schools, it's been me and Mom. And now it's just me.

Mike wipes my eyes with a tissue, his touch unbearably gentle. "It's all right to cry, Katrell. It's a horrible situation. I know you love her very much." He takes a deep breath while I try to control my breathing. "But we also need to think about the future. You need a safe environment to come home to. Your social worker wants to talk to you today, so I wanted to give you a heads-up. They've been looking into finding you a foster family—"

"Wait." I can't breathe. My heart races and cold tingles crawl up my spine. "Wait, I'm for sure going to foster care?"

"Katrell—"

"I'm sixteen." My heart monitor is beeping so fast. I'm panicking and I can't breathe. I've avoided this for so long. I was so careful. All the makeup to cover bruises. The free lunches from Will and free dinners at Benny's. Paying our bills so we wouldn't be homeless. All my hard work, for nothing. How can everything fall apart so easily? Will's horror stories reverberate through my head. The ominous feeling of bugs in my brain ratchets up and I hold one hand to my temple. "Even if Mom's gone, I can stay by myself. I pay rent there anyway, I know how."

"You're severely injured. You'll need months of care after you leave the hospital." Mike's trying to sound gentle, but that makes everything worse. The bugs drag their claws over my brain. "You can't be alone, without someone to care for you. I'm sorry."

"You can't do this." I'm gasping—Mom's gone. All my money is gone. I can't work, not with these injuries. I'm trapped.

The bugs start moving and I let out a scream.

The next few moments are a blur. Mike rockets to his feet and calls for a doctor. I writhe in pain, my body twisting against the agony of ten bugs moving and shaking in my head. Too late, I realize I'm agitated and the Revenants are on the move.

"Get out!" I scream at Mike as three nurses swarm to my side. The heart monitor beeps out of control. As hands hold me down and Mike tells me to stay calm and nurses mess with the IV, all I can think is that if I don't do something about the Revenants soon, tonight, Mike is dead.

46

I wake up in a cold sweat, weak, my sore chest heaving. I look to my left for Mike, but he's not there. I look to my right for Will.

Five is standing next to my bedside.

I'm paralyzed by shock. She's smiling down at me, her eyes glinting in the harsh hospital lights. Her green top is smeared with blood. My blood.

"You're surprised," Five says. "I came to visit you, Katrell. Will didn't tell me to stay in the apartment, so I don't have to. I can do anything I please."

My mind catches up with my situation. Five is here, probably to kill me. Shit, is there some kind of panic button I can push, like in movies? My heart rate increases and the monitor next to my bed starts beeping faster. If I get too scared, will nurses hear the machine and come? But if they do, am I putting them in danger?

Five puts her hands behind her back. "You're frightened. Don't be afraid. I'm not here to harm you."

"Then . . ." My voice fails me. I try to swallow, but my throat is dry. "Then why are you here?"

Five strolls around the room, looking with interest at the TV and Mike's get-well-soon basket. "You were upset, so I came. The doctors said you had a seizure. Amusing, isn't it? Nurses always know more than doctors do. Trust me, I know. As usual, the doctors don't know what they're dealing with."

My stomach fills with ice. "No. No, you can't be here for Mike. He didn't mean to—"

"Mike has betrayed you twice now." Five is still looking at the balloons and gift basket. "First when he called the ambulance, and then when he called DHR. Foster care? Us? In a home full of potential Geralds?" Five picks up something from the basket—a stuffed dog. "I grow weary of killing Geralds, you know."

"Five, stop." I'm trying to sound commanding, but my voice is a pitiful whine. "Mike didn't even call them, the hospital did. You're looking for an excuse to hurt him."

Five doesn't answer at first. She examines the toy in her hands, then carefully starts to unstitch one of the button eyes. "All men hurt you in some way, Katrell. Even Mike. Especially Mike. You were careless. You got too close to him and now he's ruining everything. You should just be alone. Then no one would get hurt."

"Five—"

"I know what you know," Five says. The button clatters to the floor and she starts on the next one. "It's not my fault you're weak, Katrell. You called Will weak, but look at you. Dying in a hospital room while Will plans to burn pieces of you. You don't know your own heart." The second button falls to the floor and rolls under the bed. "I came to ask you for Mike's address. I need you to think, to remember."

I try to think about anything else, but memories of Mike surface. His too-big suit. His faded pep-talk posters. The way his eyes are so focused when he catches me in a lie. I see a messy desk, a photograph of him and his husband, a framed college degree on his wall.

No address.

Five clicks her tongue. "Disappointing. But I suppose you wouldn't know where your counselor lives." Five pulls out the stuffing from the dog's blank eyes and drops it to the tile below. "I'll have to find some other means. Conrad has a pretty good nose, don't you think?"

"Don't do this," I whisper. Tears gather in my eyes and I can't blink them back. It's all out of control again. Maybe I was never in control.

Five jerks the head of the dog and it comes off in one clean piece. She drops the stuffed animal and smiles at me.

"Come and stop me, then."

She leaves the room, shoulders back, a small grin on her face.

I wait for three agonizing seconds and then jump from the bed. I have to get out of here. I have no idea what time it is, but I have to protect Mike. So many have already died. Not him too.

I almost collapse when I put weight on my feet. I haven't used my legs except to shuffle back and forth to the bathroom, so they're shaking. Shivering, vomit climbing my throat, I rip out the IV and press down on my arm so what little blood I have left doesn't escape. Next, I rip the heart monitor off my chest and the sticky things from my temples. One of the machines emits a shrill noise—gotta hurry. I take one more deep breath and pull the short tube from my nose.

The difference in my ability to breathe is drastic. I'm suffocating; I can't get enough air. I bend at the waist and take several shallow, painful breaths. But I can't stop—I have to end this. It has to be me. I've messed up so completely—no money, no mother, no home. I can't let Five take Mike too. If I don't do something, where will it stop? They'll kill everyone. Mom left me. Julio cut my hours. Will's mom called me out on my suspicious car.

Will and I had a horrible fight.

I stumble toward the door, determination and fear the only things keeping me standing. I glance at the basket Mike brought. Balloons, chocolate, a card—and peppermints. I take one and squeeze it tight. Shaking, I open the door and leave the room.

There're usually doctors everywhere, but today the hallway is empty. Someone is shouting from far away—Five? Is she helping me escape? I ease past the deserted nurses station and find a staircase. I huff and wheeze down two flights. When I push open the door at the bottom, I step out into the night.

Apparently, it's easier to sneak out of a hospital than I thought. I look around, disoriented, and my heart leaps with hope when I see the street I'm on—Watters. Two streets over from Will's.

Barefoot and wearing a hospital gown, I stumble to Will's house. The cold pavement freezes my feet and I tremble in the chilly air. My breath comes out in painful, thin wheezes; my head's spinning from lack of oxygen. But I can't go back to the hospital, not with Five and the rest of the Revenants on the loose. I have to stop them.

I stagger to Will's bedroom window and tap on the glass. Her shadow rolls over, then sits straight up in bed. She hurries to the window and opens it, moonlight illuminating her face. She's not happy to see me—she looks pissed off.

"Trell, what're you doing here?" she hisses. "You're going to die if you're not—"

"Mike's in danger," I say, my words tumbling out in a rush. "He came to the hospital and wants me to go into foster care, but I don't want to go and the Revenants know and Five came to my room—"

I start coughing and it's hard to stop because I can't breathe. Will reaches out the window and I hold her hand until I can breathe again.

"Okay, okay," Will says. "Hang on. Come in first."

Will practically lifts me through her window, like a toddler. I stand in the middle of the familiar room, shivering. Will fusses over me, bringing me a change of clothes and shoes. I pull them on shakily, savoring the soft fabric of the new hoodie.

"Sorry about your other hoodie," I say. "It's gone now. I don't know what happened to it. All my clothes are gone."

Will hesitantly touches her hand to my cheek. She shakes her head. "Trell, you're burning up. Let me take you back to the hospital."

"No," I bark, half cough, half forceful disagreement. "Will, Mike isn't safe. I don't know where he lives, so he's maybe okay for now, but Five is after him and she'll find his address and it'll all be over. I felt them moving—they're restless. It has to be tonight."

Will bites her bottom lip. "Okay, fine. But let me—"

"No," I interrupt. "No, I'm coming with you. I have to. This is my problem and I have to solve it." I pause, then look at my feet.

They're swimming lazily in a dark haze. "Sorry for talking over you. I know you don't like it and I'm working on it, I swear. I just don't want you to get hurt because of me. Not you."

Will is silent for a long time. Then, quietly, she takes my hand and intertwines our fingers.

"Okay," she says. "I'll get the car."

47

"**D**o you have a plan?" Will asks as she lugs a red can of gasoline to the car. I can't help; I can barely lift my head. She gave me some DayQuil and that's starting to work. Each breath is still a wheeze, though.

"I need to find Five."

"Do you know where she is?"

My head is a mess of pain and static. "Uh . . . no. Maybe she went back to the apartment? To recruit help?"

Will's face drains of color. "Oh God. We have to go there first. I don't know how long they'll listen to me."

"Okay then, let's go." I cough, trying to catch my breath. "We can set the apartment on fire."

Will puts the can in the backseat of her mother's car and goes back for another. "You mean set *them* on fire. We can't burn down the whole building."

"Okay, fine." I stop to cough while Will puts the second can beside the first. "Then we find Two, Three, Five, and Conrad. Okay?"

"Okay," Will agrees. She holds out the keys to me, but I don't take them.

"You gotta drive. I'll pass out and kill us both."

Will's eyes widen. "But I don't have a license."

"Neither do I." I get into the passenger seat. Will stares at me, frozen. "Come on, you're a good driver. Do or die, right?"

Will doesn't say anything, but gets into the driver's side.

I lean my pounding head back against the headrest as Will slowly, carefully, backs out of her garage. Get the Revenants in the apartment, then find Five. One thing at a time.

Will holds my arm as we climb the stairs to the apartment.

I'm wheezing, barely able to breathe, and it's just the second flight. Can I make six?

"Trell, lean on me more," Will says, her voice soft and comforting. She puts one arm around my waist and I lean into her side. We climb slowly, one step at a time.

"Sorry," I pant at the top of the fourth flight. "I'm so sorry, Will."

"It's okay," Will says, her voice soft. She hugs me closer and we ease up a few more steps. "Just breathe. I'm here. I'm here to help."

I don't deserve her kindness, her gentle understanding. And she's touching me, something she's been struggling with for years. This has to be agony for her. I want to thank her for putting up with this, and me, but my breath is too short. Instead, I try to use as much of my own strength to climb to the sixth floor, where my Revenants are waiting.

The door to room 6C is open. Will and I peek in cautiously—they're all here, even the ones who had still been with their families, except for the four Will said were missing. Every head swivels in my direction.

"Welcome back, Katrell," Taylor says. She's staring through me, her eyes dull, her hands clasped in front of her blood-splattered dress. "You didn't die. Are you disappointed?"

"Hey, don't be mean to her," Will says, emerging from behind me. One gas can dangles from her right hand.

The room brightens immediately. Shoulders relax, everyone is all smiles.

"Hi, Will!"

"Nice to see you, Will!"

"We stayed put like you asked. Are you happy?"

Will wades into the room and stands in front of me. "Nice to see y'all again too. Trell and I have to talk to you."

"Sure," Six says. He has his hands in his bloodstained pockets. "What's up?"

I step forward, shivering. "I need you to disappear. All of you."

There's a thick silence, then everyone starts talking at once.

"It's not fair—"

"We shouldn't disappear, you should—"

"There's no way—"

"Stop," I command. They fall quiet. "You're all out of control. You're attacking Mike and other innocent people. I don't want this."

"We only do what you want—"

"Stop saying that." Frustration builds and I just want to hit them. "I get why Gerald died, and even Marquis, but enough is enough. You can't just attack anyone who gets in my way."

"Why not?" Four's eyes burn like fire in the low light. "What's the difference between Gerald and Mike, really? We've already crossed the line. Murder is murder. So many are dead already."

My head is pounding, aching. It's like a hammer is driving between my eyes.

"Don't say that," Will says forcefully. "Mike is good and has been nothing but kind to you. I mean, to Katrell. There's a big difference between him and Gerald and you know it."

A wave of shame courses through me and the Revenants lower their heads sheepishly. I wipe some snot from my nose and meet each Revenant's eyes, making sure they're listening.

"Will told me I have to be better."

A crippling amount of sadness floods my chest, so much I have to lean against the wall. Some Revenants are crying, wiping tears from their cheeks. Some sink to the floor while others let out sad wails.

"We don't deserve her loyalty."

"Will is too kind to us."

Will backs up, undoubtedly freaked out, but this is good. I'll take crying Revenants over violent ones.

"Will is all we have left," Nine says, his head lowered. "If she wants us to disappear, we have to."

"I want to disappear," Taylor says. She looks at me, her dead eyes filled with a hint of emotion. "I want to see Daddy again."

Guilt prickles at my skin, but Will steps forward with the can of gasoline. "Ready?"

The Revenants nod, and Will and I carefully coat their hair and skin in gasoline. By the time we're done, the fumes have made me light-headed. The Revenants stand in a circle, dripping wet, like a bunch of kids playing a game. A twinge of sadness that's all my own shoots through me.

"It's okay, Katrell," Six says. "You hate us, but you're sorry for us now. That's a good sign, don't you think?"

I don't know what to say. I nod and Six grins at me.

"Ready?" Will asks softly. She has a lighter. I reach for it and she drops the cold plastic into my palm.

"It won't hurt," I say, more to myself than to them. "You'll feel better dead. I shouldn't have brought you back at all."

They don't answer, so I light Six's sleeve and step back.

It's like writing a letter—the fire ignites immediately and consumes all the Revenants at once. They burn, the flames orange, then blue, but the fire doesn't spread to the rest of the apartment. The Revenants stay still, silent, all eyes on me. In thirty seconds, nothing's left except for ash.

I'm suddenly overwhelmed with emotion: sadness, anger, guilt, regret. Memories that don't belong to me surge through my brain—Six watching TV with his family, Nine being kissed by his wife, Marquis hugging Taylor and crying. Then, like smoke, it's all gone, and it's just me. Six bugs in my brain disappear, like someone blew out a candle.

Four bugs left.

48

"**D**o you feel better?" Will asks. We've left the apartment and we're driving around aimlessly, trying to find the remaining four.

"My head does, but—" I'm cut off by a thick cough. "But everything else hurts."

"Did it hurt when they . . ." Will trails off.

"When they burned? No. But I got some memories and emotions. It's like . . ." I want to say, *It's like I lived part of six other lives,* but that's not right. It's like six people lived my life and I glimpsed theirs. "Never mind."

Will looks at me out of the corner of her eye. "You know when I said 'be better,' I didn't mean it like that. I don't want you to change, I just didn't want you to do resurrections anymore."

"I know." I lean back wearily. "I know, but I need to change. I killed six people, Will."

"No, the Revenants killed six people."

"I practically told them to." Tears fill my eyes when I think of Mike's screaming. "I don't want to talk about it."

Will frowns, but thankfully stays quiet. She drives around for so long I nod off. I jerk awake when something touches my forehead.

"Sorry," Will says. She pulls her hand back. "I wanted to check your fever. It's high, Trell."

"I'm fine," I grunt. The car isn't moving anymore. We're parked in front of the school. "What's going on? Did you find one?"

"I think so." Will stares straight ahead. I follow her line of sight and my stomach lurches. The back door to the school, the one not connected to an alarm, is wide open.

I exchange a look with Will. I expect her to be scared, but her mouth is set with grim determination. "I'll get the gasoline," she says.

We exit the car and creep toward the building. My heart pounds sickeningly against my ribs. *Don't let Will get hurt* runs through my brain hundreds of times.

Will and I shine our phone flashlights on the lockers and empty classrooms. We make a lap around the school, but no Revenants.

"Maybe they've already left?" Will whispers. Her voice carries in the silent hallway.

No. Now that the bulk of the Revenants are dead, I'm thinking clearer than I have in a while. If they're essentially me, they think like me. If I wanted to hurt someone and didn't know where they were, I'd look for information. . . .

"Mike's office." As soon as I say it, I know it's true. Images, quick, faint, flash before my eyes—files, a messy desk, a photo of a man. A Revenant is in there.

Will and I tiptoe to the front office, where the door waits, wide open. We shine our flashlights into the dark and Five is illuminated, flicking through a stack of files in her hand.

"Hello, Will, Katrell." She doesn't look up. She pages through a file marked JUSTIN WIGGINS. "Did you know Justin's mother died last year? That's around the time he started requesting the letters."

As she says it, I can see the information in my mind. Justin's address, phone number, emergency contact. He lives with his grandmother. Mike's scribbled a note: *self-destructing*.

"Should we look at yours?" Five picks up a file I recognize, one with my name on the label. She opens it and thumbs through lazily. My flashlight catches dried blood under her fingernails.

"Katrell Davis, high-priority case. Homelife is bad. Abuse?"

I can see Mike's scrawl in my mind's eye as she reads.

"Closed-off."

Troubled.

"Dip in grades this semester."

No support system.

"I am very worried." Five smiles at the file. "Mike's sweet, isn't he?"

I get one more image—Mike's home address in black ink on a school form.

"Too bad he has to be punished."

"Why are you doing this?" My voice is scratchy with fear and sadness. "Mike hasn't done anything wrong."

"He's ruining everything." Five studies her nails. "You have to protect yourself, Katrell. You don't need anyone in this world, especially not a man who pokes his nose into everyone's business. Mom has abandoned you. You're all alone, Katrell. Everyone should just leave you alone."

"You don't really think that, do you?" Will asks me.

I don't know. I don't know what I think.

"I know your heart, Katrell," Five purrs. She takes a few steps toward me and I back up, out of Mike's office. "You are broken, beyond repair. Doesn't the guilt eat at you? All these people, dead. All this rage burning everyone around you."

"Trell, don't listen to her," Will says.

But I am listening. Guilt and confusion and a deep, raw sadness rips through me. My head's killing me. I'm so tired.

"You're trapped, aren't you? In a nightmare you can't wake up from. Everything's fallen apart."

Five reaches into her pants pocket and pulls out Marquis's gun.

Will gasps, but I'm frozen, trembling. I should have known they'd know where I hid the gun. They know me. They are me.

Five smiles, pointing the gun straight at me. "You're dying, Katrell. If you die, the Revenants will too." Her eyes are bright orange. "Don't you think that's easier than chasing your mistakes around all night?"

"Stop," Will commands. Five's smile slips into a frown.

"Will, please. Katrell is so tired. I'm doing her a favor." She looks at me again, her orange eyes boring into mine. "Aren't you tired, Katrell? I can do this for you. We know how to use it. A handy gift Marquis gave you, isn't it? We should get some use out of it, don't you think? It's the least we can do, since we killed him."

"Okay, enough." Will steps in front of me, scowling, shielding me with her whole body. I can't even see Five anymore. "I'm not gonna listen to this. I'm gonna burn you and you're gonna stop hurting Trell. Got it?"

I peek around Will cautiously. Five studies her for a long,

agonizing moment, glaring into Will's eyes, her teeth gritted. Then she sighs and her face smooths into a mask of calm. "I'll allow you to burn me, Will. Only you. Will's the boss—she always has been. Katrell fancies herself a kingpin, but she's never been a good leader. She's not strong enough."

I watch, numb, while Will pours a little gasoline on Five's arm. Five looks at me, her eyes still bright orange.

"You know the address," Five says. "So they do too. Good luck, Katrell."

Will lights her on fire.

The flames eat up Five's arms, then her torso. The fire spreads quickly, hungrily, like she's made of paper. Her orange eyes are the last to disappear. She stares at me the whole time. When she's nothing but a pile of ash, I get a small memory—Five holding a baby and cooing. Then there's nothing but confusion and regret.

And the knowledge that Two, Three, and Conrad know where Mike lives.

49

Will and I sprint to her car. I'm out of breath by the time we get there, but Will's already reversing out of the school parking lot, scrambling with her seat belt with one hand.

"What's the address?" Will asks, her voice shaking. Her breath is just as short as mine.

"Breathe," I gasp. I fumble with my phone. "Stay . . . calm. Think good . . . thoughts. We'll make it."

Will is silent, her eyes wide. She's probably saying a prayer.

I type the address burned in my mind into my phone's GPS. Ten minutes away. We're gonna make it. We're in a car and the Revenants are on foot. I try not to think about the fact that Conrad can really move when he's motivated.

Will follows the GPS instructions silently. She's speeding, going so fast I almost miss the shape of a man running. No, not a man . . . a teenager.

In a red letterman jacket stained with blood.

"Will, that's Three!" I point to him frantically. He's speeding toward Mike's, his long legs eating up the distance between him and Mike's house.

"What should I do?" Will brings one hand to her mouth and tears at the skin around her nails. Her nails are already bitten to the quick by nervous teeth.

He's almost there. Mike's house is at the end of the street and Three's halfway there already. We have to stop him.

"Run him over."

"What?" Will shrieks. She's slowing down, her free hand gripping the wheel tightly. "I can't do that! I—"

"If you don't, Mike's dead! It won't hurt Three, we just have to stop him until we can set him on fire." A vicious cough tears from my chest, and I double over in pain. "Do it," I croak, my head between my knees.

There's silence, and then the car accelerates.

I look up in time to see Will slam her parents' car into Three. He sails through the air, then crashes to the pavement behind us with a sickening thud.

Will stops the car with a harsh jolt. Panting, she looks at me, her eyes wild and terrified.

"It's okay! He's fine. Let's go." I open the door and stumble out of the car. Three lies a few feet behind us, his body crumpled and twisted in an unnatural position. His legs are bent the wrong way and one arm is crushed, but there's no blood. Will gets out of the car and stands next to me, trembling.

"Wh-what if it's the wrong person?" Her teeth are chattering.

"It's not." I watch grimly as Three's bones crack and pop as they return to normal. He gets to his feet, his eyes burning orange in the dark.

"You maniac," Three hisses. "You hit me with a car! I hope there's a dent in it. You're unhinged, Katrell."

"Well. Desperate times and all that."

Three bares his teeth at me, like he's snarling. "Why are you trying to stop us? Isn't this what you want?"

"You know it isn't." I cough into my arm and pant, my breath making thick white clouds in the air. "Just let us burn you. Don't fight."

Three inclines his chin. "I won't let you stop me. Mike should be punished. You should be punished."

"Don't," Will says softly. His head swivels toward her. "Trell is sick and she just wants this to be over. Please."

"How dare you," Three snorts. "They may fawn over you, but I know the truth."

"Hey," I bark. "Don't talk to her. Shut up and let us set you on fire."

"Will has everything," Three says, ignoring me. "Will has everything and she squanders it all. A mom, a dad, a nice house. She gets sandwiches every day. Katrell eats peanut butter from the jar."

"Stop," I warn. I was afraid of Five, but Three's pissing me off. What does he know about eating peanut butter straight from the jar? The Joneses spoiled him, alive and dead.

"She has a nice hobby and Katrell protects her at school. A perfect existence, right? Is it fair for Will to have everything when Katrell gets nothing? Especially since Will doesn't appreciate it."

Will looks at me, hurt. I grit my teeth. "I said stop."

"Everyone else has everything," Three says. "Mike has a nice house in a nice neighborhood. Chelsea lives in a mansion. Even the people in the projects have families who love them. But what do you have, Katrell? No Mom, no home. Nothing." He grins, a huge one that splits his face in two. "Since everyone has things you don't have, we should just burn everything to the ground. That'll even the playing field, right?"

I grab the gas can from Will, unscrew the cap, and fling the contents in Three's face. He stumbles backward, but it's too late— his jacket is soaked in gasoline.

"Don't talk about Will like that," I growl. I fish the lighter out of my pocket. "The only one I'm burning down is you."

Three's grin turns into a feral snarl and he lunges at me. His hands connect with my throat and he pushes me against the car. Gasoline from his jacket smears on my chest.

"If I burn," Three says, his orange eyes glaring into mine, "you burn too."

Will's watching, paralyzed. Three's hands are around my throat and the lighter's in my hand, but if I do this, I'll die too. Is it worth it to protect Mike? Is Mike worth dying for? No, I'm thinking about this in the wrong way. If I do this, all the Revenants will disappear. Five said so. Everything will disappear.

Even me.

I grit my teeth, wrap my hand around the lighter, and poise my thumb to light it.

Suddenly, Will shoves Three from the side, causing him to stumble. I jump back, wheezing, and light the lighter. I throw it on him and his body is engulfed in flames.

He screams. None of the others screamed. Will and I watch in horrified fascination as he writhes, his skin burning at an alarming rate. He reaches for me, trying to say something, but his words are a garbled mess. Soon, he's still and his body has turned to ash. I get a memory, but it's too faded, too fragmented to piece together. I'm overcome with a sense of bitterness that lingers long after Three is gone.

I cough. Gasoline has soaked my new hoodie and the smell makes my head hurt. Two left. Two more, and it'll all be over.

"Are you okay?" Will asks.

I meet her eyes, exhausted. "Yeah. He was sort of a jerk when he was alive too."

"No, I mean . . ." Will hesitates. "The stuff they're saying is scaring me, Trell."

Hurt leaps into my chest. Will's afraid of me, on top of everything else? This nightmare never ends. I can't wake up. I swallow, my throat sending pain all through my body. "Let's check on Mike, okay? Two and Conrad are still out there."

Will nods and we walk to Mike's house, a cute two-story brick house at the end of the street. The glow of a TV flashes in the living room. Will and I peek through the window.

Mike's sitting on a couch, his laptop on the table in front of him. He's leaned to one side, talking on his cell phone. He jumps to his feet and starts pacing, biting his bottom lip. A man, the one in the photo on his desk, comes into the room holding two steaming mugs. The man sits on the couch and watches Mike pace, then pats the space beside him. Mike sighs heavily, but sits next to him. The man offers him a mug and Mike accepts it.

"He's okay," Will whispers in my ear.

I watch them, my heart aching with longing for the simple kind of peace I'll never have. After a moment, I unstick myself from the window and turn to Will. "Two more left."

50

W ill and I hang around Mike's house for a couple of hours, but there's no sign of Conrad or Two.

I'm half-conscious. My breathing keeps getting worse and worse, and I'm dizzy. Five's words reverberate through my brain: it would be easier to die. We'll never be able to kill Conrad. Should I keep struggling? Or should I end everything?

"Hey," Will says. Her voice is far away, like she's in a cave. "Hey, Trell? You okay? Trell?"

I feel her hand on my forehead and she curses. I pass in and out of consciousness, having a nightmare (or is it reality?) about orange glowing eyes.

Suddenly, I'm lying in the backseat, my head in Will's lap. I look up at her, stunned. Her face is scrunched, like she's in pain.

"Trell, wake up. Come on, stay with me."

"I'm awake," I croak. My voice is almost gone. "Where . . . where are we?"

Will's face smooths with relief. She touches my forehead with something cool. "Gas station. I got some water. Trell, we have to go back to the hospital. Your fever is bad, real bad."

"I'm okay." I can't keep my eyes open. "I can do it, I promise. I have to end this. I have to."

Will is quiet for so long I almost fall asleep. She strokes my hair tentatively, easing me further into sleep.

"You don't have to do everything by yourself, Trell."

I blink groggily up at her. She's upside down, and her face is hazy, but she's not lying. I can tell. Will is a terrible liar.

"What Five said back there, it's not true. You're not all alone. I'm here. And M—Cheryl is willing to help too. So are Mike and Allen. You're not by yourself. Don't let them tell you that, because it's not true."

I blink back tears because I want to believe her, I do, but Mom told me I was a monster. And six people are dead. And Conrad broke Mike's arm. I deserve to be alone. I don't deserve Will at all.

"Thanks," I manage. I close my eyes again.

"You're not listening," Will huffs. She presses a cold water bottle to my forehead. "I'm not kidding. You're my best friend and I love you, okay? I'll do anything you ask. I just want you to be happy."

I don't know what to say. How can that be true? I don't have anything left. No money, no home. No family. How can Will stand the sight of me? I can't stand the sight of myself.

Will and I sit in silence for a long time. I nod off, my head still in her lap. Images flash through my brain. My room, destroyed, feathers from pillows floating in the air. Two big paws stained red.

A graveyard, where it all began. An empty grave. Two's bare feet and the hem of a once-pretty blue dress.

My eyes pop open and a burst of strength surges through me. "Two's in the graveyard," I tell Will, sitting up. "And Conrad's in my room."

"Trell..."

"Come on," I urge, climbing into the passenger seat. Will reluctantly climbs into the driver's side. "We need to hurry. I feel better, promise."

Will doesn't say anything. She puts her seat belt on and pulls out of the gas station, heading for the graveyard.

We find Two next to her grave.

She's kneeling, her eyes closed, her hands folded in her lap. She doesn't move when we approach, even when I'm right in front of her.

"Two? I mean, Rose?"

Two opens her eyes. They're orange, like the rest, but sad somehow. "Hello, dear."

Will and I exchange an uneasy look. She's so still, unmoving. She's always been like this, even from the beginning. She didn't attack me when the others turned on me. I kneel beside her, and Two looks down at me. Her hands remain folded in her lap.

"It's a beautiful night," she says, her voice hushed. "Maybe our last."

I stay quiet.

Two closes her eyes. "It doesn't seem worth it, all this trouble.

Even though we fought hard, for years, everyone is gone. Gerald. Conrad. Mom." Two looks up at the sky. "Charlie. Everyone is gone. It may be time for us to disappear too."

I don't say anything, because I'm fighting the tears welling in my eyes. I'm a monster. I hit my own mother. I hurt Mike. I fought with Will. I'm trying so hard to fix this, but I can't breathe and I'm so tired. I just want it to be over.

Will puts a hand on my shoulder. I turn away, trying to hide the tears running down my cheeks.

"Don't cry," Will murmurs. "We don't have much farther to go. It's almost over."

"Yes," Two says. She looks at the sky again, her face smooth and peaceful. "It's almost over, Katrell. You can stay strong or break. There is no in between anymore. But for me, I am weary."

Her eyes lose their orange glow. "I want to see Charlie again. Please."

Still sniffling, I nod and pour the remaining gasoline onto Two's white curls. She smiles at me gently as Will gives me the lighter.

"Good luck, dear," Two says. She puts a hand on my arm, her touch light and soft. "And goodbye."

Two burns up quickly, much quicker than the rest. Like the others, I get a quick memory—the famous Charlie, dressed in a white tuxedo and framed in sunlight, his wizened face split into an enormous smile. Then there's nothing, nothing but a sense of calm. Stay strong or break. I close my eyes and breathe in, as deep as I can.

"Let's go see Conrad," I tell Will.

51

Will and I sit outside my house, silent. I can see Conrad through my bedroom window, methodically ripping up the new comforter I bought last week. He shakes feathers from the blanket, his teeth bared. What little air I have left in my lungs turns to cement.

"Maybe we can just leave him?" Will suggests. "Call animal control?"

"If you want dead dogcatchers, then sure."

We sit in silence for a few more minutes. Conrad finishes with the comforter and moves on to the TV. He knocks it over with his paws and the crash reverberates through the area. My neighbors close their blinds and turn off their lights.

"What is he doing?" Will asks.

As soon as she asks, I can see the answer in my mind. "He's

destroying all the things I bought with the money I made from resurrections. So then I really won't have anything left."

Will looks at me from the corner of her eye. "You should really go to therapy after this is over."

I laugh for the first time all night.

Conrad looks up from his pile of destruction. He stares straight at me through the window.

"We can just leave," Will says. Her voice trembles in fear.

Conrad jumps out the window and stands in the front yard. His hackles raise and he takes a few steps forward.

"Oh yeah," I say as Conrad steps closer. "We really should."

Still, I get out of the car. Will scrambles out too, holding the keys like she would if she were protecting herself from a predator in a dark parking lot. I grab the second gasoline can, my heart in my throat, and step to the edge of the yard. Conrad steps closer, so he's only a few leaps away.

Then, he pulls back his lips and snarls at me.

Conrad has never growled at me. Not once. Not living or dead. The fear is purged from my body, replaced by crippling sadness. He really is gone. He's not the same dog. I have no one left.

"Conrad, easy," Will says. He ignores her and keeps baring his teeth at me.

"Come on, boy." My voice doesn't even sound like me—high-pitched, whiny. No wonder he's growling at me. "It's time to go now, okay?"

My vision blinks out for a second, and then I'm looking at myself from Conrad's point of view. Giant bags under my eyes. Buried in Will's huge clothes. Tearstains on my cheeks, face flushed with fever, a line of dried, bloody snot under one nostril. Worst of all, my expression is tortured, like someone is twisting a knife in my side. I look like a sad child who's been kicked too much. I look pathetic.

I can't stand it.

Conrad lunges at me. My vision is my own again and I barely dodge his teeth. He snaps at the air, inches from my elbow. I stumble backward, tripping over my own feet, as he snarls at me again. My breathing is shallow and shaky, and all I can see is that pitiful image of myself, orphaned, all alone, pathetic.

Maybe I deserve this.

"Stop, Conrad!" Will stands in front of me, shielding me. Conrad barks at her and growls.

Strength flows into my chest and the image disappears. I point at Conrad, a familiar burning in my chest. "No, no sir. You better not."

Conrad falters, his ears pinned against his head.

My emotions are out of control. Fury, sadness, fear, dread. I love Will and I want to protect her, but I'm so scared of going back to that hospital and into foster care, and I'm so guilty about Mike and everything I've done. I'm a monster. I want to die. I want to live and make it right. I don't know what I want.

Conrad dodges Will and jumps at me. His paws knock me backward, sending the gas can flying. His weight pins me to the ground. He snarls at Will again as she pulls at the scruff of his neck and screams. His eyes are so close to mine. They're searching my face, as if looking for a cue.

We only do what you want, Katrell.

What do I want?

Conrad opens his mouth to tear into my throat.

"Trell, don't let him!" Will screams. She's pulling at Conrad with all her strength, but he won't budge from my chest. "I'm right here, Trell. Don't give up. You survived for so long by yourself, but it's okay to lean on other people. It's okay to lean on me. It's not over, I swear."

Tears run down my cheeks. I can't control them. I can't control anything anymore. "It's over, Will." My voice is barely audible. Hot drool leaks from Conrad's mouth onto my neck. "I'm tired. I'm so tired."

"I know you are, but you can't give up. Not yet." Will's still tugging at Conrad's scruff, but he's 145 pounds of muscle and rage and he's not moving. "Listen, it's okay. Cheryl's gonna take care of you. I'm here, I'm not going anywhere. Mike's worried about you, you saw him tonight. The hospital probably called him and told him you ran away. You're not alone, okay?"

My breath wheezes in my chest. "I don't have anything left, Will. Conrad is dead. You said you're scared of me. Mom left me. It was supposed to be me and her, always. But now it's just me." I'm sobbing. It's pathetic, I know, but I can't stop. "You were right, she doesn't care about me. But what could I do? I loved her so much. I don't have anyone else. I did all this for her, but she's still gone. I don't know how to live without her."

"That's how I felt when Nana died," Will says. She gives up pulling on Conrad and gets to her knees beside me. She finds my hand and holds it tight in hers. "Losing her hurt so bad. But that doesn't mean you can give up. You said that to me, remember? When we first met? You said I couldn't just shut down. I had my whole life to live. You do too, Trell."

I nod, confusion and pain clouding my mind. "I remember."

"And I didn't say I was scared of you." Will squeezes my hand. "I'm scared *for* you. I'm scared of what they say, because they're all liars. You're not a monster. And even if you were, I'd still be here. Just like you've been here for me."

I look into Conrad's orange eyes and Will's words sink in. I'm scared, everyone leaves me, but Will has been the one solid in my life for four years. Even when we fought, even when I was cruel to her, she accepted my apologies and has tried to help me every step of the way. She took her parents' car in the middle of the night to help me burn dead bodies who murdered six people. She's been here, with me, the whole time.

Conrad stops growling.

"Stand up, Katrell." Will lets go of my hand and stands herself, waiting. I look at Conrad and he stares into my eyes.

"Move," I tell him, my voice soft. He obeys, removing his heavy weight from my chest. I struggle into a sitting position and then to my feet, and Will wraps her arms around me.

"It's okay," she says, her breath warm against my ear. "I'm here. I'm not going anywhere."

I cling to her, unable to stop silent tears from streaking down my fevered cheeks. Conrad sits beside me, his head leaning against my legs, and wags his tail.

52

Will sits next to me on the front porch. She holds out my headphones, the red ones from before all this started.

"Thought you'd want these," she says. "It's about the only thing he didn't eat."

"Thanks." I put the headphones around my neck. Conrad doesn't stir. His head is in my lap and he's limp, inactive. He's still so warm.

"What're you going to do with him?" Will asks.

I pet his huge head. "I can't burn him. Not like everyone else."

"Then . . . ?"

I can't keep him either. He's calm now, docile, but what happens when I fight with Chelsea at school? Or someone steals something of mine? Or even if I get a bad grade on a test? I can't trust him. I can't trust myself.

I take a shallow breath. "I'll try a letter."

Will nods and hands me a pen and piece of paper.

Conrad,

You were a good dog and I loved you. I still do. But it's all over. I can't keep you here with me, because I know you're already gone. Don't worry, wherever you are. I'll be okay. Even if there are other Geralds, I'll be okay. I have Will and Mike, and I'll make it. I'm sorry I used you for my own frustration. I'm sorry I couldn't bring you back. I love you, Conrad.

Love always,
Katrell

Conrad lifts his head from my lap as soon as I finish the last *l* in my name. He looks into my eyes and a little bit of life comes back into his. He licks my chin and stands. Then fire engulfs him.

Memories crash into my brain all at once, a mix of mine and his. Me holding Conrad as a puppy. Conrad licking tears from my face. Cuddling in the backseat of a car for warmth on a winter night. Me wrapping a bandage around Conrad's paw. And Conrad's final memory, watching Gerald point a gun at him and the slow blackness that came with it.

Conrad turns into a small pile of ashes at my feet. I'm overcome with a deep sadness but also relief. It's finally all over. I was selfish, thoughtless, and I paid for it.

Will's grandma was right; I burned everything to the ground. Six lives, my home, all that money. Mom. Everything is gone. I look up at the sky, the sun rising just behind the city of Mire.

"Why do you think the letter worked this time?" Will asks.

I take a shaky breath. "Trapped people can't run. That's what Two told me. But I'm free now, right? I have nothing left."

Will hesitates for a second, then touches my hand. "You okay?"

I nod, unable to speak. Looking at my life is like looking at a wasteland, charred and barren. All that effort, all that struggling, for nothing.

Will watches the sunrise with me for a few minutes. "I'm glad you didn't give up, Trell. You're my best friend, and I love you."

"Even after all I did?"

Will looks me in the eye. "Especially after all you did. When you went too far, you stopped. And I think that's all we can do."

I don't know what to say. I really don't deserve Will. I wipe my eyes. "Thanks, Will."

"You're welcome, best friend." She smiles at her hands, her expression distant. "I wish Nana had been clearer about this. It's been a hell of a few months."

That almost drags a smile out of me. "Yeah, thanks for the warning, Clara. Lot of good that did."

Will gets to her feet, grinning. "All right, come on, back to the hospital. I'm sure everyone's panicking because you ran off."

I look up at her, uncertainty and pain swirling in me. It almost feels pointless to go back. I don't have anything left to go back to. "Hey, what'd you mean by 'Cheryl's gonna take care of you'? Were you just trying to keep Conrad from eating me?"

"No. I didn't want to tell you until it was official, but Allen and Cheryl . . . Mom, I mean, are going to be your foster parents."

I look at Will for several dumbstruck seconds. "What?"

"When you were in a coma, they got all worked up. Mom said she didn't want you to suffer anymore, and she was going to make sure of it. I heard her talking to Mike and a social worker. They have a good chance of getting you." Will shrugs, smiling faintly. "I told you, you've never been alone. Even if it felt like it."

As the sun rises and illuminates Will's face, hope surges into my chest. The future isn't a wasteland anymore. Clara's right—I burned it all down. But now I can start something new.

Will offers her hand to me. "Let's go, adopted sister. We need to get you back to the hospital before you croak."

I give her a tentative smile and take Will's hand. We walk to the car, our fingers intertwined, as the new day begins.

ACKNOWLEDGMENTS

Biggest, astronomical thanks to Grandma, who saw an angry, hurt teenager and adopted and healed me. I can never repay you as long as I live, but I hope Arby's runs, late-night laughter, and all my love bring me a little closer.

Big thank-you to my agent, Holly Root, for being a super-human and fearless champion of this book! You are my hero. And thank you to the entire Delacorte team for helping bring this book to the world.

To Tas Mollah: you are my best friend and CP, and I'm so lucky to have you in my life. Thank you for sticking with Trell from the beginning, lifting me up, and cheering for me. And also thank you for all the memes at three a.m., because, wow, I could not have survived these difficult years without them.

Thank you to three of my favorite people: Mary, Gigi Griffis, and J. Elle. Mary, you are a star and a light and I am so thankful to know you. You have loved *BWB* since we were both slugging it out in Pitch Wars, and you never let me give up. You are the best and also have the best taste in cake!! Gigi, you are *BWB*'s biggest cheerleader, and I'm so grateful for your friendship. You are smart and an editing queen, and I'm so happy to know you. J. Elle—what can I say?! Superwoman, kindest friend, loveliest human being I've ever met. Your grace and strength have pulled me through so many dark moments. I'm glad to know you, twin, and I can't wait to read all your stories.

Thank you also to Brittney Morris for mentoring me and giving me this invaluable opportunity. Huge thanks to the entire class of Pitch Wars 2018, because I truly wouldn't be here today without you.

Thank you to my many readers and friends: Emily Chapman, Meg Long, Chad Lucas, Elvin Bala, Lyssa Mia Smith, Marisa Urgo, Xiran Jay Zhao, Cas Fick, Sarah Worley, Alina Khawaja, KD Weinert, Sarah C. Street, Marith, and Sher-May Loh. Thank you so much for reading early drafts of this book, drying my tears, and inspiring me to be better. Thank you also to my writing groups, the slackers, Scream Town, WiM, and AoCs. I appreciate you all, and your chats and kindness kept me going.

Finally, thank you to young Jessica, who lived through unbearable pain so I could be here today. Thank you for staying.

ABOUT THE AUTHOR

Jessica Lewis is a Black author and receptionist. She has a degree in English literature and animal science (the veterinarian plan did *not* work out). She lives with her way-funnier-than-her grandmother in Alabama. Her debut novel is *Bad Witch Burning*.

AUTHORJESSICALEWIS.COM
@JLEW100